HARTE TOWER

Phil Wortmann

Urban Alpine Productions

The characters and events portrayed in this book are fictitious. Any similarity to real persons, living or dead, is coincidental and not intended by the author.

Rock climbing, mountaineering, and related activities involve inherent dangers that cannot be entirely eliminated. This book is a work of fiction and not intended for instructional purposes. The publisher, author, and compilers cannot be held responsible for damages or accidents.

EPUB ISBN: 979-8-9950086-0-6
PAPERBACK ISBN: 978-0-578-93162-3

Cover design by: Adele Goodwin
Editor: Tracy Hundley
Library of Congress Control Number: 2018675309
Printed in the United States of America

FOREWORD

While *Harte Tower* is fictional, the story and setting were inspired and shaped by decades of adventure throughout the American West, Alaska, and beyond. We are truly blessed to live in such a beautiful land and to inhabit a time when it is possible to explore its true heights. Thank you to all the partners who have shared in my adventures over the years. I have been blessed to meet some of the great characters of our time, who do their best to exist in that space between boldness and humility.

CONTENTS

Dedication

Boyhood can be a dangerous place.
To the patient men in my childhood who didn't run:
Maurice and David.

"The world breaks everyone and afterward many are strong at the broken places. But those that will not break it kills. It kills the very good and the very gentle and the very brave impartially. If you are none of these you can be sure it will kill you too but there will be no special hurry."

—ERNEST HEMINGWAY

HARTE TOWER

PROLOGUE

Long ago, forces yet known compelled these jagged peaks upward. And there they stood for the coming of man and his boundless pride. Each year, the earth in her might worked to bring the mountains low, throwing at them every cyclical power she commanded, and slowly, her relentless gravity worked and filled the rivers and lakes with fragments of the once formidable giants. Build up. Tear down. But mankind does not glean wisdom from this process. Instead, he rises up in futility unless, or until, stricken down by those forces he seeks to master.

But in the end, it is not success that matters. We are at our best when working to make the impossible possible. We have always thrown ourselves against mountains, real or imagined, as if knowing that, without blood, they are mere piles of stone. For it is the challenge the mountains present that gives them value. That is the true gold we seek. Tales of lore are written of those who venture too close to the edge, whether they return or not. In the end, it is the responsibility of the bold to bear both the praise of those who attempted but failed—and the scorn of those who never tried.

1903
Translated from the lost journal of Wilhelm Harte

1. FLIGHT

Brooks Range, Alaska
July 2017

Fear fluttered in his chest, but he pushed it down. *You're a Hardy. Keep it together.* A nagging sense of doom hummed in his ear like the mosquitoes harassing them as he and his grandfather loaded gear into the four-seater bush plane at the Fairbanks airstrip. He couldn't pinpoint exactly where the fear came from. But later, he wished he'd listened to it.

A green Army duffel bag was the last on the luggage cart. Ethan grabbed one of the worn straps and heaved it onto the back seat for Sandy, their bush pilot, to stow with the rest of the supplies in the cargo pod behind the back row. Ethan's father had given him the bag when he was small enough to fit inside it. That was many deployments ago.

"That bag has seen a few things," said Sandy, nodding to the tears and stains on the duffel.

Ethan pulled out his phone and shot a quick text to Camila. *Flying out in a few minutes. Wish me luck!* Then added, *I'll text when I get back. Stay safe, watch out for creepers.* He thought of promising to message from the satellite phone, but he knew it cost his grandparents money each time, so he decided against it. Instead, he sent one last line. *I'll miss you.*

"Well, I think we've reached peak skeeter season," Sandy said, swatting the whining bugs off her sweaty neck. Her gray-streaked ponytail hung over one shoulder like the tail of a silver fox. "Hopefully, you boys can camp high enough on the snowfield to escape these buggers."

"Sure hope so!" Joe said.

Sandy glanced back at him, now sitting on the empty luggage cart, wiping sweat from his brow. "When was the last time you were up in the Brooks, Joe?"

"Oh, it's been years. Maybe twenty? The great Brian Teale and I flew up. Got dropped off at the river and double-hauled the gear up to the Albatross. One hell of a formation. Camped two weeks beneath it and put up a new route. Saw lots of bears down low on the way out. It'll be nice to land on the glacier this time around. Avoid that mess of a hike. Hopefully, the bears too."

Ethan smirked at Joe's pronunciation of "bayers." Although his grandfather left the Ozarks where he was raised and moved to Alaska as a young man, his Arkansas twang still betrayed his roots. Ethan once thought his grandfather's accent was an accidental relic, but he'd started to believe he'd purposely kept it around like a sacred memento. A way of showing the world there were parts of him that would remain unchanged, much like the mountains that defined his life.

Sandy finished adjusting the cargo and gave them a thumbs-up. "Time to roll, boys. Jump in."

Ethan started to climb into the backseat in deference to his grandfather, but Joe stopped him. "First-timers ride shotgun. Jump in there and put the headset on."

Ethan did as he was told, closing the door and putting on his seatbelt as Sandy fired up the engine.

The prop spun to life as the engine coughed and sputtered. Sandy communicated with a controller on the radio and taxied toward the airfield. When she pressed the throttle to full for takeoff, the engine's power set Ethan back in his seat. They bounced down the runway and shot up into the air with the nose pointed high. They gained altitude quickly as the town fell away behind them, leaving them floating above the endless forest.

"If anyone needs a bathroom, you'll have a chance when we land in Coldfoot to fuel up and drop a package." Then Sandy pointed at a compartment between her and Ethan. "There's a bag in here if you need to puke."

"Oh, I'll be fine," Ethan said.

Sandy shook her head. She tapped her finger on a small placard on the dashboard that read, "PUSH BUTTON ON HEADSET TO TALK." Ethan flushed, then pressed the button. "I'll be fine."

Sandy smiled. "This your first trip to Alaska, Ethan?"

"First time this far north, but I've been to Alaska a few times."

Joe chimed in, "Don't let him fool ya, he's been on more adventures in his eighteen years than most men twice his age. He climbed Pioneer Peak with us when he was twelve."

Ethan remembered that climb well. His father took thirty days of leave after a year in Afghanistan, determined to give him his first big Chugach adventure. Their family team of five started the climb—more of a steep hike with some thoughtful scrambling—at 5:00 a.m. and summited Pioneer six hours later. It was Ethan's biggest day in the mountains at the time, and it made him think he could do that type of thing for the rest of his life. His family had continued their peak bagging adventures, even when Ethan's dad was away. He and his mom had summited six of Colorado's fourteen-thousand-foot summits. He wished things had stayed like that. Innocent and uncomplicated. Before he and his dad started to disagree on most everything. Before his troubles at school. And, before loss rearranged everything.

"What line are you boys gunning for in the cirque?" Sandy asked.

"Italian Route. South face of Harte Tower," Joe answered. "Didn't get much info on it but seems straightforward enough."

Sandy shook her head. "Sounds adventurous."

Ethan piped in, "My mom told him to scare me, but not to kill me. We'll see how far he takes it."

"Our plan," Joe answered, "is to scare him into goin' to college."

Sandy laughed.

"Good luck with that, old man," said Ethan.

Joe's quip about college betrayed the true intent of their trip. Ethan's mother framed it as a chance to reconnect with his grandparents and come to terms with his loss. Their loss. The family's loss. But Joe was not the kind to sit idle, so he offered several options to kill the time, and, of course, Ethan chose the big climb. And now, there was no backing out.

They crossed the Great Yukon, the north's broad, meandering, riverine highway. Beyond it, the landscape flattened into swamps and low-lying hills until they approached Coldfoot, and the Brooks Range began to rise in the distance. The airstrip stretched out in a valley, with the first jagged peaks looming beyond.

Alaska was unlike any of the places Ethan had lived. Big cities and military bases were littered with signs to warn you of any dangers, and an infinite number of rules were written to safeguard people. And if that failed, a police car or an ambulance was only minutes away. But Alaska didn't play.

On a short bike ride to town from his grandparents' cabin in Talkeetna, they had passed a grizzly bear in the ditch next to the road. The bear just raised his nose and sniffed the air as they pedaled by, then went back to snorting through the bushes, nosing around for berries. Joe said the bear would not likely hurt them if they didn't pose a threat. Ethan had never seen a grizzly up close. He white-knuckled the handlebars out of fear but didn't panic. It was hard for him to grasp that such a dangerous creature could just pop up randomly at any time.

Sandy contacted the airstrip, and they listened as the director warned her of strong crosswinds from the west. Ethan tightened his seatbelt.

As Sandy made the final approach, Ethan could tell something was off. They were obviously drawing closer to the runway, but the whole airplane was pointing hard to the left, so that Ethan could see the runway out his side window. It reminded him of how his dog sometimes trotted sideways with his hind legs out to his side.

When they were only a few hundred yards from where they needed to touch down, Ethan realized the plane wasn't actually lined up with the runway but was far left of it. His stomach knotted; he feared they would crash and burn on the rocky ground next to the strip. But, just as they reached the runway, Sandy straightened out the nose, and the wind slid the plane onto the strip at just the perfect time. One second too soon or too late would have spelled disaster for them all, but Sandy had obviously done this before. Ethan looked over at her with admiration and joy at still being alive. She felt his gaze and simply gave him a quick wink while she taxied them toward the hangar.

After a quick leg-stretching and bathroom break, they returned to the air with a full gas tank. The bleak surroundings of Coldfoot did not look inviting enough for an extended visit. Luckily, the wind had died down sufficiently enough that it didn't much affect their takeoff. The engine of the Cessna roared as it clawed them up and over the foothills and into the barren higher peaks of the Brooks Range. It was a clear day, and they could see mountains stretching to the horizon. Broad valleys cut by extinct glaciers resembled grooves cut by ice cream scoopers. Small ponds and creeks meandered gently down many of them.

"There should be lots of snow left up there, especially this time of year," said Sandy. "The range got more snow than any year since I've lived here. This summer has been colder than usual, too, so it's not melting all that fast." After a moment, she added, "The bears are hungry, so watch your backs. It's been a lean summer for them."

Ethan pulled out his dad's compass and watched the needle quiver from the plane's vibrations.

Sandy wove her Cessna through the mountains as easily as Ethan's mom drove through their neighborhood. Calm and practiced. She obviously knew which side of the mountain passes to stay on to avoid deadly crosswinds and when to point her nose into the wind to maneuver between peaks, sometimes getting too close for Ethan's comfort. He felt so close to the mountain walls a few times that he worried a wing would drag against them if the wind abruptly changed.

He was pleased when Sandy told him they were only a few minutes out and started descending to her planned landing strip. That relief faded quickly when he realized where they were landing. The South Glacier stretched out like a twisted snow cone below a giant granite fang. Ethan's heart raced as he understood that he was finally looking at Harte Tower.

Sandy cranked a handle next to her that looked like the parking brake in Joe's old jeep. "This jack lowers the skis so we can land on that glacier," she explained over the intercom.

Ethan looked out his window and down at the landing gear, and sure enough, he could see the big skis lowering a fraction of an inch every time she cranked the handle. Once they were down, she locked them in place and continued her descent to the glacier stretched out below the south face of Harte Tower.

The enormity of the tower hit Ethan like a punch, as his mind struggled to comprehend the scale. He'd seen big mountains and climbed long routes, but none so steep and sheer. He hoped it was more straightforward than it looked, and that his grandfather hadn't led him into something he couldn't handle.

Sandy dropped the plane into the valley bottom and crept up to the glacier from a lower altitude, slowly reducing the plane's speed. When they reached the glacier, they had slowed enough that she could gently set the plane down and use the slight uphill angle and midday snow's softness to bring them to a gentle stop.

The silence was deafening when she cut the engine and burst out of her door. She opened the tail hatch and started unloading their gear into a pile.

Joe hopped out and used a foldable probe, like a ten-foot tent pole, to poke into the snow to make sure they wouldn't walk across cracks covered in snow. "Ethan, hang tight until I get this place probed for crevasses; then, you can help us stack gear." After several minutes of prodding and poking, Joe gave the okay, and Ethan jumped down to help, his boots sinking in the upper layer of slush.

"Set those bags where Joe left the probe," Sandy barked. "Gives me room to turn this bird around and take off before she sinks."

They worked quickly, and within a few minutes, the gear was stacked, and Sandy was climbing back into the plane. "See you boys right back here in ten days!"

She fired up the engine without taking any time for lengthy goodbyes. She gave a thumbs-up as she cranked up the throttle and mouthed *Good luck!* through the window. She gunned the engine, turned the plane 180 degrees, then fully opened up the throttle. Ethan cupped his hands over his ears to protect his eardrums from the deafening scream of the engine. The Cessna darted down the glacier and lifted just as it reached the firn line. Within a minute, Joe and Ethan were alone, and the valley was silent.

Ethan stood beside his grandfather, gripping the compass in his pocket, eyes fixed on the empty sky. He knew exactly where he was, but he'd never felt so lost.

2. UNTETHERED

Colorado Springs, Colorado
7 April 2017

Even the darkest winter knows its days are numbered. Ethan had every intention of going to school that morning. But it was warm for April, and the winter had been long. An electric blue sky and warm breeze off the mountains invigorated him. The snow had finally melted, and he couldn't help feeling optimistic surrounded by the vibrant green grass celebrating spring's return from either side of the sidewalk. He realized he hadn't truly felt happiness in a long time. And almost as quickly, a pang of guilt stung at his conscience. But, he decided that a perfect Colorado day was too valuable to waste inside. Besides, going to school meant confronting the reality that he was failing every one of his classes and crushing the GPA he'd worked so hard for until recently.

His high school sat at the base of the mountains, tucked between the foothills and one of the city's oldest, most overpriced neighborhoods. They had moved into a condo in the district when his dad was stationed at the nearby Army base a couple of years ago, only because the cross-country team was the best in the city, and his parents thought Ethan would receive more attention from colleges, which they were right about.

He sat below a tree next to the football field and watched the street leading to his complex for half an hour until he saw his mother's car turn out of the townhomes.

"Bye, Mom. Have a good day, Mom," Ethan mocked.

Then he walked back home, went to his room, changed into running shorts and a T-shirt, filled his hydration pack, and threw in a few snack bars. He almost forgot his climbing shoes and chalk bag. They wouldn't fit inside the pack, but he clipped them onto the outside with a carabiner.

Ethan also packed his dad's compass. It was rugged and heavy. Built from steel, back before everything was made of lightweight plastic. Army green on the outside, with a long lanyard of strong 550 cord. While he didn't really need it for this run, since it was nearly impossible to get lost in Colorado—just go downhill like his dad always told him, and you would eventually reach a road, a house, or even a city—he felt more secure having it with him. He rarely used it for navigation these days, but he felt better having it.

He ran a slow pace for the first half-mile to warm up. Cottonwoods and blooming crabapple lined the two-lane road, weaving into the foothills along a murmuring creek. An assortment of houses, some big, some old, some new, some small, all absurdly overpriced, hugged the stream below the road and cut into the hillsides above. Ethan wondered what it would take for him to afford any one of them. A comfortable place in the hills for him, or maybe one day with his girlfriend, Camila. They wouldn't need anything huge. No personal bowling alley like one of his classmates had. Just a couple of rooms and a yard, without sharing walls with strangers in a townhome his mom could barely pay the mortgage on. *Yeah, right, keep dreaming*.

The entrance to Cheyenne Canyon was only a mile away, and he made quick time. He continued up the dirt trail that skirted the creek opposite the winding two-lane road. Red gravel crunched under his shoes. Birds sang their appreciation songs of spring. Big, golden granite walls awash in the morning sun peeked from between the trees. One hundred-year-old ponderosa pines sheltered the trail from wind and sun with their enormity. Ethan's favorite trees, white firs, hid in the shaded and damp corners, their vibrant green new growth already glowing at the far reaches of each limb.

He took a steep, rutted trail up to the prominent rock pinnacle that formed the centerpiece of the canyon. More of the chasm was revealed as he climbed above the canopy of trees. Over eons, the humble North Cheyenne Creek had cut a horseshoe around the hard rock of the pinnacle, which now soared several hundred feet above its banks. He skirted along the base until reaching the bottom of a big open-book corner. He changed into his rock shoes, clipped his chalk bag behind him on the waistband of his shorts, fastened his running shoes to the pack with a carabiner, and launched up the wall.

He learned through experience that the first fifty feet or so were always the scariest when climbing—especially when free soloing. The mind can comprehend that height, but above that, it doesn't seem to grasp. The jitters always went away by the time he reached the top of the first pitch of a route.

He stopped briefly at a good stance at a secure ledge and leaned back to take in the view, letting one arm dangle at his side. A light breeze cooled him and dried his sweaty shirt. He knew his mother would kill him if she knew he climbed alone. He also knew that's why he did it. Growing up as a military brat on Army bases has a way of pushing kids one of two ways. Most succumb to the overbearing weight of authority. Keeping their hair short and their grades up. Ethan had been that way, too, until late in his junior year, when he began asking more questions than his dad liked. Other kids rebelled against the authority by skipping school and smoking weed or partying hard on the weekends. Ethan skipped school to climb without a rope.

It was a well-traveled line, and the good holds on the lower half were polished from thousands of climbers over the decades, but they were solid enough to trust. He knew every hold for his feet and every constriction of the crack to lock his finger joints into. He felt weightless yet strong. He set his feet precisely and trusted them once planted. He passed the first anchor, two iron rebar bolts eighty feet up where most parties stopped to belay, but he didn't linger. He walked to the left edge of the ledge and headed up a wide corner, stemming carefully with one foot on each side, past several more rebar eye bolts. The section was steep, but the holds were secure, and he felt safe. Another anchor came up on his right, but he didn't slow.

Fifty feet below the top of the pinnacle, the rock quality worsened to the consistency of hard-packed gravel. The locals called it the "kitty litter pitch." He cautiously distributed his weight across all four points so that one slip wouldn't send him to his death. "Steady as she goes," Ethan recalled his mother saying the last time they climbed this route together as a family. Ethan talked his parents into taking him out as often as he could last summer before his dad was sent back to Afghanistan and his mom had to pull more shifts at the hospital.

Ethan's climbing habit was too strong for him to stop when his father didn't return, so he started scrambling and bouldering with friends from the climbing gym; he even converted some of his cross-country teammates to share a rope with him in the canyon. But their calls and texts fell off when he started leaving them on "read" a few months back. He dragged Camila out with him a few times and taught her how to belay and lower him safely enough, but her fears kept her closer to the ground for now, and Ethan always looked to go higher and faster. So, he scrambled and bouldered by himself and found he wasn't as scared of the heights as others seemed to be. He knew he should find a partner to team up with, and his parents warned him not to climb too high without a rope, but he didn't like inviting conversations these days. Besides, climbing solo was just easier, and he felt safe as long as he chose routes that were well below his ability level. No need to line up a partner and figure out schedules. No need for small talk. Just him, his shoes, and a chalk bag wandering wherever he wanted. Total freedom.

Ethan looked up at the top of the pinnacle, only a few dozen feet away, then closed his eyes and envisioned himself pulling over the final moves. Divots in the rock carved from the hands and feet of climbers over the last sixty years allowed him to keep moving up. Finally, only fifteen feet from the top, he reached better rock, although much steeper. He reached and grabbed a big fin of rock that protruded from the wall, and he followed it up and to the left, scuttling his feet under the fin on small footholds. Most of his weight was on his hands at that point, and he felt the pull of the void beneath. At the end of the fin, he pulled himself up, reached high to a good handhold, and hoisted himself to the summit of the pinnacle. He had a three-hundred-and-sixty-degree view of the canyon, opening up to the flatlands of Colorado Springs. But Ethan did little more than glance around for a moment as he changed back into his running shoes and scrambled down the south ridge of the pinnacle until he could run through the deep gravel of the gully that led down to the road.

While running, he reminisced about how the route had been a great adventure a couple of years ago, before all the pull-ups and training in the climbing gym. Now, though, it was only a warm-up. He scrambled up the base of the opposite side of the pinnacle to the start of the next route. A route a step harder than the first. The stone was well-featured and trustworthy all the way, so he felt confident in his ability to finish the route without falling.

The start of the route required squeezing his body between two rock faces. He entered the dark, damp, cold crevice, where water trickled down the back. He took advantage of the tightness to lean back against the outer wall to rest when looking for holds. The chill of the rock numbed his fingertips. He soon emerged from the darkness and out into the light. The late morning sun lit up the features of the wall nicely, but he feared the sun would likely be in his eyes on the upper pitch. He considered climbing back down. He looked into the cavern beneath him and contemplated negotiating the slick holds, but the thought of slipping and bouncing between the two walls until he hit the ground scared him. The best course was to keep going up.

His grandfather's voice echoed in his mind from a conversation they'd had about climbing. "The natural human instinct for safety is to keep your ass firmly planted on the ground. However, you'll become a better climber if you change your perspective." Ethan could still see him gazing high up the cliff, as if calling his line. "You need to view the top as your safe place. When in doubt, aim for the chains."

The thought warmed him and reminded him of the good times when he was first learning to climb with his family, when Ethan and his father still had a good relationship. Before his father became so critical, making Ethan feel he could never do anything right in his father's eyes.

"Your hair is getting awful long there, buddy." "Do you plan on getting out of bed today?" "I know it's a weekend, but it's almost zero nine hundred." "Your attitude is getting out of control, son." "Keeping your grades up is your duty right now. Last time I checked, there were no scholarships for rock climbing." "Climbing is a fun hobby, but you have a god-given talent for running, so stick to cross-country."

How could my father and grandfather be so different? Ethan wondered.

He dragged his mind back to the climb. He knew better than to overthink the situation and focused on one move at a time. The holds became thinner as he ascended, so he took his time to position his toes carefully on the small edges and transfer his weight onto them as he reached for the next hold. The sticky rubber of his climbing shoes allowed him to stand securely on holds less than an inch deep. He chose his tightest shoes that morning with this section in mind, exchanging comfort for sports-car-like precision.

The crux of the climb was a small roof lined with tiny

holds that he had led through several times with his mom and dad. The section required thoughtful movement and delicate footwork; he knew rushing through it could lead to disaster. Although excitement triggered a panic response deep in his brain, he managed to suppress it. He pushed away thoughts of what his death would mean for his mother and Camila. He needed to be fully present; otherwise, there would be no future to consider. He took a deep breath and executed each move like a martial artist performing a well-practiced kata.

Twenty feet of easy climbing would put him at the top, with nothing but an easy jog out of the canyon, and he'd be home in time to scarf a sandwich and clean up before his mom got home from work. Maybe he would go to Camila's and hang out if her mom and stepdad weren't home.

He was moving too fast to notice the thin layer of dirt that had washed onto the final holds during the last rainstorm. His left foot slipped off before he had a good left hand on the wall, and his whole body pivoted off his right foot and right hand like a creaking barn door. He palmed his left hand against the rock to steady himself and got both feet firmly planted. His heart beat out of his chest, and he took a moment to catch his breath and calm himself. He didn't look down at the void below, but he felt its pull.

Maybe I am out of control.

3. BASE CAMP

Brooks Range, Alaska
July 2017
10 days before pickup

PACKING LIST

Camping
Two-layer tent
Cooking tent
Pan, pot, utensils
Camp stove
Matches and 2 large lighters
2 sleeping bags
Bear spray
.44 magnum pistol with 12 rounds ammunition (for base camp)

Gear on climb
1 climbing rope, 200 ft
Climbing shoes, 1 pair each
Double set of cams
Set of stoppers
Dozen slings, 2 carabiners each
Belay/rappel device
3 locking carabiners each
2 thin cords, 20 ft each
Small portable cook stove with canister

1 small cooking pot
1 light cup (Joe's coffee)
2 titanium sporks
1 small lighter
1 space blanket (Ethan's pack)
1 rain shell jacket each
Rain pants, 1 pair each
1 light puffy insulated jacket each
1 helmet each
1 satellite phone (Joe's pack)
Compass and map (Ethan)

Glacier travel
Lightweight crampons, 2 pair
2 light ice axes
4 medium ice screws

The South Glacier pooled in the palm of a giant outstretched hand beneath the great thumb of Harte Tower and slid gradually, imperceptibly, toward the curled fingers of the outer Kavluk basin. Its ice melted at the lower elevations, cutting its escape between the forefinger and middle finger, and merged with icy tributaries snaking north to join polar waters. Ethan felt like this hand in which he stood, which loomed above him, around him, could easily ball up into a fist and snuff him out for good. Rendering his tiny existence embarrassingly insignificant.

"Don't go explorin' too far from the tent without tyin' in," Joe said. "Dropping in a crevasse would be a bad way to go."

The guide shop in Talkeetna had pictures of scary crevasses, and Joe had given him a lecture about them. They formed when the hard ice of the glaciers crept ever so slowly down the valleys, up and over bumps in the rocky valley floor. The upper few hundred feet were susceptible to cracks, some as small as a few inches, while others could grow to be fifty feet across and several hundred feet deep. The winter snows buried the smaller ones, leaving dangerous trap doors waiting for an unsuspecting climber. The most experienced guides knew where to look for them and had good intuition for where the danger was, but even they were just making educated guesses. The early trips, they said, were the most dangerous. Strong winds blew snow all winter, usually covering even the most enormous crevasses so thoroughly they were impossible to detect. The warmer summer temps would eventually melt out the precarious snow bridges, making the crevasses more noticeable. However, this was a double-edged sword. Teams in May often glided across the covered crevasses without knowing the dangers lurking below, but the teams in July had their work cut out for them because they had to weave around gaping chasms.

Scarier yet were the descriptions of what would happen if your team failed to catch your fall. A drop to the hardened ice at the bottom could cause serious internal injuries and broken bones, which could turn deadly if not treated soon. And, if you were not extracted quickly enough, hypothermia could take you. Ethan shuddered at the thought of being squeezed between two icy walls, creeping lower into the frozen bowels with each breath while his broken limbs lost feeling to frostbite.

Ethan scanned the surrounding area. In every direction was bright, white snow that hurt his eyes, even when filtered by his dark glacier goggles. He didn't see any signs of crevasses nearby, but he had no desire to chance it.

"You don't have to worry about me strolling off by myself anytime soon."

Joe laughed. "Good to hear. One year we guided this

CEO from California who didn't like to follow directions. Thought he knew everything. We woke up one morning and couldn't find him anywhere. I got my rookie guide to rope up with me, and we followed a pair of tracks leading away from camp over a bump, and there he was. Only his head and arms above the hole. Ass dangling in space. Woulda been a goner if he hadn't spread his arms so quick. We got a rope around his shoulder and pulled him out, but it's hard to tell how much longer he woulda held. Glaciers are no place for a maverick."

"Sandy mentioned they had a big snow year. Are you worried about avalanches out here?" Ethan thought he had a serious question. He knew very little about avalanches or what caused them, but it seemed to be something they should consider, given they were literally camped on snow and ice.

Joe laughed. "A month or two ago, maybe. Don't really have to worry about that this time'a year." Joe saw the uncertainty in Ethan's face. "This glacier faces south and gets plenty of sun. Anything that was gonna slough off woulda done so by now. Might be different if we were planning somethin' else."

Joe busied himself with setting up the camp and directing Ethan to help. First, they found a fairly level site and laid out their big cooking tent over the snow, then dragged a ski pole around it to trace its circular edge. Next, they pulled the tent aside and put on their skis to walk around, flatten, and pack the snow inside the big circle they had outlined for their tent platform. Joe then grabbed one of the snow shovels and cut out enough snow to create entrance steps going down into the circle. Next, he cut out most of the other snow in the circle into one-foot cubes and had Ethan stack the blocks outside the line, resembling the igloo blocks Ethan had seen in kids' picture books of Eskimos. When they were done, the glacier snow that Joe had strategically left behind formed seats and a raised kitchen table. The floor was now three or four feet below the surface. When they put their bottomless cooking tent over the hole and erected the poles, they had a perfect shelter to regulate the night's temperatures. The snow block walls around the tent would, Joe promised him, divert the strong alpine winds that could lift even the most carefully staked-down tents and blow them a mile away. Joe even dug a hole about fifty feet from the tent to use as a refrigerator for fresh vegetables and meat. He marked it with the probe so they could always find it.

"We'll just stretch out the pads and sleeping bags at night after dinner and sleep right here across the floor." Joe stretched his arms out to signify the space they needed. "We'll keep the small back-up tent in its bag in case we need it. Hopefully we won't."

Ethan thought about asking if he could stay in the small tent. He was already a little tired of Joe's gruff demands in camp, and it had only been a few hours. *Sleeping apart, instead of packed together on the floor of a snowy grave, might be good for us both,* he thought. But he decided not to ask.

"Why do we have two foam pads and two inflatable pads to sleep on?"

"Well, tell me what you're gonna do if you only have an air pad and you puncture it, or burn a hole in it with a hot stove or a pot. The foam is a backup. It'll keep you from freezing to death. Lying flat on ice, even on a warm night, that'll likely kill you by morning."

Unlike most people who retire, Joe looked fit and

hardened from work, and there was still a youthful sparkle in his eye even at the crisp age of fifty-seven. He had the appearance of someone who could build or fix most things. He was lean and weathered, with large hands tanned and worn from his time in the woodshop and exposed to the elements of Alaska. Even on warm days, he wore long sleeves and denim pants and an old pair of leather boots warped and whittled in a pattern unique to him alone. Ethan always felt a special connection to his grandfather, as if there was some cosmic link between them that his father had not been privileged to share. They obviously had their differences, but he felt they had a similar outlook on life.

Ethan did think the old man was a little too old-fashioned on some things, though. Joe had picked up Ethan from the Anchorage airport in his ancient '94 Jeep Cherokee. "I wondered if this thing was still running," Ethan had said as he swung his big bag into the back.

"Oh yeah, I don't drive that many miles, and I take good care of her."

"Ever think of trading it in for something newer?"

"Not at all. I don't want any of that new junk they put in those things. I can't stand all the bells and alarms going off every damn time you don't put on your seatbelt or do something it doesn't like. Besides, the new ones don't come with a tape player, so I wouldn't have anything to listen to."

Ethan held up his smartphone and waved it. "You could get one of theeeese. I can get any song I want anytime."

"Yeah, but it don't sound like the old days, kid."

The more Ethan embraced climbing, the more he looked up to Joe, who had been a high school teacher who moonlighted as a mountain guide on Denali for more than twenty summers, running one "trip" each summer that lasted about four weeks. Joe drove his family to Talkeetna on the last day of school every May and spent the next week organizing gear and rehearsing glacier travel and rescue skills with his clients before heading up into the range with them for a summit bid on the continent's highest mountain. After that trip, he would spend a month with his wife, Katherine, or, when his kids were still living at home, they would take climbing trips into the Chugach or go canoeing on the Yukon River until school started in the fall. It was a great summer tradition, and Ethan's dad spoke fondly of those times.

Joe's family was a little surprised when Joe stopped guiding trips on Denali a few years back when he reached his early fifties. He told them he felt too old to sleep on the glacier and to burden his back and knees with the heavy loads needed to climb it. Instead, he spent the summers at North American Mountain Guides' basecamp office, helping with organization and everyday operations. The way he explained it, he liked utilizing his hard-earned knowledge of the mountain to help others while still being able to sleep in his own bed every night, which would hopefully squeeze a few more years from his well-worn knees and back. He knew intimately what the climbers needed and how to set them up for the best chance of success. Some of the new guides were relatively young men and women who flew up from the lower forty-eight, sometimes with no experience in the intimidating Alaska Range. He tried his best to impart some wisdom to them and instill a healthy respect for the mountain's power in their hearts. He knew the mountain could build dangerous storms within minutes, quickly killing an unprepared team. He was always just a satellite phone call away when a guide needed advice or help.

"I'm setting the bear spray right here by the entrance," Joe said. He walked over to his gear bag and dropped the pistol on top. "I'll keep the peashooter. Better I keep that one to myself."

"You think we'll need those up here?"

"Possible. I've seen grizz tracks headin' into the Ruth Gorge before. They'll go just about anywhere if they smell grub. We got plenty of that around here."

Ethan took an uncomfortable look around the camp. He guessed it was only about a half-mile or less to the edge of the glacier, which wouldn't take a bear long to travel. The huge claws that he'd seen on a stuffed grizzly in Talkeetna would probably work about as well as steel crampons.

"Is there anything we can do to keep them away?"

Joe laughed and slapped Ethan on the shoulder. "Don't worry, kid, as long as we're milling about in camp, they'll likely keep their distance. And, if it makes you feel any better, the other options I gave you had even bigger bears than we'd find up here."

Ethan thought back to that decision, just a couple of weeks ago. One day, after Ethan had finished sorting ropes by length, Joe had brought him into the meeting room to discuss their plans for July. Joe had spread his map of Alaska across the big table where teams discussed strategy. The state looked like an elephant's head sticking out of Canada, with its tusks piercing the Pacific Ocean and threatening to gore Asia. The Brooks Mountain range stretched across the northern latitudes, from the Canadian border on the east to the Bering Sea in the west. The commanding Alaska Range punched right up in the middle of the state, with the lower Chugach hugging the coast to the south. These mountains marked the northern terminus of a continuous upheaval that ran along the spines of both American continents.

"Alright, young man, let's put pen to paper and figure out what we're doing with the rest of our summer." Joe had looked around the map as if finding his bearings. "I'm gonna throw you a couple ideas, but it just depends on what you want."

Ethan had been all ears. Alaska was enormous, and he had felt a bit overwhelmed by the urge to explore it all, while also knowing it would take many lifetimes to do so.

"Behind door one is a thirty-mile backpacking traverse in the Lake Clark." Joe had pointed to the labeled national park section on the map. "We'd get to see Proenneke's cabin on this one."

Ethan had tilted his head, revealing a piqued interest. He'd seen the videos of the old man building a cabin in the wilderness with his own hands and a few tools. He'd wondered what that would be like. To cut all ties with society and its demands. No worries about college, or careers, or affording a house in an expensive neighborhood with good schools. Maybe settle down with Camila in the middle of the mountains and raise kids to rely on nothing more than their own two hands.

"Option two," Joe had continued, "is a big rock climb in the Brooks Range, up north."

"How big?"

"About ten pitches, I'd guess."

"Winner!" Ethan had declared.

"Wow. That easy, huh?"

Ethan had smiled and shrugged his shoulders.

"Kid, I think you've been bitten by the climbing bug,"

Joe had said with admiration in his eyes. "Fortunately, I know a good chunk of stone up there to turn you loose on. But just remember, the goal of your first Alaskan expedition is to survive your first Alaskan expedition."

Joe returned his focus to the map. "Here's where we are now," he had instructed, pointing his thin finger at Talkeetna, "and here's where we're going." His finger slowly worked its way up the road system to Fairbanks.

"Once we get to Fairbanks, we'll buy some fresh groceries and wait for the next bush pilot willing to get us into Gates of the Arctic."

"Will that be a problem?" Ethan had asked hesitantly.

"Oh, no, it shouldn't be a problem at all. Alaska has more pilots than Colorado has hipsters."

Joe had then unraveled another map on top of the roadmap. It was zoomed in to a much smaller scale, and Ethan could make out steep cliffs and peaks using the topographical lines. His dad had taught him how to use these maps, and he had seen them often while growing up on a military base.

Joe then pointed to an area on the map labeled Kavluk Cirque. "These tight, round circles in the middle are Harte Tower, and we'll be flying into this valley right below it and landing on this here glacier below the south face." Joe had used his fingers to fly in like the plane would need to. "We'll set up base camp there and wait for good weather for the climb. As soon as it looks clear, we'll take the south face to the summit, then come right back down the way we came. We'll have ten days before the pilot picks us back up to return to Fairbanks."

Ethan looked at the map and thought of something but was unsure whether to ask.

"What is it?"

"The west face looks less steep and shorter, so why aren't we going down that way?"

Joe had nodded in half agreement. "Well, that's a good point, but I'll tell you why we're not. I heard from an excellent source that an Italian team climbed this face two summers ago, which means they must have left good anchors to rappel from all the way back down the route, so we shouldn't have to leave our gear. Also, that would put on on the North Glacier, which is heavily glaciated, so the crevasses would be more dangerous to cross. It's not impossible, but it'd be rowdier for sure. And once you get down the glacier..." Joe had pointed to a prominent ridge below the tower's east face, represented by tightly grouped topographical lines. It was shaped like a long rib bone. "This wall here is a couple hundred feet high and several miles long. I'm sure we could climb over it if we had to, but I'd rather not bother with that."

"And, just what does Kavluk mean? What language is that?" Ethan had asked.

"I believe it's an Inupiaq term for jagged peaks."

***

After dinner, they stretched out on their inflatable sleeping pads on the glacier and contemplated the route. Harte Tower soared above them, and their chosen line, the south face, stood out in shadows as the sun traversed to the west in its continuous summer ellipses.

It was nearly 10:00 in the evening, but the sun was still high in the sky. And, due to the highly reflective snow surrounding them, dark glacier glasses were necessary even at night. Even brief periods without glasses can result in snow blindness. The intense light can burn the corneas of the eyeballs and make it feel like sand has been poured into the eye sockets. They lathered all exposed skin with thick sun lotion and wore sun hats, hoodies, and gloves whenever possible to avoid painful sunburn while on the glacier.

Ethan could now identify the wall's weaknesses in the contrast between shade and light. Cracks and ledges appeared, giving Ethan new confidence that he could climb the wall.

Joe lay back with his hands behind his head as if in deep thought. "Well, the line appears to be ice-free and pretty darn dry. I say we hike up with our gear tomorrow and start climbing. We'll take the small stove with us to brew soup and coffee on the route. That ledge about three-fourths up the tower looks like a good spot."

"About how long do you think it will take us to get to the top?"

Joe took a deep and contemplative breath. "The hardest pitches should clock in around 5.9, I hear, which you and I'll be able to handle just fine, so I'd say about forty-five minutes per pitch, times ten pitches, so we should plan for about seven or eight hours to the top, plus about half that to get back down. We'll bring enough food and water for twelve hours. That should do it, I figure."

"Should we bring a sleeping bag in case something happens?" asked Ethan.

"Why wouldn't we just lower back down if the weather rolls in?" Joe said, swatting down Ethan's concerns. "We should be able to retreat to camp if it starts rainin'. Definitely bring your rain shell and puffy, though. That'll make it more comfortable in the event of bad rain or snow. Rain pants, too."

Ethan pursed his lips but didn't disagree openly.

"The thing is, Ethan, there's more safety in going light

and climbing faster than there is in going heavier and moving slower. If we bring a tent and sleeping bag, those pitches that should be easy for us will feel much harder with the extra weight. We'll burn more energy, which means we'll need more food and water, which is more weight. We'll also need more gas for the stove to cook more food, which is more weight. Ya see where I'm going with this?"

That night, the air turned cold, and clouds condensed around the tower. Short bursts of freezing rain blasted their tent.

Joe rolled over in the middle of the night. "That's likely snow up on the tower. Hopefully, the sun'll come out quick and dry it up for us."

Ethan retreated deep into his bag and tried to clear his mind for sleep.

You're a long way from Colorado.

4. GUTTED

Talkeetna, Alaska

8 April 2017

—Katherine—

Katherine saw Joe looking out the kitchen window as she pulled up to the cabin. His long, unkempt, gray hair bordered his thinning face. The dark shadows and cold eyes spoke of his grief. Gravel roads made sneaking up to the house an impossibility. She instantly felt a pang of guilt for realizing she had been intentionally avoiding her husband, the love of her life. But she had needed the day for herself. She needed a brief respite from the dark cloud of loss that had shadowed their lives since the call in November. Their only son lost to a never-ending war for no reason they could comprehend.

Though the loss gutted her, it seemed even more devastating for Joe. He never did well with change. The timing of the loss, coming just months after they had both retired from their teaching jobs in Anchorage and moved full-time to their Talkeetna cabin, compounded the shock. Their legs had been swept from under them as they were adjusting to new currents.

That morning, she skipped breakfast and took her

fishing pole to the river to spend a few hours alone on the ice. Fresh fish for lunch would also be a welcome change. She left a note for Joe, who had taken up the habit of sleeping late, and drove through their quiet village to the river. Her family never liked fishing, so it was her personal escape. Her quiet time. She would have enjoyed fishing with Joe, but he could never sit still for that long, nor could their son, Chris. Her daughter liked it, but she now lived far away in Minnesota with her own family. Katherine often brought her children down to the river when they were kids. They spent most summers at the cabin while Joe guided climbing expeditions in Denali National Park.

For Katherine, staring down a hole in the ice was a form of meditation similar to watching the jumping flames of a campfire. The ice spoke to her more than usual this morning, cracking and adjusting to the warmth of April and its swelling flows. Each day brought more light, and more volume, than the last. Soon, the raging torrents of meltwater from the big mountains would rip apart this serene, white cover and expose the turbulent river, temporarily contained just a few inches beneath her feet.

She heard the back door open as she walked up. Joe held it open for her with one arm, cup of coffee in the other, steam rising in the cold air. He looked alert, as if he'd been up for a while.

"How many you got there?"

She could see the corner of his mouth almost attempting to smile.

"Three rainbows."

"Nice work."

"They're not very big, but they're enough for lunch."

He sat down at the small kitchen table and watched her work. She set the fish down on the counter next to the sink and sharpened the fillet knife.

"Be careful on the river this time of year. Breakup's coming any day now, and you don't want to be sittin' out there when all hell breaks loose."

Katherine put on her left-handed filet glove and slid a fish into position. "I went early enough for it to still be cold." She inserted the tip of the knife into the belly skin and sliced up toward the neck, then pulled out the innards and slid them into the sink.

"Julia called your phone while you were out. I tried ignorin' it, but she kept trying. So I answered."

She lined up the blade next to the gill plate and cut down to the backbone, then turned and sliced toward the tail, popping the thin ribs as she went. "How's the boy doing? Julia was worried sick about him the last time we talked."

Joe sipped his coffee. "Not great. He got suspended."

"Again?" She turned to look at him.

Joe nodded. "Skippin' class."

She shook her head while turning the fish over, repeated the process, and stacked the filet on top of the other in a bowl. "I don't know what she's going to do with that boy."

"Well, Julia has an idea."

"And what's that?"

"She wants to send him up here."

"With us?" Katherine looked back at him again.

"Yup."

She grabbed another fish. "What do you think about that?" She truly wondered how he would react to the news. Even after decades of sharing a life, he was still a mystery. A man of contradictions. His students loved him for being the laid-back teacher whose class was almost impossible to fail. But in the mountains, he was a perfectionist. A task master who lived by a strict code of responsibility to the team.

"Hell, I don't know. I don't mind, I guess. We'll see what he decides to do."

Katherine took that response as a good sign. Joe needed interaction with people again. He couldn't hide in the cabin for the rest of his life. Although she knew he would do just that if allowed to. Growing up in the hills and hollers of Arkansas molded him into a hermit from an early age, and he never did well in big gatherings. She remembered how awkward he was in his first semester of college at the University of Alaska, where they had met. He looked out of place, like he belonged in the woods with an axe in his hand. But she soon found that he knew his way around a library better than most. They both majored in English and had dreamed of earning doctorates and professoring at renowned colleges. When Joe proposed to her during their senior year, they decided teaching public school would be easier for a young family. With Joe's background in construction, which he worked to pay his tuition, he landed a job teaching shop while Katherine finished her elementary credentials.

"I told her I could get him some gofer work at the guide shop for a few weeks. It's hard to find help out here anyway," he added.

"Gofer?" Katherine asked.

"Hey kid, go-fer this, go-fer that."

Katherine smiled. "That's good. Although I think he'll be bored to death in this little town if he's staying the whole summer. You two should take a climbing trip."

He chewed on the idea for a minute. "Well, I wouldn't be able to break away until July at the soonest. Too warm to fly into the big mountains with him then. Glaciers will be melted out, so it'd be too dangerous."

"Sure, but there are other places. Besides, he's more of a rock climber than a mountaineer. You can do that in the lower ranges. What about the Kavluks? You always wanted to take Chris there." She had to stop herself from getting too excited about the trip and tipping him against it. She knew she had to let him come to his own conclusion. He was too stubborn-headed to be pushed into anything.

"Yeah, I always wanted to get back in there. Good rock. Low enough altitude. Still glaciers there, but smaller than the monsters in the Alaska Range."

"Well, just think about it."

She finished the third trout and swept the carcass into the trash can. Then she washed the filets under cold water. "Have you thought anymore about talking to that gal in town?"

She could feel the coldness in his silence. Their son was just like him in that way. Never sharing feelings or fears, or perhaps too humble to make a big deal of them. They were polar opposites in many other characteristics, though. Joe was philosophical, whereas Chris saw the world in black and white, right and wrong. One an artist at heart, the other a soldier. Both capable of throwing themselves into a task without hesitation or fear of the outcome. She supposed some would call that bravery.

"No. I guess I haven't."

"I hear she's good. We're lucky to even have a grief counselor this far from Anchorage."

Joe stared out the window, watching soggy clumps of snow melt from the trees. On the table, just beyond his now cold cup of coffee, was a small, black box holding his son's Silver Star.

"I don't need to pay somebody to tell me how I feel."

5. THE PING PONG BALL

Brooks Range, Alaska
July 2017
9 days until pickup

A thick, cold fog enveloped their camp by morning. They stepped outside the tent to look around but couldn't see more than a hundred yards.

"Looks like we're inside a ping pong ball, right," Joe said as more of a statement than a question. "Guess we're tent-bound today. Maybe tomorrow we can head up if it clears out."

They spent the day mostly lounging around in the tent, reading or telling stories. Ethan told Joe all about the best climbs he had done with his dad, and Joe seemed to listen.

Ethan didn't really take to climbing until his family was stationed at Fort Sill in Oklahoma. On weekends, the family took the short drive to the Wichita Mountains. They often camped for the whole weekend and climbed both days when his dad wasn't deployed or training. He had turned fourteen that first summer in Oklahoma and was curious about everything his parents were.

Chris spent a lot of time with Ethan, teaching him how to place and remove climbing gear in the granite cracks. At first, Chris found spots at the base of the cliff and instructed Ethan to build an anchor of two to three pieces of protection. He showed him how to pick the right-sized cam and delicately place it in the crack so the trigger could be reached easily enough to pull the spring-loaded lobe to retrieve it. He also made Ethan work on finding natural constrictions to place stoppers. Once he mastered placing the gear on the ground, Chris sent him up routes to do it live.

Ethan's mother taught him how to climb with grace and style. Chris relied on his strength and bravado to get up the wall, whereas Julia was thoughtful and delicate. She liked finding the right moves and angles to unlock the route instead of throwing herself at it. It took a particular perspective and patience that Chris lacked. Ethan watched and tried to learn from her when she climbed.

"Sorry, I'm rambling about climbing again. Camila says I do that a lot."

"Not at all, kid. Love to hear it. Reminds me of when I was young and enthusiastic. Now I'm just old and jaded." Joe peered out the door of the tent, hoping to see the clouds lifting.

"I'm sure you get excited if you're still doing it."

"Oh yeah, when I get to explore a new place, I feel like a kid in a candy shop again. But, it's different now."

"How?"

"Oh, I guess it just feels good to be good at something. Places like this..." Joe swept his hand around at the arc of mountains and walls of granite just beyond the thin fabric door of the tent as if inviting them into the conversation. "This kind of place struck more fear than pleasure when I was young. But now, I feel comfortable here."

Ethan knew the fear Joe was referring to. He had felt a palpable fear since they landed and the plane flew away. He'd pushed away thoughts of what he would do if he didn't have his grandfather here to keep him alive. "Why did you keep going to places like this if you were scared?"

"That's the challenge. Hell, it's likely the same reason you're here. But if you're patient and put in the work, then you'll feel more at home here than walkin' down a city street."

Joe brewed coffee throughout the day. He was the kind of guy who leaned on caffeine all day long and could even drink a cup right before bedtime and still go straight to sleep.

Ethan brought an old copy of a mountaineering manual to brush up on some of the skills he might need. He also spent time looking through pictures and videos on his phone. Like selfies with Camila, or ones she texted him when she was in a silly mood. She could be so goofy. That was maybe what he liked the most about her. More than liked. An out-of-focus picture of her looking out at their graying city from a dirt road in the foothills ripped him right off the glacier. He could smell her perfume. Hear the wind that blew her long, brown hair. See the curve of her hips when she lay beside him that evening his mom picked up an extra shift at the hospital.

And his face grew red as he thought about how embarrassed he was the first time he leaned in to kiss her in an empty hallway between classes, and she stepped back, surprised, and laughed at him playfully. He didn't think she would ever talk to him again, but there she was waiting for him to walk home after school.

He brought up their text chain and scrolled back in time. Her words, so direct and to the point.

"I don't mind waiting if I know you're serious about us."

Camila had been there for him. Before his dad died, and even more so afterward. During the dark times. She knew when to give him space and when to force him outside for a walk with her or a run to the canyon. She invited him to the climbing gym and asked him to teach her how to tie in, even though she didn't like climbing much at all. But her superpower was her ability to make him want to be better without lecturing or guilting him. He somehow just knew she expected more of him, and that made him wish he could do better. Rising to the challenge was well within his ability before his dad died. He struggled with it afterward, never feeling up to the task.

"It's just that my dad told me he would help me get an apartment in Dallas and I could go to the community college there."

Before, they bonded over homework. Her drive came from somewhere deep down. A need to be perfect as a daughter of immigrants. Ethan's drive came from fear of disappointing his father. Once that fear was removed, his ambitions at school evaporated, and they lost that academic connection. He didn't work on other ways to connect, though she did.

"I like you a lot. I just need to know you feel the same."

Fighting for her meant committing to an idea of himself he couldn't visualize. And if he couldn't commit to himself, then she was better off without him. He was doing her a favor by letting her move to Dallas without him.

He shook his head and returned to looking at his photos. He wanted to look through his family's shared album of climbing photos, but they wouldn't load without a signal. He took a break from scrolling for a few hours midday to charge his phone on the small solar panel unit. Joe read a copy of *Lonesome Dove*, his third time reading it.

The rain picked up, pattering the big tent. An explosion of rockfall echoed from somewhere in the valley. It started with a single boulder sliding off its perch and crashing against ledges and walls. Soon, more boulders, large and small, joined in, creating a cacophonous symphony of demolition that thundered off the surrounding cliffs, making it impossible to pinpoint the source of the violence. The dampness of the suffocating fog amplified each clash of stone. Ethan felt a surge of uncertainty about his safety, and his body responded with an adrenaline rush, triggering a fight-or-flight response.

Joe sat drinking coffee from a thin titanium cup, apparently unfazed by the calamity unfolding in the shadows surrounding them. He had developed a sixth sense of danger over his years in the mountains. "Not close enough to bother us. Must be raining hard up higher. Rain tends to loosen things up," Joe summarized, using a logic similar to that of an inner-city kid assessing whether a bully's threats were genuine or just empty words. "Katherine never could get used to the movement of the big mountains. That's why she stays down low. I tried to tell her it's more dangerous down there with all the grizz and moose, but she does just fine with those somehow. I'd rather get the chop in the mountains than gnawed on by a bear, myself."

"How old were you two when you got married?"

"Twenty-two. Right outta college."

Ethan shook his head. "I don't think I could do that."

"Think. You kids think too damn much these days." Joe winked. "That's your problem. Sometimes you just gotta do the thing."

Okay, boomer. Here we go again. Ethan had learned to tolerate these jabs at his generation over the last few weeks. He wondered if old people had always ranted like this, or if it was a new trend. He imagined cavemen sitting around a fire, complaining about lazy kids these days who couldn't even kill a lion by themselves. His grandmother said Joe had grown more cantankerous since they'd moved away from the city, and she was beginning to think the isolation was getting to him. Ethan entertained the thought of responding. Maybe pointing out that most of the world's problems were the result of decisions made by older generations, not his own. No one Ethan's age had ever started a war, to his knowledge. Still, he thought it better to avoid starting a pointless argument. Besides, he knew the old man was still grieving, and that must be affecting his attitude.

Another volley of rocks tumbled from the same direction as before. They perked up their heads and listened for signs of danger, but the slide sounded smaller than the last.

"It's not for everybody. Marriage. Pretty rare to get hitched young these days. If at all."

"Maybe you were just lucky."

Joe shook his head. "Luck had nothin' to do with it. Life hit faster back then. You kids have more time to breathe. We got thrown out of the nest a lot younger and wanted someone by our side in case times got tough."

"Having that support is probably nice," said Ethan.

"Yup." Joe readjusted the sleeping pad he had folded beneath him, using it as a seat. "Behind every successful man is a woman rolling her eyes."

Ethan laughed. "Did you just know you were right for each other?"

"We thought so back then. Now I think we were just two broken kids trying to be whole." Joe said, then peered out of the corner of his eyes at Ethan. "Your mother says there's a girl."

A sheepish smile from Ethan gave an answer but also made clear he wasn't ready to talk about it. Not there at least.

"Well, I suppose I'll have to get the details from your grandmother. I'm sure she got it out of you."

Ethan tried to nap during the day. He had tossed and turned all night, worried about the climb. He always struggled to sleep before a new climb, especially when the route was longer than what he'd done before. He seemed to imagine everything that could go wrong: ropes breaking, rocks falling, random snowstorms, and lightning.

He asked Joe how he slept so soundly the night before a climb.

"Oh, I guess you just get used to it. Or maybe you do something scary enough times, and it loses its teeth," Joe said.

"I was up all night thinking about everything that could go wrong," Ethan admitted.

"I remember doing the same thing when I was young. That just means you're smart. Your mind wants you to live, and that's a good thing. To survive something dangerous, you have to start by imagining all the ways it can kill you. Then, you work backward and see if you can plan around each of the dangers."

"But, what if you can't...plan around the dangers?"

Joe laughed. "That just means you need a little more mileage. Keep asking questions and listen for the answers. Soon enough, you'll be able to handle what comes your way. You can sleep hard on good plannin'."

6. THE RESCUE

Denali National Park, Alaska
June 1997

—Joe—

His team decided to let the Brits die. At least that's how Joe saw it and would always see it. For three days, they watched for glimpses of the two climbers through the storm that raged on Mount Hunter, the third-highest peak in the Alaska Range. A few times, the clouds rose enough for Greg to spot them with his scope, but only briefly. The upper walls of the enormous mountains surrounding them were concealed by clouds. He made out one of them in a red jacket hanging lifelessly at the end of the rope at the bottom of the McNerthney Ice Dagger, all but confirming their worst fears. Joe had climbed the route a few years prior and knew the dangers of that section intimately. He remembered the sinking feeling in his gut as he led that very pitch, constantly eyeing the icy blocks looming above.

"Was it Liam in the red jacket?" Greg asked.

Greg then spotted the girl perched on an ice ledge at the top of the pitch, at the entrance to the Tamara Traverse, which led around to the right to avoid continuing up the gulley below the mushrooms. She appeared to be alive.

"I think the girl's in her sleeping bag."

They could see it all playing out in their minds. Charlotte was the stronger climber, just off a strong winter season in the French Alps, so of course, she would be leading that section. She would have wanted to move fast through this part because it had killed before. They had all doubted her choice in partners. Her boyfriend, Liam, was a newb and clearly in over his head. They had joked about how she would have to drag him up the wall.

Charlotte and Liam were caught on the most exposed portion of the route, climbing below the "death mushroom" that always formed under the giant roofs when cascading snow coursing down the face collided with updrafts and swirled under the colossal eyebrows until accumulating into white tumors weighing several tons. Eventually, the weight would break the bonds between rock and ice, and large chunks, sometimes the entire giant snowball, would break off and crash down the wall below.

The small crowd of American climbers around him peered up at the massive wall of black rock laced with ribbons of ice. But seeing something as small as a man on that goliath of a mountain was hopeless without Greg's scope. Greg squinted harder to see through the dim light, hoping against hope to catch a glimpse of life-affirming movement, but the clouds crept back in and obscured his view once again. Within minutes, the entire north buttress of Hunter was engulfed.

The Kahiltna basecamp had a dozen parties camped out, mostly Denali hopefuls geared up to attempt the grueling West Buttress route. Joe had flown in with Greg and Roger to attempt a new route on the short, though technical, ridge between Hunter and Denali. They had thought it wise to stick with a smaller objective since they had a short weather window the week before their clients arrived. Katherine had taken the kids on a raft trip while he was in the range. The storm had arrived early and hadn't stopped for three days. They shoveled snow off the tent in shifts to keep it from collapsing. Roger had tried to talk the Brits into waiting for a better forecast, but they brushed him off. They'd be at the top of the wall in forty hours, they said. But fate would only give them twelve.

"We can't just let her die, goddammit," Joe insisted.

Roger shook him by the shoulders, gripping the rigid Gore-Tex in his big hands. "We all have kids at home, Joe. They knew what they were gambling. They made their choice."

Joe's eyes searched the camp for anyone he could rally for the cause, but he quickly realized the three of them were the only ones capable of mounting a rescue, and no planes would arrive with cloud cover this low. A rescue would require a degree of skill well beyond the basic mountaineering fitness to snowshoe up Denali with a heavy sled. Hunter's legendary north buttress stood four thousand feet tall, nearly vertical, and was webbed with steep, technical ice.

Joe slid out of his sleeping bag around midnight. He hadn't slept a wink. The air was cold and damp, but it had stopped snowing hours before. The upper half of Hunter hid in the clouds in the dim light. He knew in his bones that the snow had stopped up high. He felt it. *A little bit of fog and clouds can't kill me.*

He remembered, vividly, the Brits walking by, elated to start their climb. She was all smiles. Her boyfriend, not so much. Joe had asked her about the small, stuffed tiger cub hanging from a key chain loop on the back of her pack.

"My dad gave it to me for good luck. He always called me his tiger cub."

Joe wondered how her parents would take the news. He could picture an older couple taking the call in their cottage in the English countryside.

He quietly rounded up his gear and stuffed layers and some food into his backpack. He threw in his puffy jacket. He didn't bother to bring his sleeping bag. Continuous movement would keep him warm. And, if Liam was already dead, as it appeared he was, then Joe could use Liam's sleeping bag when he reached them. If he needed it. It was a cold calculation, but every ounce counted, and he'd have to plan smart if he was to be successful.

Joe stepped into his skis and skinned out of camp without waking anyone. Although he suspected his partners heard him but just decided not to fight him anymore. Perhaps they were glad he had chosen to head up. Perhaps it eased their consciences knowing someone was trying.

The lazy glacier steepened near the base of the wall, and Joe slid out of his skis and stabbed each firmly, perpendicularly, into the snow for the glacier to hold until his return. He donned crampons, pulled his axes off his pack, flaked the rope out loosely, and tied into one end. He brought a few ice screws to belay himself through any tough sections, but he didn't intend to do that if the ice was thick enough. He often dragged a rope from his harness when solo climbing to trick his mind into believing he was being belayed by a partner. A placebo of safety.

Before crossing the gaping bergschrund onto the wall, he put on his headphones under his fleece hat and pushed play on his Walkman. He typically listened to what his teenage son called "hippy music" when he was in the range, but for this trip, Chris had made him a mixtape of his favorite rock songs.

The blaring horns and deep bass of *House of Pain* filled his ears as he sized up the short, overhanging ice wall that led to the lower flows. He opened his jacket once again and turned the volume up as loud as it could go. The deafening cacophony blocked out the wind's unsettling howl and sealed him up in a capsule of invincibility. He matched his flow to the rhythm.

Boom, boom.

Swing, swing.

Boom, boom.

Kick, kick.

Joe followed the path of the Brits, swinging his axes into the same holes and kicking the same divots to save energy and move faster. The imaginary pull of the space below weakened the higher he climbed. He focused on the beat and the efficiency of his movement. He analyzed each swing of his picks as they entered the ice. The solid thud traveling up his arm told him to trust the placement. His tools and crampons were old friends with whom he had bonded over many battles. They knew and trusted each other well.

Climbing alone was dangerous and irresponsible. A reckless pursuit for a family man. But for an impatient man, which his wife assured him he was, it had its advantages. No small talk was ever necessary. No one to compromise with over plans or grand ambitions. It wasn't a habit he embraced as a beginner climber—only something he later came to appreciate once he had the skill and confidence. There were plenty of times when he really needed to get away and think. Climbing was a great way to chew on ideas and problems he was working on. He often got lost in his mind when climbing solo. About controversies at work. Politics. Disagreements in the family. Growing up in the rural Ozarks had taught Joe not to fear being alone. He learned from an early age that he could tackle problems without much help from others if he was smart and resourceful.

From a practical standpoint, he saw climbing partnerships as a tradeoff. There were plenty of climbs that Joe would never attempt on his own. A partner, or sometimes two, could help in splitting the weight needed on a climb. Tents, food, stoves, climbing gear, and ropes. All of this added up exponentially. If the route was big and technical, then a partner could take half of the leads while he rested and belayed. Having a solid belayer below him, rooting for him, tied to the other end, could instill just enough confidence to truly go for it and push himself beyond what he thought he was capable of.

The downside to the tradeoff was often time. Climbing with a partner just took longer, especially if the terrain wasn't all that difficult. It automatically doubled how long a climb took because each of you spent half of your time belaying while the other climbed. That wasn't the case when you were free and cordless.

After three hours of climbing, the wide and gentle ice flows of the lower wall gradually steepened and narrowed as he approached "The Prow," a hatchet blade of granite marking the beginning of the hard climbing. He guessed he was about two hundred feet below it, which he knew was roughly fifteen hundred feet above the glacier. He allowed himself to look down past his front points to the valley below. He tried not to think of how four thin points of steel, each a few millimeters thick, were all that separated him from the life he breathed and the void below that would love nothing more than to choke it out.

The runnel leading to The Prow posed a problem. The ice obviously narrowed near the top, and Joe knew it might not be thick enough to support his weight. He kicked out a small shelf in the ice where he stood to get a more restful stance and free up one hand to turn off his Walkman and store his headphones in his chest pocket. He needed to listen to what the ice was telling him. Thin ice can detach from the rock in big sheets if struck in the wrong spot. He would need to hear those hollow sounds that alerted him to gaps behind the ice.

"Alright, let's get to it," he said aloud. He tried to reestablish his rhythm, but the short break had interrupted his flow. The cold wind rustling down the wall whispered frightful, discordant tones. He took deep breaths and centered on the truth that he knew. The only move that mattered was the next one. That's it.

Swing. Swing. Kick. Kick.

Halfway up the runnel, the ice thinned to arm's width, but each swing and kick still felt solid. He hung from his left axe and unholstered his longest ice screw with his right hand. He spun his hand around the handle, driving it seven inches deep, then clipped it to the belay loop on his harness and hung directly on it. He pulled up the rope, tied a knot on the end, and secured it to the screw with a locking carabiner. That way he could belay himself up the rest of the pitch and place more screws if possible. He fed twenty feet of rope through his belay device and tied a knot on the brake strand. He would be stopped at the knot if he fell. The thought of taking a fall that big still scared the hell out of him, but it sure beat the alternative. The ice thinned on the last half of the pitch, but he was able to place shorter screws every fifteen feet and made it to the ledge below The Prow without incident. Once there, he found a piton anchor with cord to tie his rope into and lower down to retrieve his ice screws in the runnel. He brought an ascender to climb the rope back to his high point.

Joe knew the McNerthney Ice Dagger hung just above him, to the right of The Prow. He had an eerie feeling knowing that one of the Brits was likely hanging dead at the end of his rope so close above him. He thought of calling up to them to reassure them that help was close, but he knew they would never hear him over the wind, even if they were alive. The sky had brightened a little, and he knew the morning sun was up there somewhere above the clouds. He was tired from climbing all night, but he knew he needed to keep moving.

The two-hundred-foot-high prow stuck out of the wall above like a murderer's axe sticking through a door in a horror movie. When the ice ended, he torqued the steel blade of his axes in the granite crack and scratched his crampons on tiny edges of the face. He used the same system to belay himself, clipping a carabiner to each of the pitons driven into the cracks by previous parties and left behind. Clouds once again rolled in and obscured any view of the wall above or below him. He found it comforting to not see the glacier more than a thousand feet below him, nor the looming colossus above, with its hanging daggers and seracs waiting for the slightest vibration to send it careening down the wall on top of him. He found a three-piton anchor at the top of the pitch and fixed his rope. He again lowered to retrieve his gear, then ascended the rope to his high point.

Joe now had to lower and traverse to the right to reach

the Ice Dagger. He rappelled slowly, keeping a tight grip on the rope with his left hand while delicately stepping to the right, scratching his crampons for purchase and pulling on any hold he could reach with his right hand.

When he turned the corner that dropped into the Ice Dagger, he saw Liam hanging backward from the rope, legs dangling lifelessly, head and arms swooped backward. His red jacket covered in spindrift. Definitely not alive. Joe reluctantly followed the rope upward with his gaze, preparing himself for what he might find at the end of it.

At the top of the gully sat Charlotte in her sleeping bag.

"Hello!" Joe shouted above the wind.

He watched as a small, gloved hand poked out of the small opening of the sleeping bag and pulled it down, but she didn't reply. Joe was overjoyed to see the movement.

"I'll be right up!"

Joe finished lowering down to Liam's body, attached his ascender to their rope, and hung from it while he pulled his own from the anchor. He then trailed it below as he ascended to Charlotte, who silently watched. In his mind, he worked through a plan to evacuate her to the glacier. If her rope was fully intact, then he could tie it to his and get them down in fewer rappels. Depending on her condition, he could lower her from above and wait for her to place ice screws and come off the rope, while he then lowered to her and repeated the process. However, if her injuries were significant enough to render her incapable of building an anchor and taking herself off belay, then he would need to attach her to his harness while he rappelled. It all hinged on her condition.

He introduced himself softly as he reached her. "Hey

there, Charlotte, it's Joe."

She didn't reply. She didn't even make eye contact, and that worried him.

He slowly unzipped the mummy bag enough to pull it over her head. Her helmet was cracked, and the left side of her face was battered and swollen. The ice must have clobbered her while she belayed. With head trauma like this, he was surprised she was able to get out her sleeping bag at all, but that was the only reason she hadn't succumbed to the cold already. He talked to her in a sincere, caring tone, as he did with his own daughter when she scratched her knee as a child. He knew that brain injuries could make people act erratically, and he wanted her to know he was there to help.

She held her left arm protectively against her. He could tell the forearm was broken by the swelling. He would need to address that before they lowered, or else the broken bones could cause more damage, even cut a vein or artery if she were to try and use that arm to brace herself. He had no splint, so he carefully unzipped her puffy coat and the shell jacket she wore underneath, then pulled her arm out of the sleeve. He laid it against her torso and then used his small knife to cut two small holes in her shirt sleeve. He then worked a carabiner through the holes, clipped it to the collar of her shirt, and zipped her jacket and coat back up.

He thought about looking for frostbite on her feet and hands but decided he wouldn't be able to do anything about it right then anyway. It was a foregone conclusion that someone pinned down for multiple nights alone in this environment was going to lose some toes at a minimum. And even if he took the time to warm her appendages, they would likely freeze again as they descended, which would compound the problem.

"Alright, we're gonna get you out of here now." Joe talked her through his systems while he rigged the ropes and positioned her on a tether to his belay loop. He hoped his explanations would soothe her, but mostly it was for himself. Her eerie silence made him feel alone, but hearing his own voice helped ease the tension.

They needed to rappel fifteen hundred feet to reach the glacier. Their ropes would get them down two hundred feet, so they would have to repeat the rappelling process about eight times, maybe nine, depending on where he found good places to cut V-thread anchors.

Joe had to stop when they reached Liam and take him off the rope because they needed both ropes to get to the ground. He had no choice but to leave the boy there on the wall alone. He would be someone else's problem. He had to get the girl down. Cutting the rope and simply watching the boy sail down the wall was not an option with Charlotte in such a fragile mental state. He had no idea how she would react to that, or the trauma that would cause her later. Joe placed one of his ice screws just above the body and clipped Liam's harness to it with a sling. His weight still hung from the rope, making it impossible for Joe to untie, so he pulled out his small knife and cut the rope just above the knot, and the weight of Liam's body slammed violently into the wall.

The first rappel went slowly, but Joe adjusted as problems arose. He noticed that Charlotte had a hard time holding herself upright with her one good arm while sliding down the wall, so he stopped and attached a sling around her chest that held her upright when clipped to the rope. Also, her tether was too short and kept her so close below him that he had to be careful not to kick her with his crampons while lowering. For the second rappel, he lengthened her tether just enough to avoid that, but not so much that it would be out of reach if there was a problem.

At the end of each rappel, when he neared the knotted ends of the ropes, he stopped and placed two ice screws, then clipped into those so he could lower their weight onto them. Then he twisted his longest screw into the ice at a forty-five-degree angle, then removed it and cut another hole to the side at the same angle so that it intersected the first. Next he fed the end of the rope through until he hit the knot where the ropes were tied together. Once he put them back on rappel, he pulled the two screws and slowly lowered them. It took them about an hour for each rappel. Joe had to move slowly enough not to harm Charlotte any further, and he also didn't want to rush the process and make a simple mistake that could cost them time, or, worse yet, their lives. Not having a partner with him to check his systems or share the workload placed the responsibility on him alone.

While setting up for the last rappel, he heard voices from below. A dozen climbers had skied and snowshoed up to help them back to base camp. Greg had alerted the teams when he caught sight of Joe and Charlotte through his scope once they broke below the cloud line. Joe was relieved to see them, roped together in pairs, crossing the ice field. He would not have to steer Charlotte across the ice by himself in a flimsy sled for two and a half miles.

Every Christmas, Joe receives a card from Charlotte, thanking him for what he did that day. Her road to recovery was long and painful, but most of her mental faculties returned once the swelling in her brain subsided. She lost all her toes and a few fingertips, but six years later she married, and soon after that she gave birth to the first of three daughters.

Word of the rescue spread quickly through the community of mountaineers. Journalists reached out to Joe for comment, but he refused to speak of it. Of course, Joe never saw himself as a hero. He simply did what he was supposed to. What any person in his shoes with the ability to do it should have done. He knew it was the same feeling his own son felt when he ran back into the firefight to save one more. And Joe wished every day that Chris hadn't been so brave.

7. GO TIME

Brooks Range, Alaska
July 2017
8 days until pickup

The following day brought windless, clear skies. They watched the welcoming sun slough off the thin layer of snow from the upper shoulders of the tower before they left camp.

"Today's the day. How ya feel, buddy?" Ethan could tell Joe was invigorated by the coming adventure.

"Psyched." Ethan gazed at the tower shimmering in the morning sun while fighting off the butterflies in his stomach. The air seemed to buzz. This was his first climbing expedition so cut off from the world, and he was determined to do his best to prove himself. He might be a mess at school, but he could choose his path here. All the trouble he had gotten into this year was already fading into history as far as he was concerned. Besides, maybe this kind of experience could be good on a resume if he took the guiding track. He could probably get a job with one of the guide companies with Joe's recommendation, and the certifications couldn't be that hard.

Back in Talkeetna, Ethan had helped the guides in the shop for a few weeks before he and Joe left on their trip. Joe kept him busy there, and he earned a few bucks under the table while he was at it. Food had to be stripped from its packaging and boxes and repackaged into Ziploc bags to save weight and bulk; ropes needed to be checked for damage from sharp crampons and sorted by length and use. Tents needed to be set up in the yard for inspection and to dry, then to be stuffed back neatly into their bags. Every item the teams would need had to be accounted for and packed carefully because, once they were on the mountain, bringing them extra supplies would be very costly and difficult. A new team of climbers showed up each week, and the process started over: pack supplies, re-pack gear, refresh glacier travel skills. Teams would go over the trip plans, gear and supplies would be transported to the airfield to be loaded on the plane, and then the bush plane would land the climbers on the glacier for the long trek up Denali.

Ethan's main job had been to sharpen the glacier crampons with Paul, another guide. The points had to be lightly filed to remove burs but not sharpened so much that they would cut clients when they accidentally kicked them into their calves, which happened too often. Paul was an old hand like Joe. He spent three nights on a glacier once with a client when the Cessna they were flying crashed. The pilot, his good friend, was killed in the accident.

"Your grandad told me about all the routes you did with your pops. You've done a good deal of climbing," Paul said as he watched Ethan work the file.

"Thanks. Both my parents like to climb, so I was around it all the time. I've climbed a little with my grandpa, but we don't get up here as much as I—" Ethan began.

"You're one lucky kid to have a grandad like yours. You might not realize it, but he's a legend in these parts," Paul said as he worked his small file around the points like a factory worker. "Hell, I'd climb just about anything with Joe."

Ethan finished a pair, tossed them into the "sharpened" pile, and looked at Paul. "Why did he stop guiding on the mountain? He said he's too old now, but he's fitter than most of these guys half his age."

Paul stopped filing and looked at Ethan sincerely. "Kid, you've probably heard the old cliché about there being old climbers and bold climbers, but no old, bold climbers. Well, it's true. Every damn year the best in our sport get the chop, and we tell ourselves the same thing every time. 'They were doing everything right, but I guess they were just unlucky.' But we all know our time is coming if we keep going up there and pushing it."

Ethan grabbed another pair of crampons from the dull pile and put the file to the front points. "I won't push it too far. If it gets too dangerous, I'll just find something else to do for fun," he said with the confidence of youth.

"That's what we all say, but the edge is addicting. Each time we go to the mountains and come back, we feel like we left money on the table. It means we didn't go big enough. But we don't know it's too big until it's too late. The edge is out there; it ain't hard to find it if you know where to look. Only problem is you don't get to come back if you do. Your dad was wise enough to get out of the climbing game." Paul paused at this for a moment as if questioning whether he would continue his line of thought. "Chris got to see what it did to us old-timers and the number of friends we lost to the hills. Some of us just can't ration the passion like he did."

The door to the gear room swung open. "Ay kid, so you're the one who squawrreled away the crampons," Mateo said jokingly in his heavy Argentinian accent as he pulled two pair from the pile.

Mateo had a great sense of humor, and his interesting drawl made his tales of adventure sound even more exotic. His face and hands were tanned like leather from the intense sun and wind of the high-altitude peaks. The other guides loved to tell stories about Mateo's unorthodox strategies on the mountain. One such tale was of an incident the previous year involving a group of Army veterans he was guiding back to base camp after a successful summit. His climbers were all pretty tired when they reached the top of the hill above the 7,800-foot camp, so he decided they should all jump on top of the gear sleds they'd been pulling and ride them down the last thousand feet. The only problem was that the snow was much harder than he expected, and their speed got so out of control that no one could stop them. They shot past the next camp and plowed into a sizable Korean team. Miraculously, no one was hurt, and Mateo made amends by giving the Koreans the rest of his team's whiskey. A rookie guide would have been fired on the spot, but no one would ever think of reprimanding the source of so many great tales.

Mateo lived each year in the same rotation to guide the greater ranges. He spent the Austral summer months of December and January in Antarctica, guiding peaks and assisting scientific expeditions. From there, he migrated north to Colorado to ski for a month or two, then shot up to Talkeetna by late spring for the Denali guiding season. When the planes stopped flying into the range by late July, he'd bounce down to the Tetons for a month to work trips on the Grand until the Himalayan climbing season opened up in September. This was a life Ethan could see himself living.

Ethan used Mateo's interruption to enlist an ally. "Hey, Mateo, Paul thinks being a guide is a bad career choice. What do you think?"

Mateo replied brusquely, "He's right, my friend, it's a horrible choice. I love this job and the mountains, but make no mistake. It can kill or maim you and all your friends." Mateo made a sweeping gesture with his left hand as if marking everyone in the room for assured demise. "And the ones who live will share your belongings as mementos. If you really want to do this, then start with the truth and don't fall for all the glory and hero bullshit." Then Mateo lowered his head like a bull prepared to charge, peering earnestly into Ethan's eyes. He raised his arm and pointed to Ethan. "Do you know what a mountain guide's job is?"

Ethan stumbled for an answer. "Well, I guess, to get the client to the top and back safe...ly?"

Mateo kept the serious look. "Yes, my friend. And what is the client's job?"

Ethan was truly stumped on that one. He rummaged his mind for an answer but eventually shrugged his shoulders as an act of surrender.

Mateo cracked a sly smile. "To kill the guide."

***

Joe's face, typically clean-shaven, had started to grow out after two days without a razor.

"I like the beard," Ethan said with a winsome smile.

"There's a lot more gray in there these days."

Joe smiled and scratched at his whiskers. "That's not gray, buddy, that's wisdom."

They roped up for the hike to the base of the route. Joe wanted them to get up the glacier before the sun swung around and softened the snow. The harder surface would help them move faster, and they would exert less energy. Joe led out ahead while Ethan trailed behind and tried to avoid too much slack or tightness in the rope, just like he learned back in Talkeetna. He also tried to copy his grandfather's hiking technique, focusing on sidestepping as much as possible to save his calves from burning out. Ethan had to catch himself several times when he tripped on his crampons. He wasn't used to walking with the big, sharp, metal teeth on his feet, and he felt embarrassed about how awkward he moved in them.

It didn't take long for them to get near the rock wall, and Joe slowed down a couple hundred yards away from it so he could search for the beginning of their route. From this close, they could see a dozen options for where to climb, and each crack system looked about as good as the others. Joe settled on a left-facing corner near the middle of the wall and headed toward it.

"Hard to tell which crack system has been climbed. That one looks as good as any."

By the time they neared the wall, the sun had warmed up the snow, and they kicked steps easily. Ethan noted how his grandfather seemed to have timed their approach to the tower perfectly. He realized he could learn a lot from him about the mountains, and that prospect excited him for the future. He wanted to spend every summer climbing with him from now on.

While Ethan was thinking happy thoughts, his foot

suddenly plunged deep into a hole. He instinctively yelled, "FALLING!" Joe, up ahead of him at the end of the rope, instantly dropped to the glacier and drove his ice axe into the snow under the weight of his shoulder. He kicked both front points of his crampons deep to catch the fall. Luckily, Ethan had only broken through the surface with one leg and was stopped at his hip. Ethan pulled on the rope, quickly hauled himself out of the hole, and stood up. Joe sat up, relief on his face.

"Ethan, how big was it?"

Ethan stepped to the edge and peered down into the abyss. The crack was a foot wide and dropped deep enough that it was too dark for him to tell its depth.

"It was just a small one. Thanks for the catch!"

Luckily for them, the gap between the glacier and the rock was filled with snow, allowing them to walk down a short ramp to access the beginning of the route.

"Well, that didn't take long," said Ethan when they reached the rock wall. He was barely breathing hard at all.

They removed their crampons and set them on the ledge next to their ice axes and ice screws. They'd be safe there until they returned from the climb. They would need them for the hike back to the tent.

"I'll take the first lead to get us started," Joe instructed.

Ethan was relieved he could lie back for at least a pitch and get his feet under him. He loved to lead, but he'd never been in such an intimidating environment. The size of the mountain and the sprawling glacier beneath it overwhelmed his senses in a way that both excited and scared him. He felt a combination of admiration for its beauty and a healthy fear of its danger.

Ethan grabbed the rope, carefully uncoiled it, and gently stacked it so it would not tangle as his grandfather led the first pitch—he tied into the closest end and then stacked the rope on top of itself until he reached the other end of the two-hundred-foot cord, which Joe would tie into. Meanwhile, Joe worked to clip his gear on his harness while occasionally looking up to determine which pieces he would need, reminding Ethan of his dad. Years of experience enabled Joe to assess the crack's size and accurately estimate which pieces he would need to protect his lead and which he could leave for Ethan to carry up.

"It looks like a little stance up there about a hundred and fifty feet," Joe pointed out. "I'll aim for that and build an anchor to bring you up. I'll give two hard tugs on the rope to let you know I'm off belay in case you can't hear me from down here. Sometimes, the wind picks up, and you won't hear a thing if it does."

Ethan nodded while still working to put Joe's end of the rope into the belay plate. "On belay."

"That's my boy. You got me on before I could even tie in. I appreciate the hustle; that's what it takes to get big things done in the mountains. Some folks don't know how to work while listening." Joe quickly worked the rope around his harness loops and replied, "Climbing."

The old climber moved quietly and efficiently. Ethan noticed how his grandfather often lumbered and limped a little when he got up to walk, showing his years, but all that disappeared when he climbed. His movements were quiet and smooth. He briefly stopped about every twenty feet to place a stopper or cam in the crack, then set off without hesitation as soon as he clipped it to the rope. It took him only fifteen minutes to reach the stance he had pointed out.

"Off belay!" shouted Joe, and Ethan felt the two tugs of the rope follow. The air was still calm, so Ethan had no problem hearing him. He took Joe off belay, tightened his climbing shoes, and tightened the straps to his small pack as Joe pulled in the rest of the rope, brought it tight to him, and fed it through his belay device. He pulled another two tugs on the rope.

"On belay!" shouted Joe, and Ethan launched as he replied. The climbing was more demanding than he expected, and he was glad to have the rope safely pulling him up. Joe had made it look easy, but Ethan found the crack cold enough to numb his hands, and sections were soaked with melting snow from the previous night. He took off too fast, found himself laboring to breathe, and grew embarrassed by the fact that he was sucking wind. He lacked confidence in his footing on the wet granite. He had nervously tied his climbing shoes too tightly, and now his feet ached. A part of him felt like a phony. This was Alaska. The big leagues. Was he ready? *It's just rock climbing. You know how to rock climb. You've done this plenty of times. How hard is this route, 5.9? You've climbed harder. Get it together.*

He pushed on, trying to fight off his doubts. He also reassured himself that the climbing would improve as he warmed up, and that the sun would come around far enough to shine on the crack system and warm the inside. By the time he reached the belay ledge, he had gained an even more profound respect for his grandfather's skill.

"Nice work," said Ethan nonchalantly. He wasted no time placing his locking carabiner into the anchor Joe had built with two stoppers while Joe pulled off the gear from the young man's harness. Ethan secured himself with a clove hitch.

"I'll take this next pitch as well since I feel pretty spry this morning," Joe declared.

Ethan grabbed the end of the rope tied to Joe and put him on belay.

"Your dad said you're just as bad a lead hog as your grandpa, so I'll try to get mine in early before you catch your wind."

8. SENIORITIS

Colorado Springs, Colorado
7 April 2017

Ethan was genuinely gassed by the time he rounded the corner to his townhome. He loved the dead-leg feeling he got at the end of a long run, or in this case, a long run and a fair amount of climbing. Ethan saw his mom's car in her parking space. She should be at work right now. He knew what that meant. His school had reported his absence, and she had come home early to hunt him down like before. Actually, last time she had driven around the neighborhood and through the canyon to find him. No, this was different. She was probably waiting for him in there. Waiting to watch him sneak in with some excuse about why he was giving up on finishing high school strong and had likely already ruined any chance at the cross-country scholarship he was offered his junior year.

He hesitated briefly at the door, then turned the knob, accepting his fate. *Let's just get it over with.* There was a time, not long ago, when he enjoyed coming home to his parents, especially his mother, Julia. But over the last few months, their conversations began to focus more on Ethan's failing grades and lack of a plan for his future.

Julia sat at the table, still dressed in her hospital scrubs, and turned to face him when she heard the door open. He saw the stress in her eyes. The winter had been long for her, too, and it showed. Her posture was more slumped than it used to be, and she'd lost weight. He held her gaze with the boldness of teenage arrogance. She scoffed at his audacity. She looked down at what he was wearing.

"You should just take your running stuff with you next time and save you the trouble of having to come back."

Ethan guiltily looked down at his dusty shoes. "I just couldn't do it today."

Julia leaned back, arms crossed. "We all do things we don't like, Ethan Hardy." He always knew she was mad when she used his full name. "Emily had to cover half my shift today so I could look for you. Do you think she wanted to come in on her day off?"

Heat crawled up Ethan's neck. His ears turned red. "Sorry."

"What the hell would your father think of all this?" she said, not looking at him.

Ethan was tired of the guilt trip, and something inside of him snapped. "Well, he's not here. Hell, he's rarely ever BEEN here." He wouldn't be pushed anymore by someone else's expectations.

Julia stood quickly and held up a single finger in his face. "Don't you talk about your father that way! You don't know what he's been through—what he went through for us."

"For us? Are you kidding? I never once asked for him to miss half my damn childhood!"

She slapped his face hard and fast, and Ethan could

tell by her face, through her tears and the bloodshot eyes, that she instantly regretted it, but would also never back down. She had never hit him before, and neither had his dad. He had always been too scared of his dad to ever provoke him that far. It felt like they'd crossed a line and would never be able to return to where they had been, or what they had been.

They let silence hold the room for a moment. Neither knowing what to do next.

Julia pointed again, slowly but forcefully. "You don't know what the hell you're talking about," she said quietly, her voice as raw as an open wound.

Ethan didn't want to fight with her. *It's not her fault Dad didn't listen to you.* He stormed off to his room and left her to believe she was still in charge of him, pretending to still fear her out of sympathy.

He lay on his bed, put in his earbuds, and listened to music. He chewed on the events of the day, which led him back to other events over the last few months. It made him anxious and depressed.

For Ethan, climbing and the mountains almost always soothed him. Hung around his room were posters of famous climbers from around the world on beautiful routes, including the one of Lynn Hill free climbing the Nose on El Capitan in Yosemite. Her hair flows in the wind while delicately locking her fingers into the tiny crack and dancing on practically non-existent footholds. Ethan's mother bought the poster to remind him that women climbed more smoothly and smartly than men. "You guys just try to power through with brute strength instead of using your freakin' head," she had told him, and he had to agree. One day, he knew he would be climbing big routes like that. Climbing seemed less complicated than real life. Finishing high school was more demanding than any route he had been on.

On his nightstand was one of his dad's last letters. Out of boredom, he opened it and read.

Dear Son,

It's been two weeks since I've had a chance to write to you. I hope all is well and you're still helping your mother around the house. The last time I talked to her, she said you were passing your classes, but you could be doing better. Don't let that get out of hand.

The morale here isn't great, and nobody's happy with being extended in-country for an extra three months. That means most of us won't be back home until late next summer. That means I'll miss the camping season. Be sure to get in your weekly miles and listen to your coach.

I've thought a lot about our last conversation and the way we left things. We have much to talk about when I get back, and you deserve an explanation for why I push you so hard.

I know David is bummed about his diagnosis, but I'm glad he missed this deployment, and I'm happy he's there to check in on you guys. You should take him up on that offer to go climbing. He's not as good as your pops, so you'll have to lead!

Love,

Dad

October 4, 2016

Ethan closed his eyes and held his breath when, over the music, he heard the door open. He thought it was his mom coming to give him another round of lecturing.

"I brought you a soda, big guy."

Ethan was relieved to hear David's voice. David was Ethan's dad's best friend. He had been left behind by their unit on the last deployment due to medical issues he was still trying to sort out. David promised Chris he would stop in and check on them regularly until he returned. It seemed he was coming by more often lately, but Ethan didn't mind because he was always kind and willing to take him to the climbing gym.

"Your mom called and told me you skipped again." Ethan shrugged and stared at the ceiling. David sat on the edge of the bed and looked over at him slyly. "Hell, I think you got about the worst case of senioritis I ever heard of."

Ethan smiled. "I hope it's not contagious."

"Hope not," David nodded. "Though that girlfriend of yours didn't seem to catch it. I saw her walking home with her books. She's a good one. You'd be wise not to chase her off."

Ethan nodded his head in agreement. "I have a lot on my mind."

"Well, that'll have to wait. Your mom has to work tomorrow, so get your climbing gear packed up because you and I are gonna talk over a climb. I'll pick you up at 6 a.m. You'll get it sorted out, bud, don't worry."

As David turned to leave, something poking out of Ethan's pack caught his eye. David leaned over, picked up the old green compass, and turned it in his hands.

"This your old man's compass, ain't it?" David asked.

"Yeah, he sent it to me. Around Thanksgiving."

"There are a few guys who never needed a compass for direction, and your pops was one of 'em." David lightly tossed it to Ethan. "See you in the morning, kid."

David joined Julia on the balcony, where she stood leaning against the rail. The last thin streaks of red lingered above the Front Range as the sun finished setting over the mountains. "He's a good kid, Julia. He's just going through a rough patch."

Julia frowned, unsure. "They say how a boy acts at twelve is what he circles back to after the teen years. I hope that's true. He used to be so thoughtful until..."

David pondered the point. "That sounds about right."

"My job's just to get him through it," Julia added. "He reminds me a lot of my little brother, and that worries me..."

"You never told me you have a little brother."

"I don't anymore," she said quietly. "Scott died when he was seventeen. Fell in with the wrong crowd. My dad wasn't there for him. We couldn't pull him back." She hesitated. "Scott liked to party. Never thought about consequences. One night, he was racing a friend on some back roads and took a curve too fast and lost control. He got ejected, and the car rolled right over him..."

David's face tightened. "I'm sorry, Julia, that must have been rough." David put his hand on her shoulder and squeezed it gently.

"I don't want Ethan to go down that road," Julia continued. "But a boy his age can find trouble easy. Too easy."

David nodded. "It's easy to wander into danger when boundaries haven't been drawn. But I think you do that. He'll figure it out."

Julia stared past him. "There's only so much a mother can do. He needs something else right now. Someone else. I think I know who to call."

***

Ethan fell asleep while reading a chapter of Krakauer's *Eiger Dreams*. He'd been too emotionally charged from the argument with his mom to brave leaving his room and had gone to bed without dinner. Around midnight, he awoke famished. The house was dark as he made his way to the kitchen. In the glow of the streetlight through the window, he could see the empty bottle of wine on the table and a half-filled glass. He picked up the glass and placed it in the sink. In the refrigerator, he found a store-bought apple pie with two slices left. Perfect. He grabbed the pie, along with a fork from the silverware drawer, and headed toward his room, intending to eat in peace while watching stand-up comedy videos on his phone.

The dark shadow on the couch scared him at first, but he quickly realized what it was. He'd heard his mom sobbing herself to sleep several times before, but he must have slept through it tonight. He never knew what to do when she cried. Sometimes it was apparent she needed comforting. But at night it was different. He thought it better to give her time alone to process, just like he often needed. Still, he wasn't sure he was handling it right.

He set the pie and fork down quietly on the table. He looked around the room for a blanket to cover her, but there was none. He went to her room and turned on the bathroom light so he could see. He peeled back her blankets and readied her pillow. On the headboard sat a tri-folded flag in a wooden box with a glass window front. The one David and the other soldiers folded on the top of his father's casket and gave to his mother as three rifle volleys pierced the air in what sounded to him like finality.

He went back to the living room and stood beside her. Her breathing was faint; her body seemed so frail. Ethan worked his arms under her knees and her upper back, lifting her slowly. He had never lifted her like this before and was surprised at how light she felt in his arms. It was a strange role reversal for them. Not long ago, it was her carrying him to his bed after he fell asleep in his parents' room, scared to sleep alone after a scary movie. He laid her down on the cold, queen-size mattress and carefully tucked the blanket around her.

9. SLOW IS FAST

Brooks Range, Alaska
July 2017
8 days until pickup

—Joe—

Mornings weren't as easy on the old man as they used to be, but overall, he thought this one was pretty damn good. His knees and back were achy after sleeping on the glacier for two nights. But spending time with his grandson in pretty country doing what he loved most offered more than enough excitement to make him forget the pains of his age.

It felt great to lead right from the start, charging ahead at the sharp end of the rope. Joe had originally planned to trade leads with Ethan. Each leading one, then following one. But now he thought climbing in blocks of three or four pitches might work better for them. This way, Ethan could follow for several pitches and build his confidence before being handed the rack. Trading pitches might disrupt Ethan's momentum, so it was best to ease him into it and then step back to let him thrive. The kid was strong, but Joe knew by experience that climbing a big route in remote mountains was a lot different than cragging next to a road. It required a different mindset.

Ethan reminded him so much of Chris, and he found himself feeling nostalgic for the old days of climbing and camping. He felt lucky to be able to do it all again. He saw little of Chris after he left home and joined the Army after high school, and he'd always wished they'd tried harder to spend time together. But that's how it goes when you have a family. And now it was too late to call up Chris and invite him out for a moose hunt or ski trip, or anything else. What he'd give to hear his voice one more time.

Joe came to a constriction in the crack where it narrowed down too tight to get his full hand into. He placed a smaller cam, clipped it to the rope, and looked up to plan his next moves. The crack widened again to hand width about eight feet above, and he'd be able to sink his hand in for a solid jam again. He'd just have to figure out a way to get there.

"Hey, Ethan, watch me close for a minute. I'm gonna have to punch it here."

"Sure thing."

Joe glanced down to check his belay and saw Ethan looking up attentively, with both hands on the rope where they should be.

He saw that his grandson's face was paler than usual. He hoped he wasn't pushing him too far, too fast. Putting a young man into an overwhelming situation too early could have dire consequences, and he didn't want to be the reason Ethan quit climbing. He always felt that he pushed his own son a little too fast. Perhaps that's why he had to leave and find his own path in the military. Ethan seemed different, though. He could see a lot of himself in the boy.

Once he was sure Ethan was paying attention, he focused on the task. He ran his fingers into the crack above, searching for the smallest constrictions or rough patches of rock that provided a better grip. He could pinch with his thumb and forefinger and stack one on top of the other. It was painful to jam his fingers inside like that, and he couldn't hold it for long. He turned his left foot sideways, inserting his big toe into the crack at about knee height, and stood on it while he cranked his knee back up. This, too, was painful, but it took enough weight off his hands that he could slide each one up in turn to find another painful finger stack. Once his hands could balance him sufficiently, he wedged his right toe into the crack and stood up on that foot. After several repetitions, he was able to slide his right hand into the broader section of the crack he had been working toward and made a perfectly cupped hand jam.

"Ahhh." Joe hung most of his weight on his wrist and shook his other hand to get blood into his fingers.

"Looking smooth, old man."

"Thank ya. Slow is fast. Fast is slow."

Ethan had brought new light into Joe's life when he needed it most. The last eight months (had it only been that long?) had been so dark and lacking in color or hope. He didn't know he would be up for it when Julia called, asking for help. Of course, he said yes, but he wasn't sure he could put on a smile and pretend he was strong. But when Ethan walked up to him at the Anchorage airport, he realized he didn't have to pretend at all. The kid's buoyancy naturally lifted Joe and Katherine up without him even trying. It's like they'd been rafting down the stream of life but had gotten caught up in a drop hole, circling and gasping for air until a strong current came along and forced them back out into the tongue of the stream.

Joe found a natural break in the wall and decided it would be a good place to belay. It wasn't quite a ledge, but the rock was sloped and featured enough to stand comfortably, take some of the weight off his harness, and save the skin under his leg straps from getting too sore. Nothing was worse than a hanging belay, where all your weight was on the harness; the leg loops could cut off circulation within minutes. He'd done plenty of those in his time but learned to avoid them whenever possible. He had several options for placing gear and building an anchor and was soon calling down to Ethan to take him off.

While belaying Ethan, Joe previewed the next pitch. The crack was much wider than on the first two pitches, but he couldn't tell exactly what gear he would need. He thought it widened up higher, maybe to five or six inches, perhaps even seven. He knew from experience that a couple inches of width in a crack made a world of difference. Four inches was incredibly good for fist jams. Five inches and above, however, required a little sorcery.

"Ooh, that looks tough," said Ethan as he approached the belay.

"Yeah, this one might put up a fight. We'll see."

Ethan went into the anchor and started unclipping the gear he'd removed while following. He carefully handed it over to Joe so as not to drop any in the transition.

"If the Italians rappelled this route, then why aren't we finding any webbing or anything?" Ethan asked. So far, the route had shown no signs of previous climbers.

"Yeah, I noticed that. We must be in a different crack system. So many to choose from, it's hard to tell where they went."

"Should we go down and start on the right route?"

"Oh, no, definitely not."

Joe realized Ethan had always relied on guidebooks, as most climbers do when approaching routes. These days they research climbs using apps or buy books and follow the marked paths. Paint by color. Joe had done that, too, in the beginning, but eventually he started to read between the lines. He paid attention to the cracks and features to the left and right of the known paths. "We'll be fine on this one; it seems pretty solid so far, right?"

"Yeah, I think it's good."

"Damn right it is. Plus, we get an added bonus for being off-route."

Ethan squinted. "What's the bonus in that?"

"Adventure, kid. Something you miss when you stick to the topo."

Joe didn't rack the gear on his harness like usual. Instead, he clipped the cams to a sling and hung them over his neck and shoulder. He caught Ethan looking at him inquisitively. "I want to be able to move the gear to either side while I'm climbing that monster. I'll need to put my ass into it at some point, and I can't tell which side it will be yet. If I rack it on my harness, then it'll be in my way. Or, I won't be able to get to it when I need it."

Ethan put Joe on belay and grabbed the loops of rope off Joe's right foot and draped it across his own after flipping the stack so Joe's end would feed from the top instead of the bottom.

Joe stopped. "I won't be able to get into that chimney with my pack on. Neither will you. I'll have to leave mine down here with you and send my end of the rope down to haul both up when I get to an anchor."

It started off as a cruiser three-inch crack. Solid hand

jams. He placed a cam before it widened to four inches. Then, he put his hand in and made a fist with his knuckles toward the sky as if throwing a slow-motion punch. The tighter he squeezed, the more securely his flesh compressed against the walls of the crack. The foot jams were easy at this width, too. The rubber outer rands of his sturdy climbing shoes did all the work when he kicked them in and stood up.

Joe tried to pace himself because he felt that the pitch would become progressively harder the higher he got. He took an extra moment at the most secure jams to examine the chimney looming above him. It appeared smooth and immaculate, but it was still a considerable distance away, and he hoped better holds would reveal themselves as he got closer.

The three-inch cam was just below his feet, so he decided to punch it a bit further before placing the four, as it was his only one. That way, he could set it right before the crack widened to five inches. However, the risk in the plan was that the crack might widen just enough to prevent the four from seating properly, making it ineffective if he fell. He climbed fifteen feet before his fist jams became too loose, at which point he found a great placement for the four.

Joe thrived in unfamiliarity. He had no knowledge of what lay ahead and no guarantee he was on the right path. Success was uncertain. The route unfolded one move, one hold, one jam at a time. He stayed fluid in his thinking and detached himself from any fixed plans or ideologies. Each problem identified as it arose. Only then could he find a solution. At this stage in his life, Joe possessed a deep reservoir of skills.

Fist jams became too loose for his liking, so he began

stacking one fist against the other hand to fill the larger gap. He placed his right palm against the left side of the crack, crossed his left hand over it, and positioned his tightened fist behind the knuckles of his right hand. This way, he could use his flat hand to create a constriction for his fist. The only issue then was that both hands were needed to secure himself to the wall, and releasing either hand would cause him to fall. He carefully slithered his right knee into the crack until his thigh's thickness halted him. Then, he lifted his right foot toward his rear and rotated it outward, which expanded his knee's width enough to jam against the crack's sides and hold him in place. Finally, he released both hands, letting them dangle below as he shook them out and let the blood flow return.

"Nice moves there, old man!" Ethan shouted, taking a quick picture with his phone.

Joe glanced down as he gently shook his hands. "That's how it's done, kiddo."

He went back to work, repeating the same sequence for several moves. Then, he slid a five-inch cam deep enough that he wouldn't accidentally kick it out when he climbed above it. He extended it by connecting a longer sling before clipping it to the rope. The crack soon widened to where he could fit half of his body into it. He hoped to find holds for his hands and feet, anything to grip, but the walls were smooth and immaculate.

He had no gear that was big enough for this chimney. Usually, he could find a smaller crack on the sides for protection, but that wasn't the case. He took stock of his situation. Staying calm was the play. Even in the most dire circumstances, he was never completely overcome with fear. Instead, he made a conscious assessment of the consequences, followed by a detached decision on how to proceed based on that knowledge.

If he fell from this height, the rope would eventually come tight, and Ethan would be there to catch him. There was no ledge below him to strike, only a clean fall. However, his danger would increase the higher he climbed without gear. And, there was always the thought of what would happen if the last cam didn't hold. The cam could slide out of the crack if the rock was too smooth for enough friction and his fall forceful enough. The rope could also come unclipped from the carabiner if the rope crossed it the wrong way. Stranger things happened all the time.

Reason told him that pushing his limits there was unwise. They were too far from help if something went wrong. Would Ethan be able to safely lower him to the glacier from this high up on the wall and then coordinate a rescue? Unlikely. The smarter option would be to down-climb to the five-inch cam and lower himself from there. They could probably traverse to a safer, easier line. That was the logical choice.

But he didn't *feel* like that was the right thing to do. Joe felt good. He was motivated. He was climbing smoothly and strong, like a cyclist with a tail wind. He'd grown comfortable listening to his gut over the years. It had never steered him wrong. He thought young climbers these days were too obsessed with arbitrary rules and tricks they'd learned in their guide training or watched on some video. He liked the old-school ways. The more romantic version of climbing that was anti-establishment by nature. Freedom refusing confinement. There was no better feeling than doing something dangerous that you were scared to death of doing. With style. The thought did come to him, briefly, that he might just be trying to prove he wasn't getting older and slower. That he just might not be the guy he used to be. He batted away that idea; there was no room for timidity or uncertainty if he was to win the day. *When in doubt, run it out.*

"Watch me here, bud. I'm gonna hang it out."

He inched upward, leveraging the friction of the walls against his body to hold himself in place. The pitch curved slightly to the left, so he maneuvered his right leg into the crack, positioning himself to optimize traction. He forced his entire foot into the opening, gaining some friction from his toe and heel against either side, but it wasn't enough to support his full weight. He pushed his right elbow as deeply as possible, using his palm to press against the wall in front of him while wedging his shoulder in. This chicken wing configuration was quite strong as long as his palm held.

He carefully wormed and slid one foot upward at a time, making sure to maintain contact with the wall. If he made one wrong move or overextended his body, he would likely be ejected. The climbing was incredibly physical, demanding that every muscle work in unison, which left him exhausted. Still, he pressed on, squeezing and smearing his way up in desperation, breathing heavily and sweating profusely, even in the cool alpine air. Every point of contact was essential to stay anchored, as the rounded edge of the crack constantly tried to expel him.

He was well past the point of no return. He couldn't climb back down the last twenty feet to his previous piece of gear. A fall now would be more than double that distance, and he risked plummeting into the chimney, where he could be torn apart by its gaping jaws.

Joe could see that the slope of the wall eased above

him. If he could rally all his strength and stamina, he could make it. He was in full fight mode, trying to slow down to avoid making costly mistakes. He was right on the brink of falling, and he knew better than to rush it. He always experienced a weightless feeling just before he fell, almost as if an invisible hand was tugging at his shirt. Adrenaline surged through him, heightening his senses. His pupils dilated, and the world around him washed out to shades of gray and white. Tiny crystals of quartz and flakes of mica in the rock shone with microscopic clarity. The smell of his own sweat seemed to change composition, reflecting the array of chemicals and hormones at work within his distressed body.

10. EARLY SNOWS

Brooks Range, Alaska
Fall 2016

No humans witnessed the first snow of Harte Tower in the fall before Ethan and Joe traveled to the Kavluk Cirque. Warm, moist air from the Pacific pushed in from the ocean and rose to meet the high peaks on their western flanks. The storm paid a tax that all storms must pay when crossing mountains. Clouds forming in a distant, warm, ocean paradise lose energy as they climb thousands of feet, colliding with the cold granite teeth of a mountain. Their droplets begin to freeze, combine, and fall to the earth in big, white flakes of snow.

The Bear, searching for the last of the berries and roots, took the cold front as a sign to settle into his winter den. The high mountain range was his home. Years ago, his mother had fled hunters in the valley and taught her offspring the ways of the alpine bear, who traded safety for hunger. Fish were scarce above the tree line, but when the caribou migrated to higher altitudes to escape the mosquitoes, the Bear was always ready. The rich fat of marmots helped fill the gap between caribou meals. The chubby rodents were normally too alert and quick for the Bear to catch. But he easily dug them out of their dens with his big, powerful paws. Taking one last sniff of the incoming storm, the Bear turned and entered his dugout nestled in the glacial till below the South Glacier.

The loyal ptarmigan, who live among the high tundra year-round and had only begun to lose their dark summer feathers, retreated to their hideouts in the shrubs for what they hoped would be only a brief interruption in their hunt for berries. However, the snow fell heavily and without pause until the following evening, and by the time the sun set on the second day, three feet of fluffy snow blanketed the highest passes and peaks of the range.

A thick river of ice winds around the north side of Harte Tower like a corkscrew, and at the top of this corkscrew lies the western shoulder of Harte Tower, the origin point of the North Glacier. Here, temperatures remain cold in the shade for nine months of the year, and the heavy snows of winter are protected from warm spells of spring.

When the sun returned a few days after the storm, so did the ptarmigan, venturing from their nests among the boulders to investigate shrubs now drying out as fierce cold winds from the north blew the loose snow from their branches and into deep drifts in the mountain's gullies. When the wind stopped, the sun baked the upper layers into a hardened, icy crust that helped the hungry ptarmigan cross the snow-filled gullies and couloirs to explore distant willow patches for the now dried-out berries and occasional long-dead bug. The intense, cold, dry night air ripped the moisture from the frozen ground like a sponge, reshaping the deep powder within the drifts into fragile ice crystals resembling shards of broken glass that barely held the weight of the winter snow above.

Life on the mountain remained this way for many weeks until the heavy snows of the new year laid a thick and heavy blanket over the entire range, and those first drifts were entirely forgotten by the ptarmigan.

But they were there.

11. OLD AGE AND TREACHERY

Brooks Range, Alaska
July 2017
8 days until pickup

Ethan was closer to panic while belaying Joe through the chimney than Joe was leading it. Ethan fed rope slowly and thoughtfully so as not to give Joe too much slack if he fell, constantly measuring the distance between his grandfather and the ledge he currently stood on and trying in vain not to imagine how badly he would be hurt if he fell.

Finally, after an eternity, he watched Joe pull through the last of the chimney and disappear above. He heard a loud "WHOOT!" echo off the walls as Joe celebrated his send.

Back in Talkeetna, Joe and several of the guides liked to put in time on the small climbing wall in the corner of the shop. They took bites of their sandwiches in between making a go at a new problem someone had contrived among the hundreds of old plastic holds. They didn't mark or color-code the route like the commercial gyms did. In fact, the same holds had remained more or less unchanged for years, according to Joe. The only thing that changed was the new guides who came through and imagined a new combination through the maze of plastic grips and homemade holds carved out of unused stumps of old two-by-fours. Joe was still as fit and lean as the young guys and never used his age as an excuse. He kept up with his weekly weightlifting routine in his garage. The younger guides were sometimes a little stronger, and their young joints more capable of holding on to the smaller holds, but none moved as smoothly and effortlessly as Old Man Hardy.

Ethan spent a lot of time climbing in gyms growing up. He didn't always enjoy them, but they were a convenient way to grow stronger as a climber. And, there was usually a wall at the Army rec center where he could spend hours working on routes using the auto belay when his dad was out of town and his mom was at work. Julia often joined him when she could, but when his dad was home, they preferred to climb outside and only visited the gym if the weather was terrible. On the days Ethan was alone, he would try to replicate classic routes he had read about, such as Half Dome in Yosemite or the Naked Edge in Eldorado Canyon. He would look up the difficulty levels of the pitches and do his best to climb as many routes in the gym of similar grades and difficulty.

What he liked most about climbing with the guides on their little wall in Talkeetna was their team approach. They gave each other advice on movement and subtle techniques that made a big difference. He learned more about how a slight change in the angle of your toe on a hold, or using a heel instead of a toe, could change the outcome. Once they all sent the route cleanly, someone would concoct a new variation that made things slightly harder, and they'd be right back to throwing themselves at it, crashing onto the old mattresses stacked on the dusty floor until they reached the top.

Ethan packed his water and snacks away and prepared the backpacks. Soon, he saw Joe lowering out to the edge above the chimney, where he could see him again. Joe tossed his end of the rope far out behind Ethan, and the end whipped past him with a loud "POP" when it hit the wall. He grabbed the line, tied an overhand loop, and clipped the backpacks into it with a locking carabiner.

"Ready!" Ethan shouted and gave the rope a hard tug.

Joe labored to pull both packs up to him and away from the chimney to avoid them getting stuck. Within a few minutes, he had Ethan on belay.

"Alright, kid, you're on."

Ethan hiked the fist crack section and removed the cams as he went. He was impressed with how far Joe had climbed between each piece of gear he placed and knew it must have taken a calm head to do so. Ethan had read about hand and fist stacks in his mountaineering books but had never tried them. He watched Joe do it but couldn't see exactly what he was doing from his vantage point.

"Keep me tight here," he called up to Joe.

He used the stacks and shuffled his knee the best he could, but it didn't feel as secure as Joe had made it look. Nevertheless, he made it to the start of the chimney without falling. The tight rope from Joe helped.

Ethan crept into the chimney, buried his elbow into the recess, and seated his arm in a camming position just as he saw Joe do. He clumsily fished for footing on the blank walls but found nothing he trusted. His feet slipped and popped loose, but he clung desperately with his right arm wedged high. Eventually, his weight was more than his arm could hold, and he popped free of the gap and swung out in the air.

"HA!" Joe laughed. He seemed to enjoy watching someone half his age get wrecked following him.

Ethan laughed in disbelief. "How the hell did you get up that?" He used the hangtime to catch his breath before trying again. Watching the old man climb was like watching a magician.

"Old age and treachery, youngster. Catch a rest and give it another shot when you're ready."

Ethan tried several more times to finish the pitch under his own power but was spit out quickly each time.

"Feels a lot harder than 5.9, you sandbagger."

"I agree. Quite a bit harder."

"I just don't see it."

"No worries, bud. There's plenty more climbing to do today." Joe tossed down the brake strand of the rope, and Ethan grabbed it. "Go ahead and pull that, and the belay device'll capture your progress. Poor man's ascender."

Ethan pulled the loose strand and was surprised at how well the system worked, especially with Joe using his strong hands to assist the rope. He walked up, feet on either side of the chimney, while tugging hard as if pulling the engine block out from under the hood of a car with a cherry picker. "Well, that was easy. More of that treachery thing you were talking about, huh?"

"You know it," Joe said, but his attention had already moved on from the excitement of the hard pitch to the terrain still looming above. Ethan followed his gaze. They could clearly see the next block of climbing. The finger crack Joe had built an anchor in with cams traversed up and right until it joined a bigger crack system, more of a gully, that shot straight up the middle of the tower until it reached a headwall a few hundred feet later. To Ethan's surprise, the next few pitches were less steep than the last few Joe had led and looked to be fairly moderate in difficulty.

"How you feeling, bud?"

Ethan had begun to feel better as they climbed higher, and his confidence in his skills had returned. Joe's take-down of the chimney also inspired him to level up and contribute.

"I'm great. I'll take the next few."

"Ahh, the beast has awoken." Joe handed him the last few pieces of gear he hadn't placed on his lead and put him on belay. "Take it easy, and don't run it out. If it gets too hard, just climb back down to your last placement and build an anchor to bring me up."

"Okay," Ethan said as he racked and organized his harness as he wanted. They brought a double rack of cams, so he put one of each size on either side, from small to big, so he could reach them with either hand. He liked keeping his stoppers on his left gear loop because it was the least-used loop, since he was right-handed. Behind those were his longer slings for anchors and extensions. On his back, right loop were a few quick draws, a nut tool, his belay device, and a few lockers. He slung the double-length runners over his shoulder to ease the load on his hips.

Ethan looked Joe in the eye and nodded to show he was ready. His father had taught him to do that to avoid miscommunications. "Sometimes, people get in a hurry and don't hear what you say, but making eye contact is the best way to be confident they're with you," Chris had said.

"Send it," Joe said, offering a fist bump.

Ethan appreciated the warmth from the noon sun on his back. It also shone directly into the crack so he could easily see the holds and places for protection. The half-inch crack was the perfect size for Ethan's fingers. It was slanted to the right at a forty-five-degree angle and in-cut, making each finger jam feel more like a juggy hand-hold, especially if he leaned a bit to the right to keep his body weight at the perfect angle. Tiny crystals and edges populated the wall, making holds for him to walk his toes along. He used the crack's constricting nature to set several stoppers, saving his cams for later in case the climbing got harder. Another tactic he learned from his dad. "If you're at a good stance, dump a stopper and save your cams," Chris had told him often. "The last thing you want is to need a cam in a tough spot and not have one." Stoppers were more challenging to place and took a little more time, but they were as strong as a bolt when you set one right.

The overwhelming exposure no longer overwhelmed his senses, and he could focus on the climbing. He was in his own world, concentrating on executing each move efficiently, as his grandfather had. The pitch wasn't challenging, but it had incredible flow. The pattern of holds seemed sculpted by a great master route setter, and each move unfolded naturally. His fingers fit perfectly into the diagonal split and locked gently down on his joints. Edges on the face were crisp and exactly where he needed to walk his way along.

The crack dumped him out into a vast gully-like system filled with numerous smaller cracks and flakes. He considered belaying here but thought better of it and kept going to keep them on track to reach the summit before the day's warmth left them. The climbing was easy, but the drag of the rope from the hard turn into the gully became troublesome. He found a good stance, plugged two of the biggest stoppers in solid constrictions, tied off a sling to them at equal distance, placed a locker carabiner in the knot, and hitched himself to it.

"Off belay!" Ethan shouted, though he doubted his voice would carry out of the gully, so he also gave the rope two big pulls. He pulled in the slack until the rope came tight against Joe, then squeezed it through the belay plate.

"On belay!" Ethan again shouted and pulled at the rope simultaneously. He could feel the rope go loose, so he pulled in the slack as Joe climbed. He could tell precisely where Joe was through the rope. He knew the spots he moved fast and the gear he was pulling out when the rope stopped. It wasn't long before he heard a "WOOT" below from Joe as he pulled into the gully.

"That was just a stellar pitch. Good lead, you made quick work of that."

"Thanks. That finger crack was phenomenal." Ethan knew this pitch would be one he would remember for a long time.

Ethan transitioned quickly and set off on the next pitch, hoping to reach the small headwall ahead before he ran out of rope. The climbing was relatively easy but complex. He found plenty of hand cracks, and gear placements were easy to spot. In some sections, the gully narrowed into a large chimney, which he could stem across with his arms and legs stretched wide against both sides. At the top of the gully, the cracks disappeared, leading to a low-angle slab about ten feet below the ledge at the base of a headwall. He placed one last cam before the slab and carefully smeared up the thin holds, relying on the friction of his climbing shoes to do most of the work. He distributed the majority of his weight on his big toes. Ethan checked his breathing and took his time, knowing that a fall on a slab would feel like sliding down a cheese grater. His cautious movements allowed him to reach the spacious ledge without drama. He built an anchor by wrapping a long sling around a boulder, saving the cams for his lead. From the looks of it, he would definitely need them.

Ethan broke out his water to drink while he belayed Joe. Because he anchored off the boulder, he could sit facing outward instead of against the wall. The enormity of the cirque dwarfed the glacier they had slept on at the base. Steep granite walls, streaked and broken, encircled the tower. The round, barren foothills lay between the jagged peaks, still too high to grow trees in this cold expanse where the summer could be counted in weeks. Farther out was a lush green lowland that he guessed was the Yukon River valley. He could make out no sign of human development or occupation.

Ethan knew his grandfather was close, by how much easier the rope pulled without the drag of snaking over the coarse granite and through carabiners. One hand smoothly slid over the edge and into view, then another, and then Joe's head popped up with a smile.

"That was some fun climbing right there. It's good to have a couple easier ones like that."

"Agreed."

"I think it's about time we break for some lunch," suggested Joe. "What do you think?"

"I could eat."

They propped their backs against the wall and used the ledge's ample space to spread out their gear. Joe started up the stove while Ethan pulled out the dehydrated meals. The water was boiling within a minute, and Joe filled each pouch with hot water, then sealed them to cook. He poured himself a small cup of instant coffee with the leftover water, and they sat back for a few minutes to enjoy the view while they ate.

The cirque was cloudless, and the lack of wind made the ledge delightfully warm. From this perspective, more than a thousand feet above their tent, they could see most of the Kavluk Cirque. High, jagged peaks and sheer walls surrounded Harte Tower. Beyond this crown of thorns were the lower, rounded foothills, which eased into the interior plains and bogs.

"Do you ever wish you had been a full-time guide like some of the others instead of teaching kids?" asked Ethan.

"No, not really. I liked teaching."

"Traveling the world to climb mountains all year seems like a good way to live."

"Sure, but that life isn't all it's cracked up to be. You miss a lot living like that."

"Mateo seems to be pretty happy with it."

"I'm sure he is. But he probably didn't tell you about the two kids he has back home in Argentina."

Ethan sighed. "He never even mentioned he had kids."

"If a man spends his life haulin' strangers up the greater ranges but hasn't taught his six-year-old to ride a bike... that man is missin' the plot."

Joe stretched his finger toward a distant wall. "Check out that long, left-facing corner system. Maybe we can come back someday and try that thing."

"Definitely."

All around them stood walls just as immense as

Harte Tower, some steeper and more intimidating. Ethan dreamed of returning when he was older and more experienced and exploring his own line. To him, the most glorious thing you could do in climbing was to make a first ascent.

"Well, I didn't see any of the old anchors I heard about from that Italian team. I'm guessing they took a different crack system than we did. Doesn't surprise me, though, now that I've seen the wall," Joe commented. "We could have taken a half dozen variations, and it would have been fine. We can still descend this side of the mountain, but we'll have to be smart. I can sling a few of these horns on the way down, but I'll have to leave a whole lot of gear behind, which'll be expensive. That's just the way it goes sometimes. Most of these cams could use replacin' anyway."

Ethan suddenly realized they hadn't contacted his grandmother, Katherine, in the two days they'd been there. "Should we send Grandma a message from your sat phone?" he asked.

Joe nodded his head slowly in agreement. "Yeah, we should do that before we go higher. Summits tend to be cold and windy, and it's feeling really nice right here." Joe took out the satellite phone and handed it to Ethan. "You do the honors, kid. I'm no good at that texting business."

"Okay, what do I say?"

"Just tell her we're three or four pitches from the summit, and all is going well. We should be back in camp in about eight hours."

Ethan quickly typed out the text and sent it. The sky was clear and cloudless, so the message went out with no problem. He returned the phone to Joe, who stuffed it into the bottom of his backpack beside the stove he had just packed away.

Sending the message to his grandmother was the right thing to do, but it also ripped Ethan out of the moment. He was completely content and present just a few minutes before, without a care for anything outside of the cirque. But the moment he sent that message, he was filled with emotions.

12. GRANDMA'S KITCHEN

Talkeetna, Alaska
1 June 2017

—Katherine—

He has grown so much since the last time I saw him, she thought. So tall. So strong. Still thin, but he would fill out with time. They always do. It was his strength that worried her, though. She knew it was strength that always trapped men. Strong men cast aside caution too easily and stepped into danger, not knowing that if they are dealt the ultimate consequence, it would not be they who pay the bill, but the ones they leave behind. She raised her son and daughter to be strong in their own ways. Her daughter braved college in Minnesota, where she met her husband, a farmer, and raised a family. Her son grew his own family as well; then he went away to war.

"Just line up the tomatoes along the south side of the shed, Ethan. They'll get good sun there." A single prop airplane buzzed low, and Ethan looked up instinctively to watch it pass. Katherine had grown to ignore them, like the thick clouds of mosquitoes that moved off the rivers and ponds in mid-summer.

Ethan labored to pick up the five heavy pots and carry them awkwardly from the greenhouse without breaking off any of the limbs. Katherine had already evicted the kale, cabbage, and carrots out into the open air a few weeks before, but she knew her tomatoes would benefit from some extra time in the warmth that a thin layer of plastic could provide. The cool nights were good for the greens, though. Their starch turned to sugar with the temperature contrast, forming sweet from bitter.

Katherine often reminded Ethan how much of Joe and Chris she saw in him. He was lean and tall like his grandfather but had his father's brown eyes, which she liked to think he got from Katherine herself. She spoke with Julia on the phone often and knew of Ethan's troubles lately. Chris was never rebellious like that, though he may have been if he'd been raised on military bases instead of being allowed to run loose in the wilderness all summer. Katherine believed children need a physical outlet and plenty of time in nature to learn the world's mysteries. She also knew enough to know that Ethan had entered a treacherous phase in a young man's life, and she hoped his time here would help him find his true path. Few things in this world are more dangerous than a young man with no direction.

Ethan shuffled the pots around until they were evenly spaced, then tucked in a few limbs that had fallen out of the ringed cage that kept them organized. Katherine smiled at the extra care. He had always been such a sweet boy, and she was happy to see he hadn't lost that. You never know what effect tragedy will have on a young person.

"That looks wonderful." She stood back, admiring his work, and breathed in the fragrant scent of fresh tomato plants. Ethan's presence at their home this summer was something she needed more than she let on. "Alright, come inside and tell me how you like your moose cooked."

In the distance, the sun settled into the low-lying Talkeetna Mountains, where long ago Katherine took her young son and daughter on week-long backpacking trips while Joe guided on Denali. It was dangerous, and plenty of people advised against her marching two little ones into grizzly country alone, but she knew they would be fine. Better yet, they would learn lessons not taught in classrooms or cities.

Ethan sat down at the little table in the corner with only two chairs. The size of table that couples have when they don't have children, or regular visitors. A small window cast a graying light.

The kitchen was small, but Katherine didn't need much. She was like a seasoned artist who knew exactly what she needed and nothing more. Just a little salt and some herbs from the garden. She lit the gas range, set the flame to medium, placed the iron skillet on the burner, and let it warm while she got out the moose meat, tomatoes, onions, and a big block of cheddar. The fresh meat sizzled and spat when she dropped it in. Katherine poured the young man a glass of orange juice in a plastic cup with "Moose's Tooth Pub & Pizzeria" printed on it.

"So, tell me about this girl—what was her name?" Katherine asked without looking. She learned long ago that you couldn't pull truth from a boy straight on. You had to come at him from the side. She took Chris for long drives when he was a frustrated teen. There was something about sitting beside her, looking out the windshield, watching the hood eat up the asphalt rather than being locked in eye to eye, that made him relax. But for Joe and Ethan, it was food that dropped their defenses. That was ironic to her since they were both so tall and lean. She was always amazed at how much they could eat.

Ethan finished the juice and set the glass back in the same wet ring on the table. "Camila Flores. She lives a few doors down from us."

"Do you go to school with her?"

"Yeah, we had two classes together this year. I had bio with her last year, too."

She scooted behind him and opened the little window above the table to let in fresh air, as the room had grown warm with the stove.

"Well, I'm sure she's lovely if you like her." Katherine steered the conversation back to more cheerful territory. "The men in your family pick wisely, after all."

Ethan didn't look up, but she saw him smile. He had his mother's lips and mouth shape, as well as her olive undertones and darker hair. Katherine recalled the first time she met Julia. They had flown out to visit Chris at his first duty station, and it was clear their son was already madly in love. Julia had caught the climbing bug from Chris, and Katherine worried they might never have a grandchild. Their first year of marriage, the young couple spent every weekend and holiday climbing and camping. However, Julia soon became pregnant.

"Your mother says you put college on hold. She's worried, but I told her you'd figure it out just fine. Chris did the same thing after high school."

"I barely passed this last semester, so I'm not excited about sitting in a classroom anytime soon. I'd be in summer school if it wasn't for Camila."

"I like her already." Katherine used her old wooden turner to flip the patty, then placed a thick slice of cheddar on top and turned off the burner. She set the glass lid on to keep the heat in and melt the cheese without burning the meat.

Katherine plucked the patty from the greasy pan, laid it on a bun, added a slice of tomato and a leaf of lettuce, cut it in half on the plate, and then slid it over to Ethan. "If you were here a month from now, you'd have all homegrown veggies on that, but store-bought tomatoes will have to do for now."

She sat down across from him while he ate.

"It's really nice having you out here with us. The last year has been really tough, on your grandfather, especially. It's good to see him happy again." Katherine peered out the open kitchen window at the sunlight pouring through the trees and into the garden. "I've missed his smile."

"He seems excited about our Brooks trip."

"Yes, he does. You boys will have fun." Katherine crossed her arms and took a serious tone. "Ethan, I want you to watch out for him out there."

"Me? I don't think anyone needs to watch out for Grandpa, especially me."

"No, you're wrong. I know you think he's invincible, but he's not the guy he was ten years ago. Or even five. The only problem is, he doesn't seem to know it yet."

13. THE HARD THINGS

Harte Tower, Alaska
July 2017
8 days until pickup

Joe peered over his shoulder, sizing up the next pitch. "Now that's a beaut, ay?"

Ethan glanced at the wall. Their path had led them to the base of a large rock formation resembling a tombstone. A perfect crack split the otherwise smooth wall, the kind climbers spend years searching for—pure and elegant in its simplicity. It started at a finger's width on the right side of the ledge and arced upward to the left, gradually widening to hand size and likely reaching fist size at the top. The tombstone structure began vertical before kicking back a few degrees, creating a slight overhang.

"I wish we had a photographer along. That thing would make the magazines for sure," added Joe. "I think you should give it a go."

"Are you sure?"

"Definitely. You're strong enough, and it looks safe. You can plug gear in that thing all day long, anywhere you want. And the fall would be clean once you get a few placements in above this ledge. I can spot you 'til then."

"I'll give it a shot," said Ethan, but even he could hear the hesitation in his voice.

"I'm not trying to push you. I wouldn't even suggest it if I didn't think you could handle it." Joe started pulling cams and stoppers off his harness and set them on the ledge in front of Ethan. "We haven't found any gear on this line, so I think we're likely the first to ever climb this crack. Getting a shot to do the first ascent of a pitch like this doesn't come along often."

Ethan started racking the gear the way he liked it. He took long, deep breaths and moved slowly to calm himself and oxygenate his fatigued hands and arms for the fight ahead.

"I'll give it my best." Ethan looked up and mapped his course. He liked to visualize himself climbing a pitch before stepping up to it so that he had some kind of plan. He tried to imagine where he would get rests and where he could place gear.

"Give 'er hell, kid."

"I need to quit thinking and get to it." Ethan reached high and locked his left fingertips into the quarter-inch crack, his hand turned inward with his thumb down. Once his fingers were buried, he pulled his elbow down, locking in those fingers as they rotated. He pressed the rubber edge of his right big toe into the crack, stood up straight, crossed over, and locked his right hand in a similar manner. For balance, he smeared his left foot against the smooth granite face. The crack widened one move higher, allowing him to sink his fingers in up to the knuckles. He placed his first cam and clipped the rope into the carabiner.

"Nice work, kid," said Joe, obviously relieved. He had stood under Ethan for this initial sequence, with one arm stretched out toward Ethan while he belayed with the other to push him toward the wall and keep him from bouncing back over the ledge if he fell before placing his first cam.

Ethan made a couple more moves, and, to his delight, the crack widened to a hand jam. He locked his left wrist in the crack, shook the other hand below for a moment, then placed a one-inch cam chest-high and clipped it to the rope. He felt good knowing he'd likely made it through the most technical section of the pitch. He still had plenty of climbing to reach the top of the tombstone, but at least the jams should be more secure now.

"Strong work!" Joe shouted up from below. "You're not climbing like the scrawny punk I remember."

"Mom fed me good, I guess."

Ethan immersed himself in the flow. Left-hand jam. Slide up right hand to a jam below the left. Smear the left foot high on the wall. Step up, jam the right foot, and twist it. Repeat. He was tired, and the long day was beginning to weigh on him, but he still felt strong. He was in the zone. Ten feet, place gear, ten feet, place gear, ten feet, place gear. The cams he placed were excellent, and there was nothing but a clean fall below if he took a whip. He could finally see a small ledge above him, coming up on his right where he could build an anchor to belay Joe up to him. He took his time and took deep breaths in between moves. The big fist jams on the overhanging crack limited the circulation in his hands, and the lactic acid built up, making ignoring the pain impossible. He thought of giving up and calling down to Joe to take in slack. He wanted to just hang from the rope and rest. His arms and hands were killing him. He suddenly remembered an argument he'd had with Camila.

"You only want to do what YOU want to do," Camila had said to him. "When it's something you like, then you kick ass at it." That was months ago, before they got the news about his dad. Another lifetime ago. They were studying together for a chemistry exam. He wasn't sure why the memory came to him at that time.

"What the hell is that supposed to mean?" he had responded.

"I'm just saying, anytime you have to do something you don't like, you act like you're being skinned alive."

"No one likes doing things they don't like. That's kinda how it works."

"We all do things we don't like, Ethan."

"Okay, now you're sounding like my dad."

"Well, maybe he's not always wrong."

"So, you're on his side?"

Camila had sighed. "No. Ethan. I'm on your side. Not everyone is against you, ya know."

"Sorry. I'm just not a fan of chem. I stopped liking science when they put math in it."

"Well, when you do figure out what you want out of life, I hope you're able to do the hard stuff to get there."

Doing the hard stuff. He'd heard that before. From his parents. His teachers, too. And then Camila. He knew he could do hard things, though, when he thought it mattered. He just hadn't found anything he liked except for running and then climbing. He handled all the training. The long runs, weightlifting, and bouldering at the gym. He just needed to find his passion and, even better, a way to make a life out of it. That would prove he could make his own decisions, do the hard stuff, and succeed at finding his own direction.

He shook out each hand half a dozen times and felt the blood returning and the pain fading. *You can do it. Clean first ascent. No hangs.* This became his mantra, and he repeated it to himself. He placed another cam and covered the last ten feet to the ledge. *Clean. No hangs.* One last fist jam, then he reached up to a big juggy hold he could use to swing onto the ledge.

He was airborne before he knew it. There was no time to be scared or react at all. One second, he was riding the highest high, sending the best pitch of climbing he had ever climbed. Then he wasn't. The jug silently broke off, and he fell through the air backward while still holding the head-sized rock that had felt so firmly attached when he grabbed it. He instantly knew he had trusted it too soon. A seasoned climber would have tested it with a smack of his hand before letting go of the great jam he had with the other hand.

Ethan had fallen plenty of times before. At the gym or a sport climbing crag, where there were no real consequences as long as the belayer was solid. All of those falls were on bolted routes. From a half inch of steel wedged deep in the rock. And, if he were to sprain his ankle or suffer some minor injury, then he could easily hop to the car. That wasn't the case on an expedition.

Joe was watching and reacted quickly. He slammed his brake hand downward and gripped hard to apply as much friction to the rope as possible. Ethan fell twenty feet before his full weight was caught by his last cam, which fortunately did not rip out. The upward pull yanked Joe off his feet and slammed him against the rock with enough force that it would have cracked his skull had he not been wearing a helmet. It was almost enough to knock him unconscious, but he was somehow able to hold the brake strand and arrest Ethan's fall.

Ethan came to an abrupt stop as the rope came tight, and the rock in his hands slipped from his grasp, plummeting toward the very spot Joe had been standing before being ripped from his stance. The rock hit with enormous force and exploded on top of the pile of rope stacked loosely on the ledge. Tiny pieces of rock shrapnel blasted Joe's legs.

"Whoa! What the hell was that?"

"A hold blew," Ethan said sheepishly.

"Good lord. That coulda killed me."

"Sorry, I didn't check it. It looked solid."

Joe shook his head. "Well, you okay?"

Ethan looked at his hands and arms. He didn't see any blood. "I'm okay. Are you okay?"

"Yeah. I think so. Got my bell rung pretty good, though. Think you can make it back up to the ledge?"

He looked up at the ledge. It felt so far away all of a sudden. "Yeah, I can do it," Ethan said as he pulled himself into the crack. His hands were still shaking, and he had to fight to control his breathing. Although he had already climbed this part just moments before, it now felt different, like a friend who had betrayed him and whom he no longer trusted. He slowly swam his way back up to the ledge and placed one more cam before mounting the ledge again. He built an anchor of three small stoppers in a spider-webbed crack system.

"Off belay!"

Joe took longer than usual to sort his gear and start climbing.

"Everything okay down there?" Ethan shouted down. He could see Joe hunched over, working with the rope.

Joe didn't even look up to respond. "I think the rope's fried."

Ethan felt a sinking, heavy feeling in his gut. A complete reversal of fortune had happened so suddenly. He was finally settling into a groove before that one bad move changed it all. The air now felt colder, the breeze more biting. The teeth of the surrounding peaks more jagged and threatening.

"Climbing!" Joe called up. He followed the pitch and Ethan pulled up rope robotically. Joe joined Ethan at the belay after ten minutes that felt like a week. He was breathing hard from moving up the crack as quickly as he could.

"Got some bad news, kid. We lost about eighty feet, maybe more. I used my pocket knife to cut the core shots. I salvaged the short bits for anchors, but I don't think we'll have enough rope or gear to get us down this way."

"Then what do we do?" Ethan could hear the fear in his own voice. The worst part of this for him was how helpless he felt. He had no idea of what to do or how to solve the cascading problems that had just fallen into their laps. "Can we get a rescue? A helicopter could pick us up from the top if we can get there. It's close."

"That's only in the movies, kid," Joe laughed. "We don't need to ruin anyone else's day with our problem. Especially if it costs me an arm and a leg."

Ethan felt deflated. His rush of hope had been snuffed out.

"It's alright, Ethan, we can't panic. Things go wrong sometimes on expeditions, and you have to sort 'em out." Joe looked up at the summit, then back down the route.

"We can't descend the route with what we have. We'll have to get to the top and rap the west face to the shoulder. Then we'll work our way down the North Glacier and circle around to the east rib and back onto the South Glacier."

"You don't think we should at least try to go back down from here?" Ethan was terrified of descending the west face to the giant glacier on the backside. The crevasses would likely be enormous on that side, unlike the smaller, more friendly cracks they found in the south cirque.

Joe shook his head without pause. "That wouldn't be a good idea. We can't risk getting stranded a few hundred feet off the glacier with no more gear to lower on."

Ethan did the math in his head. If they had 120 feet of rope, then doubling the rope over for rappels would leave them with only sixty feet for each rappel. That meant they would have to rappel twenty-five times to descend fifteen hundred feet. They would need to leave two pieces of gear on most anchors for each rappel, which meant they would need around fifty pieces of gear or cord. They didn't have even close to that. Also, they had only one or two pieces of protection for each size. By the time they neared the bottom, they would likely find themselves in a spot that needed cams or stoppers that had already been used above. Joe had already calculated this and knew the answer. They would have to descend the shorter, more gradual west face, traverse the glacier, and hope to ascend the east rib with their shortened rope. All this with no sleeping bag and only a few snack bars left.

"Should we call Grandma and let her know?" asked Ethan.

Joe thought for a moment. "No, we shouldn't worry

her with the details. We have plenty of days left to make it back to camp and catch the plane. We'll send her a message tomorrow, and she can let Sandy know what happened as well, just in case something else happens."

Ethan thought back to the conversation they had before starting the climb. He knew they might need more equipment if anything went wrong, but Joe wouldn't consider it. There was nothing to do about that now. He glanced at their tent with their sleeping bags and food a thousand feet below.

"Look, this will only add a day to our climb. Stuff like this happens on a big trip. This is Alaska. If you get in trouble here, you get yourself out of it. We're not hurt, and you can eat the last three snack bars. I'll make you a double-decker quesadilla when we get to camp," Joe said as he nudged Ethan with his elbow.

Ethan loosened up a little. An extra day not spent sitting in camp could be a good thing. He had grown tired of lying in the tent waiting for good weather to climb, and the thought of a few more days doing that did not appeal to him. And, he remembered that he'd signed up for an adventure. He'd read books about stuff like this his whole life. Would Jack London call for a rescue? *I can do the hard things.*

"Sounds like a plan."

14. SIMMERING COALS

Wichita Mountains, Oklahoma
Two Years Prior

The pulsing, electric chorus of thousands of cicadas shimmered in waves like an inferior mirage rising from the plains. The bugs' crescendo announced midday's arrival and signaled the end of the morning climbing session. Chris and Julia chose a shaded route to start the day, but it did little to shield them from the stifling humidity that blanketed them.

Ethan topped out on the route as the noon sun invaded their refuge. He wiped the sweat seeping down his forehead out of his helmet with the sleeve of his sun shirt and looked out at the endless plains, which he briefly stood above as if in a boat in an infinite ocean of grass. The Wichita Mountains presented a brief interruption to the otherwise unbroken Oklahoma savannah reaching toward the horizon.

Ethan rappelled faster than his mother would have liked, but slowed near the ground, lightly touching down on his toes like a dancer.

Chris looked up from where he sat reclined against the rock with his legs stretched out in the dirt. "Nice work there, hoss. You'll have to call your grandpa when we get home and tell him you led your first 5.11. He'll be proud."

"I didn't think I was gonna get it. I almost fell three or four times."

"But you kept fighting," said Julia.

"Yeah, I didn't want to come back again to do it!"

"Just like your dad says, you have to believe the line will go."

Ethan pulled the rope from his device, then pulled one end and coiled it neatly over his shoulders. "I'm getting hungry."

"Sounds like someone wants us to get burgers on the grill," said Chris.

"I second that," agreed Julia.

They packed their gear and started down the trail with Ethan in the lead. They soon came to a junction where they could go straight, take a hard right, or take a slight left, and Ethan confidently chose the slight left trail to get back to camp.

"Whoa. You sure that's the way?" asked Chris.

Ethan thought for a moment, trying to remember which direction they came from. He was confused because they had climbed in four different areas that day. He looked up to the sky for direction, hoping the sun could help him gain his bearings. Normally, the late afternoon sun would be due west, but at noon, it was directly above them and offered no help at all.

"I'll just use my phone," answered Ethan. He pulled out the new phone he had bought with his allowance recently and opened the app. "I don't have service."

Chris and Julia smiled at this revelation.

"Well, ain't that a shame," mocked Chris, sliding his backpack onto the ground. He quickly pulled out the small forest service map and his old, bulky compass and handed them to Ethan.

***

The summer heat in Oklahoma was stifling even after the sun had gone down. They lit a campfire, more to chase away mosquitoes than anything else. The licking flames also gave them something to fixate on. A silence set in, broken only by the serenade of crickets and the occasional popping of tree sap in the campfire.

"Dad, do you ever get scared...over there?" asked Ethan.

His father took a deep breath, eyes still fixed on the dancing flames. "Sure, sometimes. But it's not like what you see in the movies, kid. Mostly, it's just boredom. A lot of time is spent doing mundane stuff that needs done, like fixing equipment or cleaning it. That's never-ending. Course, there are the brief moments that *are* scary, and you never really know when that's gonna happen."

Ethan half stood and scooted his folding camp seat back from the fire, retreating from the escaping embers. "I think I'd be scared if I was in a war."

Chris shrugged. "I think most people would, but many things in life are scary. Starting up at a new school every few years is scarier than anything I did as a kid. I spent most of my childhood in one state. Rarely met anyone new until I went into the Army."

"You hunted moose and had to watch out for grizzlies when you were a kid."

Chris laughed. "True, but I was used to that. What I'm saying is we fear things like the unknown or big changes in our lives. But, we can adapt to almost anything if we don't let fear lock us up."

"Dad, I looked up the climbing gym in Colorado Springs. They have a climbing team, and I wanna join it once we move there."

"Hmm. When do they practice?"

"Weeknights, a few times a week. They go to competitions all around the country, too."

"I don't see how you could do that and keep up with cross country. Or keep your grades up."

Ethan looked into the fire and sat quietly. Simmering like the red-hot coals.

15. UNKNOWN VIOLENCE

Brooks Range, Alaska
July 2017
8 days until pickup

The weight of the situation hit them as the sun left the south side of the tower, leaving them in the cold shade of evening. Although they weren't in any grave danger at the moment—the nights weren't all that cold this time of year—and they had enough layers to stay warm enough, barring a big storm, they were in for a lot more work than they initially signed up for. Joe took action.

"All right, we need to get up and over that summit. If we stay here whining, we'll get cold. We don't have enough rope to pitch the last two hundred feet, so we'll have to simul-climb." Ethan had read about this climbing style before but had never tried it in real life. He knew it would allow the two of them to move simultaneously on both ends of the rope. But, because it carries the risk of significant falls, it's meant only for easy terrain. "I'll make sure there's plenty of gear between us, but I'm not stopping to build belays. When that rope comes tight, move your ass."

Joe set off. A few minutes later, the rope came taut, and Ethan followed, trying to keep up. The final few hundred feet were easy, and they moved fast. Ethan knew he would rip Joe off the wall if he fell, and he took that responsibility seriously. It took little time for them to reach the summit, and Ethan would remember very little of it. His mind was filled with anticipation of what was to come.

High, wispy clouds moved in and blocked the sun's warmth. A light breeze blew out of the west. The fatigue from a full day of climbing settled on Ethan like a weighted blanket. For the first time in his life, he wanted to quit. Just hit a button and start over at home, warm in his bed. But, of course, there was no such button, and they would have to get themselves back to safety under their own power. He felt ashamed and weak just for thinking of giving up. What would Joe think of him if he knew how much he wanted to stop and lie down, or get whisked away magically to a pizza parlor with an all-you-can-eat buffet? Even worse, what would his father think. Ethan couldn't imagine there was ever a time in his dad's entire life when he was tired enough to entertain those kinds of thoughts. Nope, not the war hero.

Ethan had dreamt of a joyful and victorious summit with his grandfather, but those hopes had been dashed. They spent no time on the summit basking in glory. Instead, Joe found a horn of granite and tied a short piece of the salvaged rope around it for them to make their first rappel down the west face.

The more he could utilize the old rope for anchors, the more gear would be available for them to climb up the east rib when they reached it. Joe went down first, wearing the gear on his harness and coils of rope around his torso, searching for a spot to build the next rappel anchor. He hoped to find some kind of crack or stance at the end of the rope to make the most of each anchor. The sun was now approaching its lowest point in the northern sky, casting a dramatic, red-tinted glow over the surroundings. Joe swung around, cursing as he searched for a good spot. After a few minutes, he informed Ethan that he was off rappel, which meant he must have found a suitable place.

Ethan lowered himself to find Joe hanging from a crack. There was no stance for them to stand on, so they were forced to hang uncomfortably from their harnesses. It wouldn't take long for their legs to go numb in that position, so they transitioned quickly.

Once Ethan clipped himself into the anchor, he rethreaded the rope through the two cams they would be lowering from next. Joe fed the rope through his belay device and rappelled down to the next anchor. Upon reaching the ends of the rope, he began swinging back and forth to his left and right. After three or four swings, Joe reached a ledge to his far left. He put his hand into a crack to hold himself steady while he placed a cam, then a stopper, and clipped them together, and then clipped himself directly to that and took himself off the rappel. He also tied the ends of the rope to his anchor so Ethan could lower directly to him, avoiding the need to swing over.

"This is a much better stance," said Ethan as he reached the ledge, but Joe didn't bother responding. He was too busy thinking through the dangers ahead and what he would need to do to ensure they made it home safely.

"After this rappel, it looks like we can scramble a bit to the shoulder. We'll likely need to make a couple more rappels from there to put us on the glacier."

Joe rappelled again and touched down on the steep, rocky slope below. Ethan quickly joined him, and they were happy to stand on their feet once again. Joe coiled much of the rope around his torso and tied an overhand knot when about thirty feet of rope remained between him and Ethan. He clipped this to his belay loop with a locking carabiner to shorten the length of rope between them.

The mountain was still steep but not steep enough to require a rappel. If Joe had been alone here, he would have scrambled down this section ropeless, but a slip would likely be fatal, so he opted to keep a rope between them and stay above Ethan to spot him as they made their way down to where the wall again fell off vertically.

"Alright, buddy. You're in the lead. Just take it nice and easy. I'll be back here, keeping the rope fairly tight between us. Just aim down and left 'til we get to that cliff edge and try not to stumble," Joe directed.

They made it down to the cliff below them reasonably fast, though they had to turn around and climb down a few short sections too steep to walk. Joe kept the rope tight on Ethan each time, belaying him with just the friction of the rope around his waist, and Ethan felt safe knowing that he had Joe guiding him. He was in awe of Joe's skills in the mountains.

Ethan still had lingering doubts concerning their plan, but he kept trying to brush them aside. Joe knew what he was doing, and Ethan thought he'd be okay as long as he followed Joe's lead. He must have lived through plenty of adventures like this before, and he was still kicking.

He thought back to the last conversation with his grandma. Katherine had come out of the house to check on them as they were getting close to driving out of Talkeetna. She had quizzed them for details to refresh her understanding of their plan and ease her mind.

"So, when do you fly in?" Katherine had asked.

"Hopefully tomorrow or the day after. If the weather is good," Joe had answered.

"And when do you fly back to Fairbanks?"

"About ten days after we fly in. Again, if the weather is good."

"What do I do if I don't hear from you?"

"I wrote the phone number to the airstrip on the back of the map. You can give them a call anytime to check in. The folks in the office are always there to relay any info."

Katherine had nodded, then added, "And you packed the sat phone?"

"Yes, ma'am, I did," Joe had replied, "And I'll call you on the nights we have a clear sky for a signal. Don't worry if you don't hear from us, though; that could mean we're having a cloudy streak."

It made Ethan feel better just knowing they had someone out there to help if needed. He knew Katherine would move heaven and earth to get to them if they asked.

Joe tied the last piece of severed rope around a large boulder at the edge of the cliff and rappelled to the edge to look down before committing. He smiled, seeing both ends of the rope lightly touching the snowy slope below.

"Well, we're in luck. It looks like we'll be on the shoulder with this one."

Once Joe lowered over the edge, Ethan could not see

him, but he put his hands on the tight ropes and waited for them to go limp. That would tell him Joe had taken his weight off, and Ethan would be able to feed the ropes through his belay device to lower.

"Off rappel!" echoed up from below.

He was relieved to see Joe walk out onto the snowfield, smiling. He was obviously delighted to be on the glacier and have the descent behind them. They had done it without running out of climbing gear. Sure, they had a long way to go, but they would at least be on their feet now and could return to camp at the end of the following night if they moved quickly. They could find a safe place to lie down for a quick nap. It would be cold without sleeping bags, of course, but if they found a place out of the wind, Ethan figured they would be okay.

As Ethan neared the end of the ropes, Joe walked further away from the wall and onto the glacier to avoid getting hit by any loose rocks Ethan might kick down as he rappelled the final section. Joe had put on his down puffy jacket and was looking down the glacier at the next phase of their journey, likely already piecing together a plan for them in his head.

Joe looked up at the bowl of snow and ice, as if suddenly realizing he had walked into an ambush. Deep within the snowpack beneath Joe's feet lurked a monster in hiding. The weak layer of snow from the previous fall lay only ten feet below, now covered by a winter's worth of wind-blown snow that had condensed as hard as wood but was fragile as glass. If fractured at any point, the entire layer would collapse and slide. Like a buried land mine waiting to be tripped. Megatons of icy blocks would skate, break, and demolish everything in their path. It was the kind of danger that even the best of the best would often miss. The steep, north-facing slope up high where the cold persisted was a different beast than they had encountered on the South Glacier, which was lower in altitude and baked by the sun. Joe looked down at his feet, then up toward Ethan, who was rappelling down to the surface.

Joe held up his hand and shouted, "Ethan, stop!" But he was too late.

Ethan zipped down the last ten feet to the glacier and landed solidly on its firm surface. He both heard and felt a resounding "WHUMPF" come from the earth, and it all fell out beneath him. Above them, in the accumulation zone of the glacier, a crack shot across the entire width in an instant as the lower slabs broke, and the upper bowl emptied on them as if the foundation of a skyscraper had been detonated, like in one of those videos of buildings being demolished.

As he fell, Ethan looked back briefly to see Joe swept from his feet and almost immediately lost as the snow that had seemed so firm now broke apart into thousands of massive blocks as they slid down the steep valley. Ethan stopped abruptly when his belay device hit the knots Joe had tied into the ends of the rope in one final act of safety that unknowingly saved his grandson's life. Ethan dangled well above the fresh ice of the glacier that was left after the upper layer slid off.

Seconds slowed, crawled by, as Ethan caught flashes of the savage force rushing under him. A river of mayhem. Massive bricks of packed snow the size of trucks broke apart into smaller blocks, then exploded into roaring clouds of powder that veiled the true carnage from view. Far more frightening to Ethan than what he could see was the unseen. The unknown violence his grandfather was now a victim of.

Eventually the roar of the avalanche subsided and the cloud of crystallized powder dissipated, leaving tiny shards of floating ice particles glistening like crystals in the sun. The air was still, broken only by echoes of the cascade barreling down the lower reaches of the gorge, and Ethan's muffled sobs as the weight of his grandfather's death settled in.

16. OPTIONS

Colorado Springs, Colorado
8 April 2017

Ethan and David left early Saturday morning, just as the sun cast its first rays on the high peaks above. Pikes Peak was the first to turn blood red, and within minutes, the entire range was awash in that brief flood of Alpenglow. By the time they drove into Garden of the Gods, the temps had climbed into the low sixties. Great fins and spires of sandstone and limestone cut across the divide between mountain and plain like some old, dilapidated wall that once held back the barbarians but had fallen into a state of disrepair. Rock layers representing eons of time at the bottom of ancient seas and riverbeds now folded upward by the might of the Rockies, announcing that the world was now theirs. David parked in the south lot, which was still mostly empty this time of year, before the tourist hordes overflowed the park for the summer. They shouldered their packs for the hike.

After fifteen minutes of huffing and puffing, David and Ethan were at the base of their route. A two-hundred-foot crack system broke up the limestone cliff above. Birds circled the summit, protecting their nests from would-be predators.

David dropped his pack on the ground and wiped the sweat from his forehead with his shirt. He was tall, well over six feet, but not exactly athletic. Ethan's dad, Chris, was a good five inches shorter than David but was built more solidly. David's pale skin tended to burn if he was out too long, so he caked himself in sunscreen.

"Well, it's been a long week for me, kid. It's your lead today. I sure wish I had those seventeen-year-old knees of yours."

"Almost eighteen, in June," Ethan clarified.

David laughed. "Well, I stand corrected. Your lead, mister *almost* eighteen."

"Sounds good," Ethan said as he pulled his gear out of his pack. Within minutes, he had his gear racked on his harness and was tied into the rope. David was a little slower to get ready. He was new to climbing but did his best.

"You're on belay," David called out, and Ethan nodded and replied, "Climbing."

He danced up the first pitch of the route quickly. The angle of the wall wasn't steep, and he had plenty of footholds, so he needed only a few pieces of gear along the way. The first pitch was easier than the next and was well below Ethan's threshold. He was at the anchor ledge within a few minutes. He tied into the two steel bolts and shouted down to David, "Off belay!" Then he pulled up the rope until he felt it go tight and put it through the belay plate. Ethan's dad would have been climbing before the rope came tight, but David took a minute to prepare. As David eventually pulled up to the anchor, Ethan grabbed the gear from David's harness and sorted it on his own in preparation for leading the next pitch. David attached a locking carabiner to the anchor, tied in direct, and quickly put Ethan on belay. Without words, they checked each other to see if they were safe, and Ethan again launched upward.

Ethan had grown to see climbing as a balance between doing your best not to fall and trusting your partner to catch you if you did. David was one of the few people Ethan trusted to belay him outside his family. His father had constantly lectured him about the bond of the rope. He compared it to being a soldier and how you owe it to each other to watch each other's back and make sure you both make it home safely. His father met his mother at his first duty station, where she worked at the base's PX. She was an "Army brat" and had grown up on bases across the US and Europe. Her father died of a heart attack soon after retiring and before Ethan was old enough to remember him. Ethan's parents' first date was actually at the Fort Hood climbing wall, and the bond of the rope must have worked because little Ethan was born less than a year later.

The second pitch was steeper and more challenging. Ethan spent extra time searching for the best holds among the huecos, fins, and hand jams in the crack. He remembered to stay calm and breathe deeply and slowly, just as his dad had taught him, and soon he reached the anchor. He then brought David up, and before long, they were both lounging on their backs at the top of the spire.

"Your father told me one thing he liked about the mountains was their honesty. He said you're either strong enough to climb it or you're not. Mountains will never let you cheat or get away with something you haven't earned." David punched Ethan's shoulder, saying, "The only thing the mountains have ever told me is that I'm out of shape!"

Ethan liked that David didn't take himself too seriously. It made him easy to talk to.

They had earned an impressive view of the park and took a few moments of silence to soak it all in. Below them sat Colorado Springs, lazily sprawled out, with a snowy Pikes Peak perfectly framed by the foothills.

The ambiance was broken by beeping sounds from the device on David's hip. He looked down at his blood glucose reading and took out a snack bar from his pack.

"I don't know if I'll ever get used to this thing," said David.

"I thought people were born with diabetes. I didn't know it could just happen to you," puzzled Ethan.

"It happens that way sometimes. They say it's genetic, but sometimes it doesn't hit you until you're older. It was that way in my case, at least."

They went back to enjoying the view silently for a few more minutes.

"Ya know, when this happened," David pointed to his blood monitor, "I thought it was the worst luck I could have. And when your dad...well, I felt even worse then. Like I should have been there. I still feel that way, kind of. Do you know what I mean?"

"I think so."

"But, here lately, I started thinking maybe there was a reason I was left behind." David straightened up a little and said, "Ethan, you're at a crossroads right now." Ethan could tell he was trying to delicately broach the topic of his recent troubles. "The way I see it, you have three options. One is you can keep throwing darts at life and hope for the best, which will likely get you kicked out of school. I don't imagine your mom will keep supporting you in her house after that unless you get a job, but who knows.

Two, you can go to work landscaping for Bill Thomas. Remember him? Our old First Sergeant. He retired last year and started his own company. He loved your pops."

"Yeah, I remember him."

"And there's a third option. Your mom thinks you need a little direction. She wants to send you up to Alaska to stay with your grandparents this summer. Maybe take some time to make your own plan, and then you can come back and take things a little more seriously."

Ethan didn't respond right away. Instead, he gazed out at the tiny cars zipping down the roads toward the city, adrift on the high plains.

"You don't have to decide now; just let your mom know soon so she can make plans. She has Thomas's phone number if you want that job."

"Should I roll some dice?"

David smiled and shook his head. "I think you must've been a nomad in your former life."

17. ALONE

Brooks Range, Alaska
July 2017
8 days until pickup

The rope Ethan swayed from, the sole reason he still lived, shuddered violently in his hands as his weight oscillated back and forth along the exposed rock above like a string across the teeth of a saw. Knots tied at each end of the rope had sucked up against the metal plate of the belay device on his harness and had saved him from being swept away when he triggered the avalanche—when several football fields of snow broke up and rushed away beneath him. Now, he hung ten feet above the glassy ice of the freshly exposed glacier and would stay there, swinging wildly, until the jagged teeth of the mountain chewed through the rope's outer sheath and flushed him right down that river of ice with no more care than a child dropping flower petals into a quiet brook.

He could see the damage that the serrated edge had caused to the rope from twenty feet below. He knew the situation required immediate action. He needed to relieve the tension on the ropes quickly, but there was nowhere to stand and nothing to grab. The wall in front of him was smooth and featureless, but to the right, about ten feet away, there was a ledge big enough for him to stand on. From there, he imagined he could take his weight off the ropes, open the carabiner, untie the knots, and pull the rope through the anchor they had set for the rappel during their escape. Once he accomplished that, he could climb down to the glacier and formulate a coherent survival plan in his mind. He tried not to dwell on what he couldn't control; he could only focus on fixing one thing at a time.

The next time the rope swung toward the rock, he kicked with both legs, propelling himself to the left, away from the pedestal. When his pendulum brought him back to the center, he kicked again, this time to the right, getting within inches of the platform but not quite reaching it. Instinctively, he leaned into the momentum. He could feel the rock above gnawing at the rope once more. How long could it hold? Once gravity halted his swing to the left, he pushed off with all his strength. With only a little grip from kicking against the wall, he just managed to reach the pedestal, grabbing hold of the rock with both hands. His fingers turned numb from the cold stone. The vibrant orange and yellow lichen decorating the wall he clung to glowed electric.

A brutal, biting wind whipped across Ethan's face, sharp enough to freeze the tears still wet on his cheeks. Like a cold breath from a corpse. The sudden sting jolted him from his haze of fear and deep grief. The low sun of the gray Alaskan night cast an effulgent light throughout the desolate valley, where he now stood as the solitary occupant.

From his vantage point, suspended at the end of his rope and perched on a small, precarious ledge, the jagged peaks of the Kavluk Mountains surrounded him, making him feel as if he were sitting in the mouth of a giant beast, taking one last look at the world before being swallowed whole.

An overwhelming fear threatened to consume him as the Arctic's unforgiving emptiness closed in. He shivered, his breath visible in the icy air, and the reality of his situation hit hard. He was alone in the middle of the night, dangerously exposed, and facing a deadly ordeal he was unprepared to endure.

His father's words suddenly whispered to him as clearly as if he were standing next to him.

Believe the line will go.

Ethan had no idea how he would get out of the mess he was in, but he did know he needed to get off the rope and find a safe place to sit. He mantled up to a stance on the perch, which unweighted the rope enough for him to untie the knot on one of the rope ends, and he let it slide through his belay device as he climbed down to the glacier. The resistance of the rope pulling from the anchor above helped to ease him slowly. Once down to the edge of the ice, he pulled the rope hand over hand, and the end eventually ran through the anchor above and fell to him, loosening several rocks as it did. Ethan scurried to avoid getting hit and slid on the ice. He clawed desperately as he accelerated feet first in the direction his grandfather had been swept. He clung to a rock frozen in the ice and brought himself to a stop. His heart was beating so fast he thought he was going to faint.

"I can't do this!" Ethan cried out. All he wanted was to lie there, never to move again, or to be transported back home, safe with his mom and Camila. He wished he could be like those kids who did everything right. Who went to college on scholarships and never skipped class. The ones who knew what they wanted to do with their lives back in eighth grade. He could be in Colorado, working a summer job to earn a few bucks before starting his first semester in the fall. He wouldn't have needed to fly to Alaska to figure out who he was and what he truly wanted in life.

The ice was cold, so he picked himself up and leaned against the rock, standing on small rocks sticking out of the ice. He coiled the rope and placed it in his pack. He needed a place to rest and take shelter. A place where he could survive long enough for help to come and rescue him. He would die here otherwise. The adrenaline started to wear off, and he realized he was shivering from the cold or from fear, maybe both. He found a stance on the edge of the rock wall next to the glacier and took off his small backpack. He regretted putting the satellite phone in Joe's backpack instead of his own. If he had it, he could have called in a rescue right then, and he didn't care how much it would cost.

He changed out of his rock shoes and into his lightweight mountain boots, which were much warmer than the climbing shoes he'd been wearing. He thought about tossing his climbing shoes away to lighten his load but thought better of it and placed them in his backpack in case he needed them later. He had only three snack bars left and knew that would be a problem. He wondered how many days he could make it without food after that. He opened his one-liter plastic water bottle and swallowed the last of it. Without a stove to melt the snow, he would be left to eat ice and snow from the glacier. He thought of throwing the bottle down, but he packed it instead. It was light enough not to be an issue, and it could be valuable if he came across water somehow.

Also in his pack were a pair of rain pants, a space blanket, and a thin down jacket. They had been moving so quickly to get off the mountain that he had no time to get cold until now. He promptly put on the pants and jacket to preserve the warmth his body possessed.

He checked the time on his phone. 2:37 a.m. The battery was at sixty-one percent, so he powered down to save it. He wasn't sure why. What could he use it for now? Finding cell coverage anywhere in the mountain range was highly unlikely and not worth trying. The only reason he brought it on the climb was to take pictures, and he was in no mood to do that now.

He looked around desperately in hopes of finding somewhere to hide. Somewhere safer than the collision zone between rock and ice that he currently straddled. Ethan surveyed the scene below him, the direction he and Joe had planned to go, and saw nothing of comfort. Just hard ice tucked against the vertical wall of rock. But uphill from him, nearly a hundred feet away, was an enclave in the mountain. Not quite a cave, but a recess into the rock with what appeared to be a flat floor. He worked his way up, using handholds on the wall to his left and trying to avoid stepping on icy spots as much as possible. Once below the recess, he scrambled up a dirty chimney littered with gravel from rocks that had fallen from high above and broken into smaller pieces on the ledge.

He gained the ledge and moved loose rocks to the back of the recess and looked for a flat spot to sit. He rearranged some stones to make an opening big enough for him to sit down and lean back against the rock. He went back and forth on whether to lay his backpack on the floor to sit on or to lean it against the rock to ease his back. He decided to sit on it first and see how that went.

Ethan sat down, pulled his legs up against his chest, and wrapped his arms around them. It was the warmest position he could conceive. He tried in vain to clear his mind from the chaos that befogged it. Memories of the fall and the avalanche replayed, and each time, he tried to correct the mistakes they made, desperately trying to mentally alter the trajectory that led him to that ledge and Joe to an icy death. Tackling the future was impossible with so much attention averted to guilt over past mistakes.

He wondered what Camila was up to at this moment. Colorado was two hours ahead of Alaska, so she would still be sound asleep in bed. *If I'd put the sat phone in MY backpack, I could call her right now.* It would be dark there, as nights are in the lower forty-eight. He found himself homesick for his own bed, wrapped in its cocoon of darkness, in contrast to the ceaseless and unforgiving midnight sun that tormented diurnal creatures like himself. He wanted to look at her picture but knew he shouldn't kill his battery for that since he no longer had the solar panel charger.

His mind searched for someone to blame. It was his mother's idea to send him to Alaska when he lost his college scholarship. It was his grandfather, with his grandmother's encouragement, who offered to take him on his first real climbing expedition. And, of course, none of this would have happened if his father had not died. It was all their fault, and now here he was, alone and hopeless.

He wished to be that kid again, the one who did everything right. Made good grades. Went to college. Got the girl. Made her happy. He could have done all those things if he'd been stronger. More "resilient." That's the word that the therapist used, the one his mother sent him to and he had refused to go back to see. She said she worked with a lot of military kids who lost parents and that they could choose "post-traumatic stress or post-traumatic growth." It was that one word that stuck with him after their visit and angered him still: *choose*. Like any of this was a choice he'd made.

He pulled the hood of his jacket over his head to cover his eyes and block out some of the light. He fought to clear his mind and rest, achieving brief moments of peace before being jolted back to consciousness by terrifying dreams of Joe's slide down the glacier. He felt guilty for being alive. His weight had triggered the slide, but it was his grandfather who had paid the ultimate price. Would others forgive him or blame him? What would Katherine think? He was certain she would understand, but he also knew he would always carry a sense of guilt for his role in what happened.

Echoes of rocks falling far above didn't seem real at first. But when the first small boulder hit the ledge twenty feet in front of him, he had no further illusions that he was dreaming. Shrapnel from the impact peppered the walls around him, and the gunpowder smell of exploding granite filled the air. His hood and helmet were sanded, but the large rocks in front of him took the brunt of it, saving his legs. He dropped down onto his side in a fetal position while the rest of the rock slide shot over the recess and showered the outer lip of the ledge and the glacier beyond it.

It was over soon enough, but he was instantly more aware of the dangers of his position. The world around him was volatile. More so, it was hostile. Staying here and waiting for days on end for a rescue was not an option. He had to concede that no one would come for him anytime soon, and if they did come for him, they likely wouldn't find him. And, if they did find him, it would likely be too late. *I can't just wait here to die*.

The survival books listed dozens of ways he could be hurt or killed out there. Aside from being crushed by rocks falling off the loose north face above him, he could freeze to death if a storm came along. How long would he be able to sit in the cold rain and survive hypothermia, especially at night, without a tent or sleeping bag? He shuddered to think of starving to death alone on the ledge while dodging rocks.

He had to do something. The task at hand was overwhelming, but the alternative was to sit on the ledge and wait for a miracle, and that he could not do. He had to try to get back to the tent, even if it was futile. He could die either way but moving felt like the better choice. At least he would be warmer moving, and the temps should be more hospitable the further he dropped in elevation.

Before the trip, while Ethan served his five-day home suspension for skipping, without electronics or TV, he filled time with books from the library, which was close enough for him to walk to while his mother worked. He mostly searched for adventure and survival books, anticipating his summer in Alaska. One book was a military field manual on outdoor survival that detailed how to survive in various climates and conditions with minimal gear. He tried to memorize some of the more essential skills that might prove helpful if he got lost or was in a plane crash, which seemed to rise to the top of his fears. He wanted to try different ways to start a fire without matches but was worried about getting fined by the HOA. The last thing he wanted right then was to piss off his mom any more than he already had. He looked for things he could practice before he left. He focused on navigation, building shelters, and basic first aid.

The author stressed a few things above all others. One was to keep yourself as dry as possible. A person with wet clothes would quickly succumb to hypothermia, especially at night. The second was to use your resources to the best of your ability. A sleeping bag could easily save your life. But what can you use if you don't have one? The book also showed several ways two people could cuddle for warmth or use different parts of their bodies to warm another person's feet or hands to prevent frostbite.

Camila had helped him prepare by judging the survival skills he practiced, like how to use a poncho as a sleeping bag or build a snare for rabbits. She also let him practice first aid skills on her, like splinting a broken bone and dressing a wound. Camila determined the poncho wrap was not likely to keep him very warm in Alaska, and after three days of rabbits ignoring his snare, they both deemed that one a dud as well.

"I think you need to be sure and take real food and sleeping bags because you might not make it back if you rely on *that* book," she had quipped.

He remembered reading that it was crucial to make a solid plan and to follow it. He pulled out the paper map Joe had given him and examined the options. He saw the escape path they had agreed to after the rope was obliterated, circling around to the northeast down the glacier and around to the east rib. It struck him that he was standing on the shoulder west of the tower, only a quarter mile away from its high point. If he could make it there, he would be standing right above the top of the south-face glacier where their tent was still sitting. If he could rappel down that wall, he would likely return to the tent by the end of the day, as it was only a mile of hiking from the base of the wall to their tent.

Why hadn't they talked about this as an option? he wondered. It must have been because Joe was so adamant about reversing the route. They spent almost no time on a backup plan to get down. They touched on the North Glacier-to-east rib route, but mostly just to dismiss it, pointing out the dangers of that path. He needed to take a look at the wall and either choose to take it or rule it out before committing to the longer route around the tower.

Ethan packed up again and down-climbed from the recess back to the glacier. The exposed ice was slick now that the snow above it had slid, and he struggled not to slip. He quickly learned to step on small rocks frozen in the ice for friction. At the end of the ice was a ten-foot wall of snow where the avalanche had broken and slid under Joe. Like a windshield wiper clearing snow from a windshield. Ethan could climb over it on the left side, next to the rock of Harte Tower, and scramble up to the high point of the shoulder where the ceaseless westerly wind had blown the snow clear from the mountain's rocky skeleton. He could see the south-face glacier coming into view below him, so he carefully scrambled down toward the edge of a cliff that grew steeper by the step. He soon came to an abrupt edge that he could not see over.

Downclimbing was no longer safe, so he had to rappel from there. He placed two cams into a solid crack and clipped the middle point of the rope into them. He tied knots at the ends of each side so he would not rappel off the end if he forgot to watch it, or if the wall was too steep for him to stop, take his weight off the rope, and build an anchor. He'd read about plenty of accidents in the mountains where climbers rappelled off the ends of their ropes, and he didn't plan to be one of them. He coiled both ends and tossed the two identical lengths over the edge. He fed the rope through his belay device and started lowering himself. He looked down as soon as he got far enough out to see where he was going, and what he saw horrified him.

The wall below was overhung so much that his rope fell straight down without touching a thing. Instead of landing safely on the glacier, the ends dangled in the breeze. If Ethan had lowered any further, he would have found himself hanging freely in the air, unable to set up another rappel anchor. He now understood why his grandfather had not considered this way an option, though he never said it out loud. Ethan tied an overhand knot in the rope, just below his belay device. That would stop him in the event of falling while he climbed the rope hand over hand up the sloped wall back to his anchor.

That was a big waste of time. Ethan tried to shake off his disappointment, but he had let himself be too hopeful about the shortcut.

Stop pouting and keep moving.

Ethan didn't take long to coil the rope, pack it up, and return to the North Glacier. The day had warmed, so he shed his puffy jacket and rain pants and packed them away while he was at it.

From the west shoulder, the North Glacier stretched out below for what looked like a half mile before veering right, east, around the backside of the tower. The right side of the glacier, the side butting up against the tower, was erratic with big rocks, and the wall was steep. The left side, however, was gentler, and he thought he could hug that side and even walk on the rock slabs and avoid some of the glacier altogether. He would have to be innovative and pick a line across the ice that avoided crevasses. The snow he currently stood on, above the slide zone, was like Styrofoam and easy to walk on and dig the treads of his boots into. The surface of the glacier exposed by the slide was much harder. The avalanche had revealed the icy crust that had formed the previous summer, before it was covered by the fresh snows of winter.

He figured the cracks should be big enough to see that time of year, like all the others he saw on the plane ride in, and he hoped the avalanche had filled in the smaller ones. He also remembered learning in a book from the guide shop how snow from an avalanche will actually heat up from the energy of falling and will settle like concrete when it stops. He had hiked up a firm avalanche funnel with his family while climbing Pioneer Peak and remembered it felt like walking on frozen mashed potatoes.

Although the sun was now rising in the sky, it had moved off to the east and around the opposite side of Harte Tower. He was now on the shady side of the mountain, so he put on the leather belay gloves to keep his hands warm and to protect them if he fell and needed to claw and grasp at anything he could while sliding, like he had just a few hours ago. He longed to have the ice axe with him; his dad had given it to him a few years ago. A nice stick would have helped, also, but no trees grew at this altitude, especially near a glacier. Eventually, he found a sharp, pointy, slender rock that was not too heavy. He hoped to use it to arrest his slide in the event of a fall. His father had taught him how to use an ice axe to slow himself when falling on snow, and he felt he could use the rock to do the same if he had to.

What he really wanted was the set of twelve-point crampons he had left at the base of the route, now on the opposite side of the tower. He had sharpened them with Paul's help back at the guide shop. He knew he could be making significant progress down the glacier right now if he had them strapped to his feet. He had even taken the time to read the chapter about how to walk in them on varying terrain. About ways to sidestep to avoid burning out your heels. Instead, he was left to improvise, teetering on small rocks and gravel frozen in the ice and hopping between snow patches where he could get a better grip with his boots, while trying to avoid the shiny surfaces that could cause him to skid.

He slowly made his way down the glacier, alert for dangers. He knew to avoid "sagging" areas, which might indicate snow bridges covering crevasses. He made long traverses to his left when he came across any areas that seemed suspicious.

Believe the line will go, his father's voice repeatedly played in his head.

As he reached the outer edge of the glacier, he found that the granite slabs were easy to climb onto and walk along for a time. However, he soon encountered short cliffs that forced him back down onto the ice. Even on the slabs, he needed to exercise caution. The rock had been worn smooth over eons by the glacier, making it as slippery as ice when wet.

Ethan's dad had never liked rough paths and trails when they went out for a run together, but Ethan preferred them. Chris always worried about injuring his ankles or knees and getting in trouble for it at work. A soldier's body belonged to the military, and it was his duty to ensure he was healthy and deployable. Yet another reason Ethan could never see himself signing up. He liked the narrow trails with big roots and rocks to launch over.

The foothills of Colorado Springs had lots of those. Loose and fast. Sometimes, his cross-country team would run them together, but mostly, he ran them alone. He could set his own pace that way and follow some gnarly-looking side canyon that caught his eye. He always felt that he gained more from the rugged terrain, even if it did slow him down a little. It was challenging to bomb down narrow paths over and under obstacles, constantly forced to react quickly to whatever surprise was thrown at him. It required complete focus to avoid catching his foot on a branch or a root, or having a messy slip on a wet rock. He loved that kind of full engagement.

He found that he did his best thinking while running. His brain responded to pain by seeking distraction. On his runs, he would dive deep into imaginary conversations or arguments with his mom, dad, teachers, or anyone he had recently disagreed with. Occasionally, he got caught up in negative thoughts, but he learned to guide himself back to a more positive mindset. And recently, he usually did so by thinking about Camila. She was kind and thoughtful; she taught him to cook her family's recipes for dinner when his mom was working a late shift. Camila also had a way of calling him out on his mistakes, especially when she discovered his poor grades or when he skipped school, which had become quite frequent the past year.

Running was Ethan's first love. His parents had signed him up for every sport they could to give him a chance to find something he enjoyed. Something to push him. They wasted plenty of money on ball sports like soccer and T-ball, but he never could sit still long enough to take direction from the coach, and he never saw the point of it. All it took was a butterfly to float by him or a glimpse of a good stick lying in the grass at the edge of the field, and he was gone.

His mother took him to his first cross-country race when he was in kindergarten, and he ran well. At the finish line, they gave him two ribbons. A black one for participation and a green one for his place.

"Mom, why does it have a five on it?"

"That means only four boys were faster than you." She was ecstatic that he had done better than the other fifty kids behind him, but Ethan could think only of the four. The following week, Ethan took first. He rocketed from the starting line and never slowed as the others began to wobble and weave from the strain.

But running was more to him than all the medals and trophies. At least it was before it got serious. It seemed the only people he ever met who took running more seriously than he did were the coaches and college recruiters. Junior year, that's when it all fell apart.

Ethan forced the memories out of his mind and shifted his attention back to the task at hand. Where the polished cliffs pushed him back onto the ice, the glacier became more erratic. The stone walls closed in on both sides, choking the frozen river through a bottleneck, and the ice reacted much as a stream of water would. It buckled up into a frigid rapid. Ethan slowly worked his way around some of the larger waves of ice and snow, constantly worried he would fall into a hole and disappear into the icy bowels. He used the rock to stab the slushy surface and support him when he had to turn around and downclimb at several steep sections.

Eventually, he came to an abrupt drop. A cliff of ice he would somehow have to find a way around. But, slick rock walls rose up on both sides, polished smooth by the coursing ice for millennia. He dropped to his belly and crawled out to the edge, doing his best to distribute his weight across the surface to avoid collapsing the edge and dumping him down the other side.

He peeked over the edge and saw that the drop was close to twenty feet at its lowest point, directly below him. To his right, the distance increased, and the gap between the upper and lower planes of ice opened up a large, gaping hole. He scooted backward and found a place to sit far enough away from the edge to be safe. *How the hell do I get down this thing?* Behind him was a large boulder of ice, snowy on top, but bright blue ice on the underbelly. *If I had an ice screw or two, I could rappel.* But he didn't have ice screws. He felt at his harness, grabbing the cams still hanging. He stood up and made his way to the rock wall on his left, about ten feet away. The stone was smooth but had a few small cracks. Ethan found his smallest cams and tried in vain to fit them into the widest openings, but it was futile. The cracks were too thin.

I guess that leaves only one option. Ethan had studied ice anchors in his mountaineering books and remembered the "snow bollard" method of lowering when there was no other option. It required cutting an upside-down U into the ice to hold the middle of the rope and allow him to rappel from. It seemed to be the only thing left to try.

He used the rock to cut the outline of the bollard through the slushy surface. The book had defined the size he would need to cut, classified by the hardness of the ice or snow, but he couldn't remember the specifics. The ice below the surface was solid, so he reasoned he only needed to cut it a few feet across at its widest point. He began chopping into the ice with the rock, alternating hands as they grew cold and tired. He quickly warmed from the activity and stopped to take his puffy jacket off and place it in his backpack. He bashed away for almost an hour as he created a well-shaped bollard nearly a foot deep. He pulled out the rope and flaked it at his feet. He found the middle point, dropped it into the icy grooves, and pulled it back and forth to settle it into position. The exposed ice warmed and softened from exposure to sunlight, making it easier for the rope to cut into it.

Man, I hope this works. Ethan yanked the rope downward to test its strength, and it held firm. He fed the rope strands through the belay device and locked it. He lay down on his belly, trying his best to stay flat and not to pull the rope upward, which would surely dislodge the rope from its groove. He took several deep breaths and watched the bollard closely as he applied his weight to the rope. He tried to think light thoughts as he lowered himself, feet first, still sliding on his belly, with his hand out to the side holding the brake strands. He thought he was going to vomit from fear as his legs went over the edge. He was fully committed now and could not reverse his course of action. He tried to lower slowly over the edge, but the edge broke apart under his weight, and he fell backward into the air, entirely on the rope. He held his breath, anticipating the collapse of the bollard and his plunge to the glacier below. But that didn't happen. It held. Ethan lowered himself to the glacier before the anchor changed its mind.

"Oh my god, I can't believe that worked!" he shouted aloud.

After another hour of picking his way through the cryptic boundary of ice and stone, he came upon the avalanche debris. It had piled up at a flat spot on the glacier where Ethan assumed the ice was rising over a bump in the valley floor far below the glacier before descending even faster as it wrapped around the north face of Harte Tower. The rock walls on both sides were now too steep to be of any use to him. The snow was firm and stable, and he could finally walk without sliding, although he had to dodge some of the larger chunks of snow.

The morbid thought that his grandfather must be buried somewhere beneath him dawned on him. Joe could be anywhere, maybe even under his feet. Ethan started to walk more thoughtfully and scanned the surface for clues of where his grandfather could be buried, though he wasn't sure he wanted to find his body. He thought it might help him to move on if he knew for certain he was dead instead of constantly wondering what the end was like for him. *No*, he concluded. *I don't want to see him like that.*

At the far end of the debris field was the most colossal crevasse Ethan had encountered so far, and he could see a vast series of crevasses beyond it. He scanned back and forth, looking for a way around the deep gash and settled on the right side. He followed the right edge of the debris field to take advantage of the firm snow of the avalanche's runout and followed it to the edge of the crevasse. He slowly and carefully stepped toward the edge to get inside but did not step close enough to collapse the lip and get swallowed. As Ethan got closer, he was elated to see that the right side, where it got close to the rock wall that made up the north face of Harte Tower, wasn't so deep, and he could easily climb through to the other side if he used the rock he carried as an ice axe. He found the shallowest point of the crevasse, stepped to the edge, peered down into it, and plotted a path across. He could tell the avalanche debris had filled it, and he wondered how deep it had been before that.

He glanced left, deeper into the crevasse, primarily out of curiosity, when something caught his eye. By that point, Ethan had been awake for well over twenty-four hours, aside from the short naps he had taken in the recessed wall, and with all that had happened, he was beginning to feel reality slipping away from him. The line between real and imagined was fading.

18. FIRE FROM WITHIN

Colorado Springs, Colorado
20 November 2016

The wind rattled the windows all night as the edge of the cold front rushed down the foothills. The compression warmed the air, making for a pleasant, though breezy, walk to school. However, things changed in the afternoon, catching many by surprise when the wind shifted and brought a cold, arctic chill from the north.

"You really don't have to race today, Ethan. Just make sure you take care of yourself." Coach Driscoll sat beside Ethan on a bench, neither of them noticing how cold it was for early November. A strong cold front was forecast to hit later in the day with a chance of snow. Everyone hoped it would hold off until after the meet. Countless teenagers nervously paced, awaiting their heats and adjusting their layers to the changing weather.

The front-range schools of Denver, Fort Collins, and Colorado Springs made up the majority of entrants, but small schools from the mountains and deserts of the western slope also sent their best. The city boys were known for their audacity; the mountain boys for their grit.

Ethan was numb to the size of the crowd. "It's State. I feel like I have to try." It had been less than two weeks since they got the knock on the door they always worried would come but hoped never would. The knock that now tore apart the fabric that wove their daily lives. Julia would have to work more hours to pay for their everyday needs. "Thank god for your scholarship. I don't know how we would afford your college otherwise, kiddo," she had said, not knowing how much pressure she put on Ethan to perform that day. "Your father insisted we use his GI Bill money to pay for my nursing degree. I wish we could have saved it for you instead, but we didn't have much choice at the time."

"You just tell me what you want to do, and I'll support it," his coach assured him earnestly. "But, you should probably get to the line if you are running today. You only have a few minutes."

Ethan waded through his distracted thoughts and the sea of teenage harriers to the back of the starting line. Cocky alpha males threw sharp elbows to earn the front row. A light snow began to fall. He mulled about unfocused until the starter pistol pierced the air, and only then did he realize he hadn't stretched. The front-runners got the jump on him, and he struggled to maintain a position at the front of the main pack, knowing that he would have difficulty passing them when the course narrowed as it entered the forested hills. The first mile was relatively flat, which was not Ethan's strength. He was better in the hills. That's where he would make his move on the leaders if he could hold off the mob on the flats.

But slowly, the insidious mob passed him one by one until only a few stragglers remained.

His father's voice still played freshly in his mind, and Ethan worried how long it would take for those clear memories to fade. Like how he said "pacificly" instead of "specifically." Things like that. But it was their last conversation—argument, rather—that haunted him most. *He has to know I didn't mean that.*

A deep sadness pervaded Ethan's thoughts, overpowering his will to move. He couldn't find the right gears. Runners floated past him effortlessly while he faltered. His mind raced with doubts and despair until he pitied everything about himself. Clouds darkened overhead, and the snow fell more heavily, reinforcing his feeling of desolation. Everything in his life was falling apart, and he could see nothing good. College was slipping away. His family was shattered. He resented being placed in that position. What did he do to deserve it? He had always been a good kid. He followed his dad from base to base without argument. He lost friends, made new ones every few years, and didn't complain. He couldn't do it anymore. No, he shouldn't have to.

Again, their final words came back to him.

"Son, I love you more than you can know. And that's why it's so hard to watch you slack off like you have been."

"Watch me slack off? Since when did you watch? You're never here. You've been gone half my life!"

A brisk, cold headwind shot out of the north and struck the runners like a sandblaster. He saw the boys ahead tuck their heads to shield their faces from the icy slap. But Ethan didn't turn from it. He embraced the sting, and it ripped him out of the dark hole he had dug for himself like a grenade fragmentation. This was an element he could fight against. A tangible opponent to throw his shoulder into. He was angry at all of it. His losses, his mistakes, and the faceless storm parading down the high plains from Canada to disrupt the State Finals. His fire warmed him from within, and he fed that conflagration with the fuel of as much pain and self-hate he could cast into it. The cold stare of the soldier at the door. The college recruiters who would be disappointed with the losses he was sure to rack up. His mother having to pick up night shifts to make the mortgage. He threw every bit of it into the fire.

He didn't notice much about the first runner he passed, nor the second. He ran in a rage. A blind fury. He passed a dozen within a few minutes and entered the hills in a stronger position, but he knew he was still way behind the leaders. The average pace slowed as they climbed, but not for Ethan. He plowed ahead with the same steam. The trees seemed to fly past. Several runners tried to hold him off, but few remained when they hit the last switchbacks before gaining an open, rocky ridge. His fingers numbed, and tears froze on his face. Ethan passed the third-place runner as the boy slowed to pull on a windbreaker jacket that had been tied around his waist. Ethan's arms reddened, but he hardly noticed.

The rest of his last conversation with his father came back to him.

"I'm here now, son. I'm here right now."

"Yeah, for how long?"

The trail dropped precipitously at the end of the ridge and again entered the tight forest. He bombed down at a reckless speed he should not have been able to maintain, riding the thinnest line between disaster and victory. He deftly strode over rocks and roots and dangerously cut corners inches from mature aspen trees that would have crushed his shoulder on impact. The second-place runner was only a few turns ahead, and the boy heard Ethan's monstrous strides closing in. The boy made the mistake of lengthening his own stride to maintain his position. His toe caught a tree root, and he went down. Ass over teakettle. Ethan flew past without looking. Normally, he would look to see if the guy was okay, but today, he was different.

Ethan broke from the trees into the meadow in a blinding snow squall. His assistant coach shouted from the side of the trail, "You're in second, Ethan! One more to catch!"

Ethan knew the trail was flat and straight from here to the finish. Only half a mile left to hunt down the leader. He pumped his hands in small circles in front of his body. His dad called it the wheel of power, some ancient practice he had read about somewhere. "The way it works is you imagine your fists as being like the gears of a jeep, and you turn them in a tight circle at the pace you want, and your feet will follow at the same speed. It's a natural relationship."

Snow gathered in his hair and on his clothes and in his eyebrows. His lashes gained a coat of icing. He squinted through the storm in search of first place. His lungs screamed, and his legs burned, but he refused to relent. Then Ethan saw him. The orange shirt appeared between gusts of snow. Ethan leaned further forward, risking an embarrassing fall on his face. He was closing.

Ethan could almost touch the boy's back when he broke the tape.

"It's my last deployment, Ethan. I'll be back by Christmas."

"Don't bother."

19. FLUSHED

Brooks Range, Alaska
July 2017
8 days before pickup
—Joe—

Joe realized what was happening the moment he felt the ground shift beneath him, and he was instantly angry with himself for missing the warning signs. He had just taken a moment to remove his pack and put on his down jacket, and as he put his pack back on, he let himself get distracted by the tracks of ptarmigan in the snow. Three distinct toes. Like the feet of tiny dinosaurs.

The steep snow slope behind him and the protected, north-facing aspect were clear indicators, if he had been looking. However, no one would have expected a slab avalanche that late in the summer. Harte Tower was much farther north than the mountains he had climbed most of his life, and every mountain range has its own unique set of rules, which can be unforgiving. Second chances are not guaranteed for mountain travelers. In the colder temperatures of the high Arctic, buried weak layers can remain concealed longer than in other mountain ranges. *I couldn't have known.*

He had been in smaller slides himself and lost a few friends to the viciousness of big avalanches. He knew he would likely die soon in one of two ways. Either the snow would bury him and slowly squeeze the oxygen out of his lungs, or the weight of the white monster would smash him against rocks and ice walls until his body was broken. However, if he was lucky, alert, and fought hard enough, a third option might reveal itself. He just needed to stay vigilant and look for an opportunity.

Joe made a quick turn to point himself downhill just as his feet were swept out from under him, and he was laid out on his back. He sat up, extended his arms, and paddled as if he had been thrown out of a boat on a whitewater rafting trip. He kept his feet out in front of him to bounce off rocks or ice blocks. The snow slab was disintegrating into ever-smaller pieces, and he kept sinking into the snowpack, only to be launched back to the surface when he struck something significant at the bottom of the flow. Each time Joe went under, he inhaled large amounts of snow and ice crystals, and he thought he would surely suffocate if he wasn't beaten to death first.

But more than the snowpack had fractured. A deep quake shook Joe's soul and separated all convictions from their moorings. His unshakeable, though never spoken, belief in himself as a master of the mountains evaporated. Poof. Seconds before the slide, he stood anchored in that identity, which he'd built brick by brick and others helped cement, supplying the mortar. Then, in an instant, all of it, foundation on up, cascaded down the valley toward a certain finality. That impenetrable fortress was nothing but a wooden movie prop, toppled by a slight breeze. The truth was revealed in an instant. Competence was a lie. Safety an illusion.

The slide down the glacier took an eternity, and he fought to stay conscious. He knew that to survive, he would have to be on top when the snow came to a stop. If he wasn't on the surface when the snow settled, then he would be trapped with no way to budge even an inch as the cement-like snow firmed up around him.

He sensed the slide beginning to slow. He fought hard to stay up top, but an invisible hand seemed to pull him down. His head crept below the surface, and his lungs felt as if they would burst as he fought for air, but he only pulled snow into his lungs. He desperately reached his leg down as deep as he could, hoping to find something to kick and propel him back to the surface, but there was nothing there. He sank deeper.

This is how it ends, he thought. His mind raced to his wife getting the call. Poor Ethan wandering the glacier for a week, hopelessly lost. But just as he lost hope, the flow widened as it emptied into a large crevasse, and his foot reached the hard bottom. He kicked hard, propelling himself to the surface of the flow. He dumped over the edge into the crevasse, riding atop the white beast, and was ejected to the far side, where he hit with such tremendous force that it knocked out all the snow and what little air he had in his lungs. He fell hard onto an ice ledge below and felt his right leg snap on impact. Through all the pain, he still had the wherewithal to cling to the ledge on which he found himself. Below him, the snow rushed two hundred feet down to the bottom of the enormous crevasse. After another minute, the snow came to a standstill, and then there was only silence. He coughed painfully and vomited. The world was spinning, and there wasn't one part of his body that did not radiate pain. *Dinosaur prints.* His last thought before he collapsed onto the platform face down and passed out cold.

"Daddy!" Chris pointed his little hand to the ancient bedrock beneath his feet. "Big chickens!"

They'd spent Christmas break that year road-tripping the desert southwest for two weeks. Camping in the sand and cherishing the high-altitude sun and crisp, clear nights. An escape from the dark Alaskan winter. The kids were five and nine that year. Chris was so innocent then. So fragile. So curious.

His big sister laughed. "Those aren't chickens, dummy. They're dinosaur prints."

It was a long hike, but they didn't mind. They wanted to soak up as much sun as they could before returning home. Katherine wanted to see the prints so badly that she carried Chris the majority of the way. And finally, there they were. Four prints of different sizes, but the same shape.

Chris pointed to each in turn. "Daddy. Mommy. Sissie. ME!"

The boy's voice was so clear in Joe's memory of that moment long ago. It had distracted him. No. He let himself get distracted from the dangers around him. He'd lowered his guard. Something he never would have tolerated from his fellow guides or climbing partners.

***

He had no idea how long he had slept, but he was jolted awake by violent convulsions. His core had grown so cold that it reacted with deep shaking in a last-ditch effort to warm him. He was soaking wet. Snow had invaded every layer of his clothing during the slide, and now it had melted against his body. The ledge he was thrown to sat on the shady side of the crevasse, but the sun's blinding rays showered the opposite side just a few feet away. He lifted himself up onto his arms and was seized in pain.

"Oh, good lord," Joe said through a tightened jaw. It was apparent to him that he had broken a few ribs when he hit the wall, as well as his right leg. He gritted his teeth and tried again, this time crawling to the edge on the uphill side and using his momentum to slump down into the crevasse full of settled snow from the avalanche. The blocky texture made it easier for him to grab and pull himself up the gentle slope toward the sun. Ten minutes of extreme pain and exertion brought him to a relatively flat spot in the sun, where he collapsed. He could feel the warmth against his skin, but he needed more, and he remembered he had a mid-layer fleece in his backpack. He reached for the buckles to unsnap but couldn't find them. It dawned on him that his pack must have been ripped off by the avalanche. There was no telling where it had ended up.

We're in for a real adventure now. He quietly laughed to himself. He always had a talent for finding humor in dire circumstances, though this was probably the most dire he had ever been in.

He rolled over onto his back and cherished the warmth of the full sun on his face. He unzipped his jacket to dry out his mid-layers, and steam rose from his body as the moisture evaporated into the dry air.

Reading survival stories had always been a favorite pastime of Joe's, and he always wondered how he would handle those scenarios. Doug Scott had crawled for nine days on two broken legs to descend The Ogre. Joe Simpson had crawled for three days without food or water with a broken leg as well. Would he have a powerful enough survival instinct to overcome his situation? He hoped so. The thought came to him that neither of those men had their grandsons along to worry about. And, he was no longer the young man he had been when he'd read those tales.

Joe tried to call out for the boy, "ETH—" but pain stabbed his side.

The idea that Ethan was left on the mountain alone broke Joe's heart. How did he react to the avalanche? He may have tried to hunker down at the west shoulder and wait for help. If so, then he would be there a long time. Joe couldn't remember exactly how much food Ethan had in his pack, but it couldn't have been more than a few snack bars. The nights would be cold, but it was still summer, so he shouldn't freeze to death this time of year and at this elevation. He wouldn't be comfortable, that's for sure. If Ethan tried to make his way down the glacier, then that was a whole set of problems of its own, and the kid had minimal experience with crevasses, or ice, for that matter. Ethan had read a lot about it over the past few weeks, so maybe he could piece together a plan and make it work.

Joe had to keep faith that Ethan would be okay and get back to taking care of himself for the time being, or he wouldn't be in a position to help Ethan if the chance arose. Joe knew that to survive, he would need a plan, and to make one, he would need to have an accurate assessment of his situation.

He had survived a large avalanche. That was good. He felt like he had multiple broken bones. That was bad. He didn't seem to be bleeding internally. That was good. He could not walk on his leg. That was bad. He was certain Ethan was still attached to the ropes when the slope slid, so he would have survived the avalanche. That was good. Ethan was alone in the mountains above the Arctic Circle with limited resources. That was bad. Ethan had a copy of the map, knew the path back to camp, and would likely pass through close enough to see him. That was good. The satellite phone was lost in his backpack. That was bad, too. If he couldn't get out of the crevasse in time, Ethan might pass him and continue without him. That was *very* bad for both of them.

"Alright, but what can I control?" he asked himself out loud. And then answered himself. "I can crawl out of this god-forsaken hole to get a look at where I am." He winced in pain as he craned back over his shoulder to spot a path out. "And maybe Ethan will be able to see me up there." It appeared to him the snow had filled in the crevasse enough that he could crawl up the ramp to where it reached the surface, about two hundred yards away. He could only hope there was no steep wall at the end for him to climb out.

Planning his next step was complicated by the fact that he didn't know where Ethan was or what he was doing. Once out of this hole, should he head up the glacier to join Ethan? Joe wasn't confident he could physically do that. Any number of obstacles could stop him cold. Crevasses being highest on the list. Also, ascending the glacier would be more taxing on his body than descending, where he could use gravity to help slide down. He knew Ethan might not come down the glacier, or worse yet... no, he couldn't dwell on that fear if he was going to survive. He had to move.

He could only crawl for five minutes before tiring and needing rest. Three crawling sessions got him halfway to the exit, so he felt he deserved a short nap. After all, he hadn't slept the night before, and it was catching up with him. Just a few minutes of rest, and he'd get moving again. Just a few minutes.

20. REUNION

Brooks Range, Alaska

July 2017

7 days before pickup

In the crevasse, someone who looked like his grandfather was only a hundred feet away, crawling around blocks of snow and ice. Was this a ghost? He was surely dead because no one could have survived that. The apparition then looked up and locked eyes with Ethan. Then slowly smiled.

"Took you long enough, young man."

Ethan rushed to Joe and helped pull him up to a wider spot. "I can't believe you're still here!" Ethan had to choke back tears as he helped flatten a spot for them both to sit.

"I can't either. I'm sure happy to see you, kid."

"How the hell did you live through that? I thought you were done for!"

"I did too, but I just fought to ride on top of it. Got damn lucky when I got spit out over that edge." Joe pointed at the top of the wide crevasse. "I kicked off the bottom at just the right time, and it flung me against the wall over there. Liked to have broke me in half."

Joe looked at Ethan quizzically. "How was the hike

down?"

"One star. Wouldn't recommend." Ethan shook his head. "Oh! Do you have the sat phone? I think we have a good enough excuse to call for help, now."

Joe shook his head and looked down. "Pack got ripped off in the slide. All I got's the clothes on my back."

Ethan tried not to show his disappointment. He had made the mistake of getting excited. "At least you made it."

"Help me get turned around."

Ethan pulled at Joe's right arm, and Joe gave an instant "AHHHH!" in response.

"Where all are you hurt?" asked Ethan.

"Think I cracked some ribs on that side when I hit the wall. My leg hurts like hell so I know it's broke too."

"You sure that's it? Have you checked?"

"Not exactly. But I know where I hurt." Joe's sentences were short and choppy as he struggled to breathe deeply enough due to the pain in his ribs. "Let's take a look. Fix what we can. I ain't dyin' down here in this damn hole."

Joe zipped down his coat and looked around for blood, but there was none. Then, he slowly ran his fingers over each of his ribs and winced in pain.

"That's good news. They're fractured, but they ain't broken all the way through. They'll hurt, but I won't have to worry about them comin' apart and puncturing a lung. That'd kill me out here. Sure as anything. Help me get that pant leg up so I can see the damage."

The pain in his ribs made it hard for him to lean over. Ethan pulled the right pant leg up slowly so as not to bump Joe's leg around and hurt him more, which was practically impossible.

"See any blood?"

Ethan pulled down the high sock to get a better look. He was surprised to see a white stick of jagged bone protruding from Joe's shin.

"There's only a little blood...but you have a bone sticking out."

"Damn it to hell. That's what I feared," replied Joe softly. "Alright. Put me back together. My leg's gettin' cold already."

Ethan pulled the sock back up, lowered the pant leg, then sat back quietly, waiting to hear what Joe thought of his condition. He didn't want to push him too fast because he knew he was in a lot of pain, but he knew time was not on their side. The sun was already making its way around to the south side of the tower at its midday height, leaving them in the cold.

Having Joe back was a gift Ethan never expected. Watching him disappear from sight as the avalanche broke apart and swept him away was the second most painful moment of Ethan's life. The feeling of complete isolation was so powerful and overwhelming that he knew he would never forget it, no matter how long he lived. With Joe back from the dead, Ethan didn't know how to feel, especially since Joe was so severely injured. It was clear to Ethan that Joe's condition was worse than he was letting on. The thought of losing him a second time was unbearable.

Joe lay back and looked to the sky, breathing deeply. "Alright. Ain't the end of the world. Some fractured ribs and a broken tibia. Let's get that leg wrapped with something and get moving." He sat up slowly to avoid sharp pains from his side. "Hand me that backpack of yours."

Joe emptied the pack and took stock of what resources they had left. He felt around the inside. Then, he found his pen knife that was safely zipped away in his back pocket. He used the knife to cut away the lining in the pack, then pulled out the thin back pad. The pad was ten by eighteen inches and almost half an inch thick. He folded it around his right calf and wrapped the whole thing with the climbing tape. Inside the back frame of the pack, on either side of where the back pad had been, were two aluminum rods that kept the pack stiff. He pulled both out and carefully ran them up either side of his calf, underneath the taped pad, and left them sticking out the bottom on each side, next to his boot. Then, he used more climbing tape to secure the stays to his boot. He hoped the makeshift cast would keep his ankle from moving abruptly while crawling or hopping, because any ankle movement caused severe pain in his leg as those muscles moved along his broken shin. "I'd kill for some gauze," Joe said. "And some strong pain killers," he added.

"Shouldn't we try to put the bone back in? I read something about traction in my survival book."

"Wouldn't work in this case. That sharp end would just move around and cut up everything. Veins and arteries. Once you pull it apart, you must keep it in traction. We don't have that option out here."

Ethan was glad Joe knew what he was doing because he genuinely felt out of his element. He knew he wouldn't have known what to do if he were alone and it were his own leg.

"We need to figure a plan to get us out of here. What do you think, kid?"

"Should we just stay here and hope someone flies over so we can wave them down?" asked Ethan, looking down at his grandfather's swollen leg.

"If we had food and a tent or a sleeping bag, I might

agree. Mostly 'cause the pain I'm in. But very few planes fly through these valleys. 'Specially not close enough to see us down here wormin' our way through crevasses. We have a good chance of freezing and starving out here just waiting," Joe answered.

Ethan considered Joe's reply and asked, "Do you think Sandy would find us if we *did* stay here until our pickup date?" He couldn't imagine an alternative scenario to sitting it out. Joe couldn't walk; hell, he could barely crawl, it seemed.

Joe looked tired and irritated. Like he had already calculated these scenarios and was irritated by the need to spell them out for Ethan. "If she does show up on time, that's several days from now, and she's not likely to look on the north face since we told her we'd descend the south face. And if we did wait here for a week for her to find us, and she didn't, we'd still be faced with the same trek back to camp, but we'd be many days weaker by then. And even if she did see us out here, she would have no place to land and would have to go back to town and organize a rescue anyway. We're in this ourselves, kid. Superman ain't comin'. Unless you have an S on your shirt."

Ethan was not in the state of mind to laugh at the wisecrack. "Can we follow the same plan we had before the avalanche? I still have enough gear to lead the headwall, and that's the shortest way."

Joe nodded reluctantly. "I'm willing to try it, but I'm not sure if I can climb on this leg. If I can make it work, though, it'll definitely save us a day or two."

"Shouldn't we get started?" asked Ethan. He was nervous about spending the night on the ice.

Joe thought for a few seconds before responding. "No,

it'd be smart for us to sleep right now while it's warm, then move during the night. We don't have sleeping bags, so we'll likely freeze to death if we try to sleep on this ice at night, when it gets the coldest. And it's safer to travel across the glacier when it's frozen the hardest in the middle of the night. The heat softens things up too much in the day for us to cross snow bridges. We're both whupped. Let's huddle together in the sun and sleep until it gets too cold. Then we'll get moving."

Ethan stomped out their spot and leveled off seats for them both. He also used the rock to cut out a platform for their feet below them. Joe told him to spread the rope out for them to sit on so they had some insulation from the snow. Ethan helped Joe get settled on the left side of the bench so he could extend his right leg out higher to the side, and he packed some snow to form a perch for it to rest on that was almost as high as his heart to keep the swelling down.

They huddled close together for warmth and covered themselves with the space blanket from Ethan's pack. Both passed out in minutes from exhaustion. Their sleep was deep, and they didn't move for hours. Ethan's dreams were vivid and haunting. His every step in the dream world seemed to be off a cliff, and the ground below him kept suddenly sliding off and dragging him into darkness.

They were too exhausted to feel the cold until their shivering woke them. Ethan woke first and could not remember where he was. It took a few seconds for the horrors of the last day to come back.

Joe woke rather quickly. The pain in his leg was more potent than a shot of espresso, and he was instantly alert.

"Welcome to the night shift, partner. Better get movin', I suppose." He gave the pack to Ethan to put back on. Next, he instructed Ethan to tie into one end of the rope and coil the other half around his torso, under his right arm, and over his left shoulder until he was at the half. Then Ethan tied an overhand knot in the rope and clipped it to his belay loop with a locking carabiner, the same way Joe had done the night before while descending the west face. Joe then tied the other end into his harness. Part of the rope had been frayed when Ethan swayed on it during the avalanche, but the core was still intact, so they ignored the damage.

"Alright, kid. You're the lead man from here on. Keep this line tight. Pick out the smoothest path that'll get us out of this god-forsaken hole."

Ethan was ready to get moving and warm up. The chill of the glacier had zapped his core temperature in the few hours they rested. He thoughtfully made his way out to the edge of the crevasse. He dodged around the bigger chunks of ice and tried to stomp down the parts Joe would have difficulty crawling over. He found the most accessible exit from the lower side of the crevasse and took a strong stance at the top. His father had shown him how to use a "body belay" before. In fact, it's the way Chris belayed Ethan when he was small and light enough that he didn't need a mechanical belay. Ethan pulled the rope tight, then strung it over his left shoulder, down his back, and into his right hand. He used his left hand to pull up the slack while his right hand, down low, worked as a break. The friction over his shoulder provided enough resistance to arrest any potential slide Joe might take. Ethan firmed up his stance even more when Joe approached the short exit wall of the crevasse. The wall of snow was only four feet high, but it could be tricky to get over with only one leg and busted ribs, and it would be the first test of their system.

“Alright, Ethan, here we go.” Joe prepared himself for the pain and slowly rose up on one leg. He ignored the shooting pain from his ribs as he mantled up onto the flat ice of the glacier and flopped over on his face, breathing heavily. Only then did he allow himself to yell out in pain.

After a few moments to catch his breath, he motioned for Ethan to continue.

“Ever onwards.”

21. FOR THE BOY

Brooks Range, Alaska
July 2017
6 days until pickup

They continued until late morning when the temperature rose and the sun swung around to the east and shone on them with all its glory. It had been a long night.

This section of the glacier was steeper and littered with crevasses. Unfortunately, they were not filled with snow from the avalanche, so Joe and Ethan had to be very careful. Ethan walked ahead slowly and sought the most straightforward way across. Often, he had to backtrack after finding out his potential path was a dead end or was too deep for Joe to climb out of. They tried to find a safe spot to set up Joe before Ethan made his way down into or over the crevasses, but it wasn't always an option. Joe tried to belay him around his waist from a sitting position, but they both knew that a significant fall would likely pull them both into the dark bowels of the glacier. Still, somehow, the thought of his grandfather holding the other end of the rope gave Ethan enough false confidence to venture out.

They found a nice flat spot on the glacier next to a large boulder that had long ago fallen onto the ice from somewhere on the north face of Harte Tower above. Ethan pulled out one of the snack bars and split it between them for breakfast. They had two more left. Ethan wondered if they could make it back to camp in two days. Thoughts of cooking up chicken quesadillas in the tent were about the only thing keeping him going at this point. He was already feeling weak, as the last couple of days had really worn him out.

Ethan peered down the glacier. The wall of rock on their right still blocked the view, but he felt like the east rib must be around the corner.

"How much further do you think we have until we're off the glacier?" Ethan asked.

"Hand me that map."

Ethan produced the folded and worn paper from his pocket.

Joe traced the contour lines on the map with his finger, glancing up several times and squinting at his surroundings, working hard to match the real world with its white, green, and brown depiction. The glacier was clearly marked as a white tongue, half-circling Harte Tower and terminating on the northeast side. He assumed the glacier had retreated some since the map was made but didn't know how much. The east rib ran for several miles past the terminus. A crossed pick and shovel marked an old mine shaft at the base of the rib. Joe thought of mentioning it as a possible shelter but decided against it. It had likely collapsed, and he didn't want to raise the kid's hopes.

"Not much further. About a half mile. We're actually

not far from the east rib. I think we'll make it there in a few hours from here after we get some rest."

Ethan felt a sense of relief upon hearing that. He knew they still had a long way to go, but walking on solid rock and dirt sounded luxurious after spending so much time precariously shuffling on ice.

He was amazed by how well Joe had managed despite his injuries. Ethan doubted he would have handled the situation as well if he were in Joe's condition. Perhaps the older generation was raised differently, or maybe it was just an Alaskan thing.

"Have you ever been in this tough of a jam in the mountains?"

Joe was adjusting his makeshift leg splint and took a moment to consider the question as he sifted through the haze of his fatigue. "Yeah, I guess I have," Joe lied.

"Were you hurt that time, too?"

"No, it was a client that time. I was a young guide on Denali. Your father was home with his mom. A few years younger than you are now. Two guys fell in a crevasse. One of 'em died. Guy in the lead. Fell eighty feet to the bottom. Cold, hard ice broke him up. Other fella was lucky enough to live. But both his legs were broken. It took a lot for the two of us who weren't hurt to get us all out of there..." Joe trailed off. "This is a new role for me, kid. I'm supposed to be the one helping. Not being rescued."

Ethan felt he needed to guide the conversation back to practical ground. "How long do you think it will take us to get back to camp from here?"

"Can't be certain. We could make the wall tonight. Then to the top of the wall the next day. From there it'll take another night to traverse the South Glacier to camp. So, that's three, three and a half days. If everything goes right. That'll give us a day or two of flexibility. If things don't go exactly as planned."

Ethan contemplated that. Then, reluctantly added, "Do you still think you'll be able to climb the rib?"

"That's the million-dollar question." Joe looked out over the glacier to the distant peaks of the Brooks. "It's gonna hurt like hell. More than anything in my life. Physically, at least. I know that for sure. Stumbling along the base of that rib for an extra day or two. That'll likely hurt even more. I think if we take our time...and find the easiest route...and you break it up into short pitches...I should be able to grunt my way up it. If not, then we'll have to descend the valley. Make our way around the rib at a lower point."

They found a mostly flat spot on the ice and laid the rope across the frozen floor for them to sit on, but it didn't provide much warmth. They sat down back-to-back as the day started to warm, trying to relax. It was very bright, and Ethan had a hard time falling asleep. He pulled his hood over his eyes, but it didn't provide much relief from the blinding reflection of the glacier. If it weren't for his sunglasses, he would likely be fully snow blind by now. Joe had lost his glacier glasses in the avalanche and was really suffering. He squinted as much as possible since losing them, but the arctic night was still harmful enough to cause him pain. It felt to him like someone had sprinkled sand in his eye sockets, but it would have been worse if they were traveling in the daytime when the sun's rays were truly debilitating.

Ethan dozed off and snored lightly from being hunched over. Joe whispered to himself. "You have to make it for the boy. His mother wouldn't survive it. Neither would your wife."

Ethan had several short but vivid dreams throughout the night. In the first, his mother lectured him about cleaning his room, pointing to his clothes scattered across the floor. After that, he sat with Camila at the park, and she told him to be honest about why he kept getting in trouble. He asked her what she meant by that, but she repeated the same demands, her face growing increasingly agitated each time. Then he saw his father walking away from them, across the glacier in his Army dress uniform. Ethan cried out for him, but Chris didn't hear. He just walked away as if out for a quick stroll without a care in the world. The dream was so clear Ethan could make out the medals on his chest and the sharp creases in his pants.

Joe gently shook Ethan awake. "Time we head out, Rip Van Winkle." Ethan could see the shadows were long, and the day's heat had come and gone while they slept. The sun had set gently behind the outer ring of peaks to their north, leaving them shaded and the north face of Harte Tower glowing pink and orange. "The ice'll be good to go," added Joe. "Let's get ourselves off this glacier. It'll take me a while to get up that wall."

"How are you feeling?" Ethan asked.

"Broken and old."

"Ha, ha. I meant, how's your leg?"

"Stiff. Hurts like hell when I move it. It'll warm up a bit once we get moving. I can work out some of the stiffness from the night."

They gathered up the few things they had and started out again for the second time since the avalanche. They were approaching the end of the glacier now, and things were more convoluted than ever. The ice was harder and bluer, and the crevasses were more frequent but not as deep. Ethan stayed on the far right side, where there were numerous rocks and plenty of gravel that had fallen onto the ice. This gave enough texture for him to walk on and kept Joe from sliding, although it was rough on his clothing when he had to crawl. There were many sections where Joe was able to stand up and hop along on one leg for a distance with Ethan's help.

An hour after leaving their bivy, the wind shifted. They had enjoyed an easterly wind that brought dry, warm air from the interior of Alaska for the past three days, but now it blew hard out of the southwest, carrying moisture from the Bering Sea.

Joe knew what that meant. "We might get some weather. Let's figure out where we're headed before it gets here."

They peered up at the long wall of the east rib that had finally come into view once they rounded the north face. It was broken up by countless crack systems. The steep wall, undercut by the glacier's advances and retreats, and the rock above clearly fell into the valley regularly, leaving a litter of large boulders and gravel below the ice's terminus. Joe pointed out a long, ramping corner system that was not as steep as the rest of the wall. "Let's head for that. I think I could climb that."

But Ethan had his doubts once he saw the wall. It was steeper than he had hoped. Sure, it would be easy for him to climb, but it was hard for him to imagine Joe getting up it in his state. He thought of arguing for the longer walk, but he wasn't confident enough to question Joe.

Ethan did his best to wind his way through the edge of the dying glacier. The bright, blue ice helped him see depth as the sky above him grew darker with the approaching storm. Eventually, he found a wide crack that led left down a groove and ended on solid rock. They were almost off the glacier. He looked up at the east rib above him to keep his bearings so as not to lose the corner system they would have to climb. Snow was beginning to fall and swirl at the top of the wall. Within minutes, the storm was upon them.

22. GHOSTS OF THE EAST RIB

Alaska Gold Rush
1880-1903

—The Harte Bros.—

Karl and Wilhelm Harte were the youngest of six sons born to a poor farming family in Austria, a country with many people but little land. Centuries of subdividing estates between sons left the farmers of eastern Austria toiling small plots with no capacity to feed their large families. The boys learned to rise early and ignore the pangs of hunger. Their mother believed their strong bond enabled them to survive the famine of 1889. By some miracle, the two youngest, along with the eldest, held on while three of their weakened brothers perished of cholera. The meager family plot was left to the eldest brother and his pregnant wife when their parents passed.

The youngest boys, Karl and Wilhelm, were determined to build a better life, so in 1898, they left Austria with dreams of building a fortune. They labored for two years in Berlin's booming steel mills, enduring six-day workweeks in dark, grimy factories and squeezing into overcrowded tenements, saving every mark they could. Nefarious characters mistakenly judged the boys to be easy targets but quickly found the Harte Brothers to be ferocious fighters when together, and they were never apart.

Their sights were set on a new beginning in the New World. But when they finally made the grueling journey halfway around the world to Alaska, they were told they'd narrowly missed the Nome gold rush. Low-paying jobs were plenty, but the prime claims were taken, and they had not come that far to fill another man's cup.

They pressed farther north and east, deep into the Brooks Range, chasing the next big strike, hoping to earn enough gold to land wives and live the rest of their days rich in America. But those aspirations withered like willow leaves in that cold, gently sloped Kovluk valley beneath the glaciers of the shining tower. They dug with the reckless boldness only youth knows until the iron of their picks and shovels wore as thin as their bodies. Desperation kept them longer than wisdom would allow, and well beyond the amount of time their meager supplies could sustain their grueling effort. Yet they refused to turn back, unwilling to return home as beggars.

The increasingly cold nights eventually broke their resolve. Ice lined the riverbank by the time they abandoned their meager camp and all their mining equipment and loaded their few belongings into a small boat. Starvation ate out every ounce of ambition the Harte brothers had brought with them, and when their boat met the exposed rocks common to the late season, they had no fight left. Hunters found pieces along the shores of the Alatna River in the spring, but the brothers were never seen again. Harte Tower would forever bear their name in homage to their valiant, though altogether unsuccessful, attempt at taming the untamable.

Decades later, the trickle of fortune-seeking miners like the Harte brothers gave way to extensive corporate operations that scaled up on rich deposits in the easier-to-access lower altitudes, where roads could be built to send the rich metals to all parts of the world for big money. The high, remote peaks returned to the quiet subsistence hunters and were eventually shared with the adventure-seeking climbers and kayakers of the modern age.

23. SHELTER

Brooks Range, Alaska
July 2017
5 days until pickup

The pudgy marmot moved cautiously among the boulders at the edge of the glacier. He stayed close to the safety of the rocks, constantly aware of where to hide from the ever-present birds of prey that migrated to the northern range during the summer months. Throughout the day, he had been munching on young shoots of grass and tender leaves sprouting from small shrubs, but as evening approached he foraged for bright green and yellow flakes of lichen clinging to the rocks. His fur was so thick he barely noticed the temperature dropping rapidly as a cold front moved into the valley.

Also unbeknownst to the marmot, a golden eagle hovered far above, waiting for the fat rodent to venture further from safety. The marmot would make a nutrient-rich meal for the eagle's partner and three chicks waiting at their nest. With one of the slowest metabolisms in the animal kingdom, the marmot stored an immense reserve of calories for any predator that was quick and fortunate enough to catch him. The eagle began his dive, hoping for one last catch of the day before the approaching storm put an end to its hunt. The marmot lay exposed, stretched across the surface of a boulder, licking the golden lichen flakes, making him an easy target.

Suddenly, voices echoed from the glacier, and the marmot froze. The sound of Ethan sliding down an icy slope and launching into the gravel bed startled the big rodent, prompting him to hide, just as the eagle swooped past.

The sound of terra firma crunching under Ethan's feet was supposed to be a joyous occasion, but the anxiety caused by the storm postponed any celebration. He looked back toward Harte Tower, but it was already obscured by clouds. Ethan donned his hood and zipped up his jacket to block the wind. Joe slowly scooted down the chute, his busted leg crossed over his good leg for support and protection. It was obviously excruciating, for he winced in pain the entire way. He finally gave up trying to control his slide and let himself skim down the last ten feet and skid out into the loose gravel next to Ethan.

Joe lay back with his eyes closed for a moment. "God damn, that hurt."

"Sure looked like it." Ethan wanted to empathize more with his grandfather's pain, but the storm worried him. "These clouds rolled in fast."

Joe opened his eyes and blinked at the stinging flurries. "Yeah. Better find a bivouac. Hunker down for a bit." He slowly sat up on his left arm and looked around for a place to sit that offered some kind of shelter.

"It's not exactly rock climbing weather," replied Ethan.

"It might be cold. But at least it's windy. Let's hobble down. Find a hiding place. In that boulder field."

Joe's sentences were short and choppy.

The ice had terminated just above a valley full of erratic boulders and rocks either emptied there by the glacier or calved off the north wall of the east rib. Ethan propped Joe's right arm over his shoulder and held onto his left hip by his belt to guide him as they slowly made their way through the maze of the mountain's detritus.

They spotted several large boulders that looked promising and aimed to find one with a cave or overhang to block the snow. The first was the size of a house, with a big cave underneath, but the floor was too steep to be comfortable. They decided to hold out for better accommodations and moved on to the next. The second boulder was smaller but had a sizable roof over a gravel bar that would be better for them. It offered a dry spot to sit and would block most of the wind if it didn't shift and blow from the north.

They were about to settle in when Joe tugged lightly at Ethan's elbow. "Look up there," he said.

Ethan followed his gaze up the hill to what looked to be a mineshaft at the base of the rib. Old wooden beams clearly held up the open mouth. A rusty, weathered pickaxe leaned against the wall just inside the entrance. The sudden appearance of man-made materials in a vast, empty wilderness was a jolt to Ethan's weary brain, and he had a hard time comprehending the meaning of it.

"How the hell did that get there?" he asked.

"I suspect that would be the Harte boys."

While Ethan's mind made the connection to the tower's namesakes, Joe started his slow hop toward the mine. "Let's check it out. Might be drier in there than this damn place."

They stumbled their way up the hill to the entrance.

The snow and rain mix intensified. Ethan raised the hood of his jacket.

"How far ya think they hauled those beams?" Joe asked.

Ethan peered out over the valley in the grayness. "Must have been quite a ways."

The mine was no more than fifteen feet deep. The entrance was almost tall enough for them to fully stand, but it narrowed down quickly to a crouch in the back, where a few old wooden boards were stacked. Ethan opened the book, which appeared to be a personal journal.

"What language is this supposed to be?" questioned Ethan, holding the book open toward Joe.

"Looks like maybe German. That's my guess."

"Do you know how to read it?"

Joe did his best to stretch out on his back on the dry dirt of the cave and control his breathing. His heart beat out of his chest from the hike to the cave and from the increasing pain in his leg. "No, sir. I do not."

Ethan tossed the book back into the corner. "We could use the pages to start a fire if we had a lighter."

"A fire would be nice. Not sure any of that old wood would burn, though."

Ethan found a flat spot to sit between Joe and the cave wall and used his hands to smooth out a good spot to lie down. His palm uncovered a wooden handle, which he pulled up to examine in the light. "Take a look at that," he said.

Joe looked at it with squinted eyes. "An old rock hammer."

Ethan rubbed the tool against his pant leg, which he couldn't imagine getting any dirtier anyway. He cleared away much of the dust and grime. The steel head was rusty, but not to the point where it couldn't be used.

"That thing would make a decent ice axe, Ethan. Throw it in your backpack. Could be handy on the South Glacier."

Joe's legs stretched out in front of him. Ethan shook his head at the mess that Joe's meager splint had become. The tape had gotten wet in the rain and had loosened all around. Fresh blood wet his pant leg.

"We gotta fix this up somehow," said Ethan. Joe was too tired to respond. Ethan opened his backpack and pulled out the roll of climbing tape and his pocketknife. He crawled to the back of the mine and retrieved the leather bag the journal had been stored in. The bag was much bigger than the journal, and Ethan suspected it had stored more than a book at one time. Perhaps clothing. It had a flap over the top, much like a saddle bag. He cut the flap off and set it aside. He ran the blade along one side, so that he now had two closed ends and two open ends.

Joe grew curious about Ethan's intentions. "What do you have there?"

Ethan wrapped it around his own right foot for good measure. "A boot. We can set your foot in it and maybe use a couple of those boards to run along the sides of your leg to stabilize it. Then we'll tape it all up tight."

"Damn, kid. That might work."

After Ethan fixed Joe's splint the best he could, he sat back and watched the freezing rain falling in the early morning light. Joe lay on his back, obviously in pain. His breathing was shallow and quick. Ethan worried about what that meant. It could be the broken ribs, he thought, that pained him too much to take deep breaths. But maybe shock. That worried him more. He didn't know much about shock. *What are the symptoms?* he wondered.

He could only guess.

"Do you think it'll get infected? Your leg, I mean," Ethan asked.

"Eventually. Yes."

"How long do we have?"

"No idea. No fever yet. We'll see."

Ethan wanted to have some plan for it if it happened, but he couldn't think of one. They had no way of keeping his leg clean. No soap. No antibiotics. Not even a Band-Aid.

"What can I do?"

"Hell. You're already doing a lot. You practically carried me here from the glacier."

"I don't mind it." Ethan truly meant it.

"Thank you." Joe patted Ethan lightly on his leg. He seemed to barely have the energy to lift his arm. "If it gets infected. It'll get tougher for me to move. If the fever gets bad...I could lose my head."

Ethan tried to assure him. "You're tougher than anyone I know. I'm sure you can limp it out to the plane."

Joe shook his head. "I'll try. But there might come a point. Where you have to go alone."

Ethan didn't want to think of ever leaving Joe. He decided to change the subject.

"This weather's gonna set us back a bit, isn't it? I really hoped we could at least start up the wall today, but this isn't looking good. What will we do if the storm doesn't stop anytime soon?"

"Can't climb in the rain. We'll have to head down the valley if so," Joe replied.

Ethan pulled the empty water bottle from his pack and opened the lid. He was dehydrated and needed some real water, not the splashes of snow or bits of ice they had been chewing on while traveling the glacier. He found a spot to set it where water dripped over the lip of the boulder.

They sat together and huddled again to keep as warm as possible under the circumstances, watching the rain mixed with snowflakes just beyond their feet. It was too warm to collect; it melted as it hit the ground.

Joe sighed, "I don't think we'll get much sleep today. Gonna be a cold one. You should do some jumping jacks every once in a while to keep warm." They were wearing all the clothing they had brought and had no more to put on.

"I'm cold already," replied Ethan.

Joe looked at Ethan and sized him up. The boy's attenuated frame made his jacket appear oversized. "I've lost a little fat already. You look a little trimmer, too." The same lean build that allowed them to climb so effortlessly, especially compared to those with bulkier physiques, also made them more susceptible to the elements. "I had to tighten my belt a notch. We're burning through insulation pretty quick."

Ethan had noticed his pants were fitting loose, but he figured they had stretched from all the exertion of the last few days. Camila always laughed at him for not having enough ass to keep his pants up. He didn't have much to spare.

"Good thing we ain't up high in the Alaska Range," said Joe. "Small storm on Denali could bring you three feet before morning. At least we're not likely to get that here. We can be thankful for that."

Ethan studied the patterns of yellow and green lichen on the rock roof. He wondered if there was any nutritional value in eating it. Would they get that desperate?

"Did you ever get caught in a big storm on a climb there? On Denali, I mean."

Joe took a breath to ponder the question, digging through his archives. "No, I guess I didn't. Plenty of times while in camp. But not on a climb." He picked up a handful of pebbles from the gravel floor. "I'd like to say I had a pretty good sense for avoidin' trouble. I'm sure there was a lot of luck involved, too." He slowly tossed the pebbles, one by one, as he spoke. "Once, I started up the Valley of Death with Rob Shepherd. Headed for the Cassin. A liiiittle cloud over the summit bothered me for some reason. I couldn't explain it. I demanded we turn around. Rob was so damn mad. Weather service called for several days of clear skies. But I didn't budge. My gut told me it was wrong. We skied back to Kahiltna base camp. Snowed for three days straight. We got five feet out of that damn storm. We were up every few hours shoveling snow off the tent so the weight wouldn't break the poles and collapse it. Can't imagine what would have happened if that storm had hit us on the route."

"You guys really lucked out," replied Ethan. "Why do they call it the Valley of Death?"

Joe tossed another pebble. "It's a narrow valley. Big walls on both sides. Avalanches sweep the whole glacier that runs down the middle of it. Quite a few climbers are sealed up in those crevasses."

Ethan started to ask something but stopped.

"What is it?" asked Joe.

"I was just gonna ask if you knew anyone who died there," said Ethan reluctantly. "But that's probably not a polite thing to ask."

"That's alright." Joe scooped up another handful of pebbles. "I knew Mugs well. He spent a lot of time on the mountain."

"I don't think I've heard of him."

"He's a legend." Joe tossed a pebble. "He was way ahead of his time. He soloed stuff no one thought possible. Put up a lot of good routes. Last anyone saw of him was..." Joe paused. "Hell, I got that wrong. He died coming down the south buttress." Joe tossed another stone out into the gray. "It's hard to keep straight where they all died. And how."

The heat of the day, which had previously blessed them with warm naps, never came. The snow transitioned into a cold rain. Sometimes the rain would let up and almost stop but then would rally and pound the valley in sheets. Still, they dozed off briefly until the shivering woke them again. Ethan stood and paced when he got too cold. He did some jumping jacks to get his blood pumping. He tried to make it to one hundred each time but didn't have the energy and would tire sometime after fifty. Joe had it especially hard since he couldn't stand on his leg and move around to warm himself. He shifted his weight back and forth from one ass cheek to the other but found little in the way of comfort.

By late afternoon, they had grown restless and had gotten little sleep throughout the day. Ethan wondered when they would be able to travel.

Joe watched as Ethan paced. Eventually, he spoke up. "This weather changes things. Traveling at night only makes sense when it's not cold. And wet. We'd get hypothermia going out in this mess. Now that we're off the glacier, we don't have to worry about the soft ice. We'll have to wait 'til mornin'."

Ethan stood under the rock roof, surveying the storm. He could see only about one hundred feet. Although he thought he could remember where the corner system they were planning to climb was, he wasn't confident he could find it in this weather.

"How long should we wait?" Ethan hated the idea of wasting a day and a night away in the cave.

"Guess it depends. We don't have much time to fiddle around. If we wanna catch that plane. But leave too early and this storm picks back up...we'd be in trouble out there."

"I can't believe I'm worried about snow in July. That's just crazy," noted Ethan, primarily to himself.

"Happens on them Colorado peaks, too."

Ethan shook his head. "Yeah, I guess you're right."

The cold seemed to make Joe's leg ache even more, along with the sedentary day he'd spent lying on the hard ground. He took a glance at his wounded calf, which he had avoided doing most of the day. It was still swollen, and he didn't see any good coming from opening up his pants again for a closer inspection.

"What a damn mess," Joe muttered disappointedly.

"No one could've seen that coming."

"Broken bone is nature's way of saying you messed up. Bad things happen when we get comfortable. I let my guard down. Little things kill ya in the mountains. Same goes in war. I reckon."

24. THRESHOLDS

Colorado Springs, Colorado
10 April 2017

—Camila—

She spotted him on the grassy hill beneath the shade of an elm shortly after the school bell rang to announce the end of the day. He wasn't supposed to be on school grounds during his suspension, and she figured that was why he had pulled his hat down low over his face. He sat leaning on his knees in the shade of the tree. Typical Ethan, showing up only when he wasn't supposed to.

She smiled as she walked up behind him. "Hey, creeper."

He turned, a little surprised. "I thought you might want company on your long walk home."

"You look like you're about to kidnap someone. All's you need is a sketchy van."

Ethan laughed as he got to his feet. "Yeah, I'm not supposed to be on school grounds. I'm going incognito."

Camila raised her eyebrows. "So, you won't go when they want you to, but you'll show up when they don't. You're a silly boy."

"Girl, you talk more trash than anybody."

She knew that tone, half joking, half vulnerable. She liked to tease him. It was her way of forcing him out of his tough-guy shell. She liked the humble Ethan more. The Ethan she felt only she got to see. "I'm not judging you, silly boy." She wrapped her arms around his neck, and they hugged softly as loud, careless teenagers sped past on their way out of the parking lot. Ethan reached for her hand, and they headed to the crosswalk.

"School isn't as fun without you there."

Ethan smiled. "I'll be back next week." Then frowned. "I have a lot of catching up to do if I'm gonna graduate."

"You'll be fine. It pisses me off you can pass tests and barely have to study. It's not fair." Camila punched him playfully. "I heard from your mom that you guys got in an argument."

"When did you talk to her?"

"A few days ago. When your mom pulled up, my mom and I were walking to the car so she could take me to work." She squeezed his hand. "She's worried about you, you know."

"Yeah," he said lightly. "I'm not that great at following rules. Unless I like them."

"My mom says you military brats like to rebel against authority," Camila said. "Kind of like being a preacher's daughter."

"Your mom is almost as funny as you are." He nudged her with his elbow. "I just don't know what I want right now. I just know I don't want to move to some random state and waste years on a degree I might not even use."

"So you won't be following your dad into the Army, either?" she asked, as they neared their complex.

"Hell, no, that's the last thing I'd ever do."

The sun was brutal, even this late in the afternoon, so they settled onto the shaded steps of the one of the many identical townhomes. Camila watched the light flicker through the leaves, thinking about everything she hadn't said yet.

"Is it school you don't want," she asked carefully, "or do you just need more time? My friend Lacey is taking a gap year."

Ethan scoffed. "Lacey's filthy rich. Of course she is. My mom can't send me to Europe to 'find myself.' I'll need a job this summer or school…or both."

Camila inhaled slowly. This was her opening, and suddenly it felt terrifying.

"Well," she said, choosing her words, "if you don't want to go full-time, you could just take one or two classes to start. It's cheaper, and…" She hesitated, heart pounding. "If you had to move out, we could split an apartment in Dallas. Help each other with rent and everything."

She waited for his reaction. Silence stretched between them, heavy and uncomfortable. She told herself not to overthink it, but she already was.

After a moment, Ethan shifted. "So…how are things in Driscoll's class?"

The change was obvious. Intentional. Why were boys so immature? She thought of her own father marrying young and coming to America with no more than the clothes on his back and desperation in his heart. He worked two or three jobs at a time so his two daughters could get an education. But he worked so much that they never saw him, and they grew apart. His work trips got longer until divorce permanently crumbled the foundation of their family. Camila's older sister seemed to take it the hardest. She dropped out of high school her junior year, pregnant and unmarried. Camila promised herself she would succeed no matter what. She would finish high school and then college. The first in her family with a degree. She felt she was the last hope, but she also wanted a partner on that journey and hoped Ethan could fill that role. If only he wanted to. She wouldn't—no, she *couldn't* —force his decision.

"Ugh," Camila said, forcing a smile. "SO boring without you. Time doesn't go as fast without you joking around."

They got up and continued walking toward her place, and she filled the space with school gossip. Who got caught cheating, who broke up, who might not graduate. Anything to avoid the knot forming in her stomach.

When they reached her building, Ethan stopped. "Hey," he said quietly, staring at the ground. "I decided to spend the summer with my grandparents in Alaska. We won't be able to hang out before you leave like we thought."

The words hit her harder than she expected.

"Hold up. What?" Camila stepped back, pulling her hand away. "Where did this come from?"

"I'm sorry, Cam, I really need to get myself together. This year's been such a setback, and my mom thinks, and I think, working with my grandpa and maybe doing some climbing will give me time to figure things out."

"Well," Camila said, forcing sarcasm to shield the sting, "if you don't pass your classes, you'll be 'figuring things out' in summer school."

He grinned. "I only need to pass two to graduate. I'll get them up to a D, no problem. Especially with the cutest study partner in school."

She didn't laugh. She couldn't. His hands slid to her hips, and he tried to pull her closer, but she resisted.

"A little too soon there, climber boy," she said. "That's quite a bomb you just dropped."

He blushed, suddenly shy, and for a split second she almost softened.

"Will you be gone all summer?" she asked.

"Most of it. My grandpa might get me some part-time work so I can earn a little money."

Camila glanced at her front door, then back at him. "I'll be working all summer, too. Trying to save for college. So I guess we wouldn't have hung out much anyway."

"Are you okay?" he asked.

"Yeah," she said, looking away. "I'm fine."

"You don't seem fine."

She met his eyes, steady and sharp. "Well, I am. And I have to go."

"Okay," he said, clearly confused.

She turned toward her door, then looked back and smiled tightly. "Have a nice trip, Ethan. I hope you have a great time climbing."

She crossed the threshold and shut the door behind her. Inside, she leaned against the door and told herself to stay strong. She couldn't let her emotions steer her. She wanted Ethan more than he could know, but she would not sacrifice her own future for someone who didn't take his own seriously.

Ethan hesitated for a moment outside, then turned and walked away.

25. COMPLICATIONS

Brooks Range, Alaska
July 2017
5 days until pickup

They lay next to each other, side by side, and watched the light rain until they nodded off for a while. A little after midnight, Ethan awakened Joe with a light elbow.

"I think the rain stopped."

Thick clouds still cloaked the high peaks, but the rain rose several thousand feet above them. Joe looked at his watch; it read 12:27 a.m. It would be pitch black in the lower latitudes, but the midnight sun still grayed the sky. "It'll be cold. But we should take advantage of this. It'll take me a while to hop up there."

They had little to pack up, so it took them no time to prepare for their day. They simply tossed the rope onto Ethan's pack. He then carefully helped Joe rise to his feet, and they found their positions, with Ethan under Joe's left arm. They had tried the other side briefly the day before, but that position stretched Joe's ribs and sent excruciating pains down his side that were unbearable. Having Ethan on his left, the same side as his good leg, set him off balance, but they could do little about that. He yearned for a good walking stick. Unfortunately, no trees or tall shrubs were growing at this high altitude.

Ethan tried to look ahead and guide them through the best terrain for Joe to hop through. Sometimes, they had to stop for him to crawl over rocks in the way, and each time Ethan was uncertain where to take them, he found a place for Joe to sit while he walked ahead to find the way.

After several hours of hiking, they reached the open-book corner system just as morning arrived, brightening the sky enough for them to make out the details of the wall. It looked to be an easy enough climb, one they would have really enjoyed in better circumstances. If they were at a roadside crag and well-rested, it would have been a one- or two-hour climb. But he knew success was far from guaranteed for them today.

They collapsed, already exhausted, at the base of a gentle, gravelly slope. Joe was obviously in excruciating pain and grimaced through it the whole morning. Ethan also felt the effect of pulling his grandfather along. He was still too slender at his age to bear such a physical burden, but he did so without complaint.

They rested for a few more minutes, but as soon as they caught their breath, Ethan sorted the rope and prepared himself for the climb.

Ethan looked down at Joe, seated on the slab. "How you feeling?"

Joe shook his head. "Like shit."

"Ha. Same. And hungry."

"If I had my .22 and a bundle of wood, I'd pop one of

these fat marmots. Fry 'em up right here."

Ethan curled his nose. "I don't know if I'm that hungry yet."

Joe looked up at him judgingly. "Hell. You don't know what's good. All that fat. It's gotta taste good."

"Have you ever eaten one?"

"Not yet. One of the few animals I ain't."

"What's the best-tasting animal you've had?"

Joe smiled. "Arkansas snappin' turtle. Hands down. Slow movers. Tender as all get out."

Ethan peered up at the route. He was too tired to worry about whether he could do it. His thoughts were on Joe and whether they were making a mistake. If Joe couldn't climb, then this was a waste of time and energy, and they had neither in surplus. Joe could also get hurt worse trying to climb. That was followed by the thought that Joe could get hurt just as badly by hiking down the rib further. There truly were no good options for them.

"Are you sure you wanna try this?" asked Ethan.

Joe looked up at Ethan. "Yeah, let's do it."

Ethan tucked away his doubts. Joe was a rock. He knew what he wanted and would have said so if he thought this was a bad idea. He had to trust that the old guide knew what he was doing.

Ethan had the climbing gear already on his harness, which had not come off since the climb. He tied into the top of the rope stack, then handed the other end to Joe for him to tie in, which he did slowly. He then put Ethan on the belay. Ethan removed his boots, changed into his climbing shoes, and put them in his pack.

Ethan started up without saying he was climbing. He was too tired to check if he was on belay. Of course, Joe picked up the rope and slid it through his belay device and locked him in. Ethan wanted to make good time but was too tired to move fast. He took many breaks and placed more protective gear than he otherwise would have on such easy terrain. The rock was still very cold, and he had to warm up his hands often by sticking them in his armpits when he had a stance that was good enough to balance without his hands.

"Don't go up too far," reminded Joe, "Break it up...so I can rest more."

Ethan found a nice ledge about fifty feet above and surveyed his options. This whole wall seemed to be nothing but stacked blocks, with cracks running between them. He built a belay by placing two hand-sized cams in a crack, equalizing them with a sling, pulling up the slack until it came tight, and putting Joe on belay.

"That's me. I'm moving, Ethan."

Joe struggled from the beginning and yelled loudly when he hit his injured leg on the rock or had to reach too high and pull down, straining his ribs.

"AHH! Keep the rope tighter!"

Ethan was pulling as hard as he could, but the dynamic nature of the rope had enough stretch that Joe slid down several feet every time he fell. After an hour of constant swearing and yelling and desperate climbing, Joe collapsed on the belay ledge next to Ethan. He crumpled up his face in agony and frustration, not able to talk for several minutes. Though he was mostly silent, tears of desperation managed to escape Joe's eyes, and it was the first time Ethan could remember that happening. The old man's body shook lightly as he struggled to control the pain. Ethan kept the rope tight and waited for Joe to work through it; he felt horrible for not being able to help him. He would give anything to make this easier for him but was helpless to do so.

"I can't do it. It's a waste of time. We have to head down," Joe gasped.

But Ethan didn't move to rig for the rappels. He looked up to the top of the rib. It was so close. They could make the top in two or three more short pitches. Even if they took an hour for each pitch, they would still save time compared to hiking down the rib and hoping to find easier terrain, which was no guarantee.

"I really think we should push it," Ethan declared. "At least we know what we're up against here. We don't know what's down the rib."

Joe looked up to him incredulously.

But Ethan stared back coldly. He believed this was the best way for them, and he didn't want to back down again. Something in him was turning. Something that had been building for days, maybe longer. He was losing confidence in his grandfather's judgment. He couldn't keep it in any longer.

"I wanted to bring more gear on the route, but *you* disagreed, and so I let it go!" he exploded. "I wanted to make a phone call after the rope was destroyed, but you shot that down too, and again, I backed down! And didn't I ask you several times if you were up for climbing the rib, and you said you could do it?" Ethan shook his head angrily. "And now we're here, and you want to back down and waste more time and energy we don't have!"

"Kid, I just can't do it," Joe said, shaking his head.

"It's only a couple pitches. I'll pull harder this time, and you can take as much time as you want."

Joe sat, still shaking his head. Something in him was breaking as well. "I wish I could, kid. I wish I could."

"Damn it!" Ethan erupted. He beat the wall with his

fists. None of this was fair. Nothing. And all of his frustration with the world and with himself released at once, as if a dam had broken. Multiple nights with little sleep or a hot meal tore out his filter.

"I just want out of here!" Ethan kicked at the wall, then hunched over on the anchor and began to cry. "I want out of here."

And when it was over, he felt remorse. Joe sat at his feet, lightly sobbing. Ethan slowly realized they had both been broken by the trip, and by the loss that came before it. Suddenly, it didn't matter whose fault it was. Or that it was unfair. They had to help each other out of this.

Ethan was devastated, but he had to admit defeat. If they continued up, only to fail and retreat later, that would be a waste of more time and energy. Maybe Joe had the wisdom to make the rational call and cut their losses.

Ethan tried to clear the disappointment from his voice. "I'll rig the rappel."

Joe shook his head. "You'll need to lower me. I won't be able to do it." Joe reviewed with Ethan how to rig his belay device for a lower, which was more complicated than a standard belay. With Joe's direction, Ethan ran the rope through his belay device and then directed the brake strand through a carabiner on the anchor. When it was ready, Joe sat up, scooted to the edge, and prepared for the ordeal he knew it was going to be.

"Okay. Take it easy, Ethan. I'll have to scoot down. On my good side. 'Til I get to a spot I can kick out on my good leg."

Ethan hesitantly lowered Joe off the ledge, scared to inflict more pain on him than he was already suffering. The pitch was at a low enough angle that he could see each obstacle Joe was avoiding and could adjust the speed he was lowering to help him. It took only a few minutes for Joe to be safely on the ground, collapsed again, back where they had started. Ethan then untied his end of the rope and tossed it down, leaving both ends to rappel from. He had to leave two good cams in the anchor, which he usually would not do. The gear was expensive to replace, but he had no choice. He just hoped they could find an easier way across the rib that didn't require the gear he was leaving behind.

Ethan rappelled to the base and pulled the rope, coiling it up in one hand as he pulled with the other. Joe rested for another minute before slowly sitting up. He reached over and took out Ethan's map, which he still had in his own pocket, and ran his finger along the contours that characterized the bottom of the east rib's north face. He gazed at his watch, his wheels obviously turning as he calculated.

"Take a look," Joe said to Ethan, who was standing above him, stuffing the neatly coiled rope into his backpack. Joe pointed to a spot just along the long ridge that protruded east from Harte Tower and curved around like a rib bone to the south as it worked away from it. The rib lost prominence the farther it went, meaning they would have less to climb if they continued following it in search of another break. "I think we're here. At the base of the wall. If we follow it down. About two miles. The angle of the wall starts to break up. I think we can cross over. To the South Glacier here."

Ethan followed his logic and agreed it was a solid plan, although dragging Joe across two miles of this terrain sounded like an eternity. But, if they could cross the rib at that point, they should be able to come in below the South Glacier, where they would hopefully find a way up to the tent and await Sandy's arrival.

"How long do you think that will take us?" asked Ethan.

"Half mile per hour. Maybe less. Only thing more broken up. Than me right now. Is that boulder field," Joe said as he pointed at the chaotic maze of rocks and gravel bars stretched below.

Ethan whispered the distances to himself to be sure of the plan. He could tell that his brain wasn't firing very quickly due to his lack of sleep and food. "Two miles at a half-mile per hour pace, so four hours if we're lucky, but maybe six or eight if not."

Joe looked up at the dark sky. The cloud level remained a couple thousand feet above them, and there was only a slight breeze out of the west. "We should be able to get around there today. While it's warmer. That cloud bank will drop on us this evening. When the temps drop. Along with the dew point. I wanna find something to crawl under. Before it does. I don't know if we'd survive. A night out in the rain. As weak as we are," Joe said with labored breath.

Joe's comment about their chances of survival hit Ethan unexpectedly hard. He suddenly realized he had been pretending to be confident about their odds, assuming Joe had no doubts. However, Joe's admission of their vulnerability planted a seed of doubt in Ethan's mind, growing like a dark cloud that overshadowed his certainty, and he struggled to shake it off.

He sat down next to Joe on the cold rock. He was still warm from rappelling and coiling the rope, and he knew he would get cold quickly if he sat there, but he didn't want to move. He just wanted to rest more. He'd lost the momentum he'd had before they tried and failed to climb the rib.

Finally, Joe broke the silence. "We better get."

Though exhausted, they started off. Joe said the terrain might be gentler if they went back downhill for a few hundred yards before traversing along the base of the rib. He also hoped the sidestepping would be less steep. He tended to painfully catch his right foot more often on the ground when it was slanted upward to his right. A flatter surface helped him avoid that awful lightning bolt coursing up his leg.

They retraced their path from the mine, then turned hard right when Joe felt it was an excellent spot to do so. Ethan worked hard to support him, and they both looked ahead and scanned the sea of boulders for the best path. They made good time when they had open land between rocks and the ground was firm. In other places, sand and gravel diminished their footing and made it hard for Ethan to hold up his grandfather. Sometimes, they encountered large boulders stacked precariously; they tried their best to skirt around those. They found themselves trapped a few times and had to hop and crawl through the best they could, but it took much longer than they wanted. It also zapped them of the little strength they had left. By noon, they were exhausted and needed a break. They shared the rest of their water, then lay out for a nap on a soft, sandy patch, hoping for the sun to peek through the clouds, but it did not comply. The day never warmed up much beyond the previous night's lows.

They slept hard for a few hours until they grew cold. Joe sat up and rubbed his arms for warmth. The sun never penetrated the cloud cover.

"Too cold to sleep much," Joe said as Ethan stood up to pace around.

"It sure is," Ethan agreed. "Should we get going?"

"You're my ride. I'm ready if you are."

"What time is it?"

Joe pulled up his sleeve to see his watch. "Almost 3:30...p.m."

They continued their stumble through the labyrinth of house-sized boulders. Ethan was still lethargic from his nap and had a hard time regaining his alertness at first. Still, he put one foot in front of the other and did his best to look ahead and stay focused on the task at hand.

They passed a boulder with a natural bowl on the top, which still held water from the previous night's storm. They sipped the clear water slowly so as not to disturb the sandy bottom. It was cold. Tasted of iron. Ethan thought his eyes in the reflection looked gaunt and scared.

Ethan drank twice as much as Joe.

"What's wrong, you holding out for coffee?"

Joe half-smiled. "Water's for children."

They continued on.

"Looky there," said Joe, nudging ahead with his nose. "Grizzly bear dig. Looking for roots or rodents. Most likely." When they got closer, Ethan could see the claw marks in the soil where the beast had scooped several square feet of dirt out of the half-frozen ground.

They could tell the hole had been recently dug, but neither mentioned it, in fear of admitting more danger into their already impossible situation. Their eyes darted about the boulders as they stumbled on, and they took more care to be quieter in their movements. They would not mount much of an opposition to a bear attack in their weakened state.

They began to see the east rib lose its height on the skyline above as it transitioned from the world of jagged peaks and joined the lower land of valleys. They felt optimistic that a path through it would soon be revealed. They just had to keep moving.

That path arrived as the long light of evening approached. A long, deep gully cut through the wall and flushed out to a fan of broken rock and pebbles at the base. The boulders strewn on the path were brighter in color than those on the surrounding wall.

"Those are new rocks. Must have been a big rockfall," Joe pointed out.

"Can we take it up, or will it be too unstable?" asked Ethan.

Joe took in the weight of the question. "We have to try. No telling how far. We'll have to go down. To get up on the rib if we don't. Further we drop now, the more we'll have to climb later. To get back up to the tent."

"How long do you think we have until it rains?"

The cloud level was already down to the top of the rib, only a thousand feet above them.

"Not long. Let's have a look at the boulders," said Joe as he leaned forward impatiently.

They headed for the largest gathering of boulders, about one hundred feet ahead, and lucked out. The big stones stacked on each other in ways that left big, angular tunnels and caves between and underneath them. At the bottom edge of the most immense boulder, about the size of a school bus, Ethan found a small opening leading to a dark hole with a soft, gravel floor. "We might stay dry here and out of the wind." Ethan smoothed the gravel with his feet in the dim light and pulled out a couple rocks to flatten a bed. Then, he pulled out the rope and uncoiled it, laying it carefully across the floor to make bedding to insulate them from the cold ground.

“This’ll have to work,” said Joe. “Unless the bear tries to join us.”

Ethan didn’t laugh at the attempt at humor. He replied, “I’m sure he’s already holed up somewhere. Staying out of this storm.”

As Joe predicted, the rain grew heavier as the evening wore on, and the temperature dropped. They could hear the rain falling just outside the cave. Eventually, drops started to run down the inside walls of the boulders, and Ethan took the space blanket from his pack and hung it from cams he placed in the spaces between the big chockstones suspended above. He found a spot under an edge of the blanket to prop the water bottle so that it would catch the rain. They would need water for their push up the rib.

“I’m sorry about how I acted earlier,” Ethan said.

“It’s okay,” Joe said. “Sorry about this mess, kid.”

“Me too. I hope this rain doesn’t stick around for a few more days and delay our plane,” Ethan worried.

“Always a possibility.”

“Did you ever get stuck in the mountains like that?”

“Oh, yeah, quite a few times.” Joe stopped to cough, then continued slowly. “Some glaciers. Are more prone to it than others. I got stuck on the Tok. Below Huntington once with a team for a week. We had a great forecast. But the day after we flew in, we woke up in pea-soup. Stayed that way the whole time. That’s typical for the Tok. That pocket of the mountain. Tends to trap the clouds. We didn’t want to risk climbing in that. We just sat there in the tents and played cards. Probably got three or four feet of snow,” Joe recalled, then laughed to himself, painfully. “Then, when the sky cleared. We all threw on our skis. And skied up and down the runway. To pack down that new fluff into a strip. For the plane to land. If you’re not careful, an airplane will sink in fresh snow. You'll never get it to lift out. No matter how hard you lean on the throttle."

Water pooled in the floor's shallow spots, and they did their best to avoid them, but that got harder as the night progressed.

26. CRAVINGS

South Glacier, Brooks Range, Alaska
July 2017

—The Bear—

The Bear's ears twitched toward the sound of the big, shiny bird. He'd heard its roar before, but rarely this close. He was a cub the last time one flew so close. He remembered the urgency of his mother and how she bit his neck and ran with him. The loud roar of the bird was louder than the growl of the loudest grizzly. But this time, there was nowhere to run. He was in the open with no place to hide. He backed away, head lowered and teeth snarling, his heart beating in anticipation of the fight.

But the big bird roared past.

For days, he smelled the food. Intoxicating smells he had never smelled before, wafting off the ice and mixing among the boulders. His belly pulled him to the edge of the ice. But another smell stopped him from continuing onto it. His mother had betrayed the ways of the alpine bear when hunger pushed them down low and right into the sights of the man with the stick that brought thunder.

The man had smelled different than other animals. Not caribou, not pine, not rain. His smell burned like a strange fire. The salty, fatty, and oily sweat of the man mixed with smoke and an unnatural flower. Danger.

Hunger drove the Bear. It steered every thought. All other desires were secondary to the need for calories. Without enough fat stored, he would perish before the following spring. In the tug of war between cravings and fear, cravings would eventually win out.

His belly pulled him to the edge of the ice for three days, but he did not enter. The odor of the two-legged animal who carried thunder repelled him. But on the fourth day, the smell of danger was gone, and the only scent was of fresh meat somewhere on the ice. He stood up high on his hind legs and sniffed once again at the air and swiveled his ears forward to listen.

27. FEVER

Brooks Range, Alaska
July 2017
4 days until pickup

—Joe—

Joe's leg swelled and throbbed hard enough to wake him. He awoke with a fever, shivering helplessly. He tried to go back to sleep, to get the rest he would need to fight hard again the next day, but the pain and feverish delirium and the drip, drip, drip on the space blanket made for the most hellish night of his life. So far.

He sat up and tried in vain to find a position that would elevate his leg and ease the swelling. He pulled up his pant leg and tried to assess the wound. But the light was dim in the cave, and the only thing he could see was the soft glow of a white pus oozing from the hole in his leg next to the protruding bone. A rancid smell backed up his suspicion that a nasty infection was setting in.

God damn it.

Joe did his best to wrap it up, then he lay back down, but sleep eluded him. A deep dread set in as he wrestled with the reality he and his grandson were now living. An infection like this was dangerous, not only for him, but for Ethan as well. Joe had enough first-aid training as a guide to see down the road ahead. Fever would plague him until he got antibiotics, which he wouldn't get until he was flown to Fairbanks. If the fever became severe enough, he could become delirious and confused. That was especially dangerous in this environment, where he needed all his mental faculties to survive. There may come a point when he would become too much of a burden for Ethan and need to be left behind. He only hoped that Ethan would do so if that time came.

He thought a lot about Ethan's outburst on the rib. The stress of the last few days probably contributed to it, but he knew there was more. The boy—he still thought of him as a boy—*had* wanted to bring more gear. Of course, they never could have done the climb with that much weight in their packs, but Ethan didn't know that. He didn't have decades of experience on big routes to learn from. But Joe had to admit that the boy was right about them making a phone call after the rope was destroyed and their plans had changed. If they had told Katherine about their new descent route, then Sandy would have known where to look for them if they didn't make the rendezvous on time.

As for the climb on the rib—he should have known better than to even try. What the hell was he thinking? He'd always felt invincible in the mountains, and it was difficult to let go of that concept. No matter how difficult his objectives had been, he'd always been able to pull them off. Just throw his shoulder into it and not give up. He always figured he'd be able to crawl and fight his way out of any predicament, but his confidence had been shattered over the last few days.

By morning, the drizzle seeped from everywhere above them and dampened the ground all around. The sound of drips on the space blanket had made it hard to sleep, but at least it kept their clothing mostly dry.

28. NOPE

Brooks Range, Alaska
July 2017
3 days until pickup

—Ethan—

Ethan rolled over in the early morning hours and opened his eyes to see Joe staring back at him.

"It wasn't the Hilton…but it beats being out there," said Joe.

Ethan ran his fingers through his matted hair. "How'd you sleep?"

"I didn't." Joe took as deep a breath as he could without hurting his ribs. "Fever hit last night."

"Infection?"

"Looks like it, kid."

It's what Ethan had worried about the most. He'd hoped they could make it to the glacier at least before an infection hit. "Once we get to the top of the rib, we should be home free."

"If," replied Joe. "I think we'll still have a ways to go even then."

"Well, we have to try. I can't just leave you here."

"We'll try. Just can't promise I'll make it."

"I'll make sure you get up it."

"I like your energy. But you can't control everything."

"I'm not leaving you here for the bears."

"Alright. Let's pack up."

Joe looked at his watch. It was 6:32 a.m. In a low voice, he said, "As good a time as any. Hopefully, the clouds'll rise with the temperature again today. Cross your fingers."

Hunger hit Ethan, tying his stomach in knots. He had a hard time not thinking about food, especially the groceries they had in camp just a few impossible miles away.

They crawled out of the cave and into the light rain. Ethan pulled the hood of his rain jacket tight and waited for Joe to join him. Joe's leg was stiff and swollen, and it took him a minute to wriggle out of the cave's low exit. Ethan helped him to his feet when he emerged from the dark hideaway. Even the dark, gray skies appeared bright compared to the poorly lit hole they had huddled in.

The gully they needed to climb to reach the top of the rib stretched southward, most of it barely visible through the fog and drizzle. A long ramp littered with ominous stones and loose gravel flushed from the rib like a collapsed wall of a castle. From below, it appeared as a hellish stairway into the leaden sky. Ethan felt for Joe. He knew the obstacle would make or break their escape, and he had an idea of the agony in store for him. It would be like going into surgery without anesthetic. Their lives likely counted on him making it to the top. At least from there, Ethan could see the South Glacier and know how to get back to the tent, even if Joe could not.

"Time to clock in," said Joe, more to himself than to Ethan.

Ethan put his arm around Joe, and they proceeded with the same process as before. Ethan half-dragged Joe as he hopped on one foot and tried to avoid hitting his broken leg on rocks. Occasionally, he did and let out a loud bellow, which Ethan grew to ignore out of necessity. They had to get out, no matter how bad it hurt his grandfather. The hunger and deprivation had numbed Ethan's emotions in a primal response to better his chances of survival.

The gully was a nightmare of loose gravel and fist-sized rocks that often slid and rolled when stepped on. It seemed they took two steps forward just to slide back a step. The going was slow, and they rested frequently, typically when they found a larger, more stable rock to sit or stand upon. Ethan no longer looked far ahead to plan a path. All options were equally bad. By midday, they were a bit past halfway up the gully. Exhaustion pulled at them, and they couldn't climb for more than a few minutes at a time.

Ethan grew fatigued from hauling Joe up each step. His arm burned from pulling all day, and his fingers were numb from gripping Joe's belt so hard. They came to a big step up to a ledge, and Joe thought it would be better for Ethan to climb up first, then pull him up once Ethan had a good stance.

Once in place, Ethan instructed, "Alright, I'm good. Give me your hand."

Ethan grabbed Joe's hand and wrist with both hands and pulled as Joe pushed himself up onto the ledge with his other arm. He was almost to the top when he threw his good left leg up and over the edge. Ethan wasn't expecting the motion, which pulled hard on his arm, and he lost his footing. He used his right hand to catch himself, and Joe slipped from his grip. Their weakened, sweaty hands were unable to hold.

Joe crashed onto the ledge in the worst possible way, landing on his broken leg that dangled below him when he slipped. Ethan heard and felt the pain in Joe's screams and hopped down to help, though there was little he could do.

Joe writhed in pain, tears in his eyes, for several minutes. Ethan felt for him, but he was also happy that Joe hadn't slid down the gully in his fall.

"I can't, kid. I can't."

"It's alright, I'll push from below this time. You go first."

Joe shook his head, eyes closed. "I can't. Leave me." His exhausted lungs still breathed hard even though he was lying down.

"I'm not gonna do that. You know that."

"No choice," Joe answered, still sprawled on his back, eyes closed.

Ethan looked up at the rest of the gully and guiltily entertained the idea. If he left Joe here, the old man could crawl his way back down to the boulder where they had slept and wait. Ethan could make it to the tent in a matter of hours if he didn't have to drag Joe. He could eat. Tonight. *But the glacier by myself will be dangerous,* he thought. Though maybe he'd be okay. He did make his way down half of the North Glacier alone, and without being roped. If he stayed vigilant, then he believed he could find a path around potential crevasses. And when the plane picked him up, he could lead them to Joe.

He looked down at the boulder field. A plane would never be able to land there; even Sandy couldn't find a spot in that maze to set down. They'd need to call in a helicopter. How much more time would that take?

"Nope," Ethan said decisively, then took off his pack and sat on a rock next to Joe.

Joe opened his eyes and squinted up at Ethan, blurred by the gray sky. "The hell you mean 'nope'?"

"I'm not going anywhere without you. I'll just sit here 'til you're ready, old man."

Joe closed his eyes again and lay his head back in the gravel. "You stubborn son-of-a-bitch."

In the early afternoon, the clouds parted a little, allowing the sun to shine briefly. This did much to improve their spirits. A sudden boost of energy came their way, and they did their best to ride it to the top of the gully. The upper half of the draw was rockier but had less gravel for them to contend with. The rocks were also less precarious and more trustworthy underfoot. Ethan paused for fewer breaks, and they pushed on to the top of the rib by early evening.

The long ridge line of the east rib was nice and flat, like a gently sloped field. They collapsed on the flat ground, elated to have defeated the most significant challenge on their return to camp.

"That was. Too much," Joe proclaimed as he fought to catch his breath. "Didn't think. I'd make it."

Ethan noticed the furrows on Joe's face were more profound, and his eyes sank in. He seemed to have aged years in just a matter of days. Joe had always stood tall and strong for his age, but for the first time, he appeared frail and wizened to Ethan.

Ethan shook off the observation and smiled proudly at what they had accomplished, though he was still dazed from the exertion. The sun shone brightly upon them at the moment. Still, everything appeared hazy in his depleted state. He sat up and looked around. He had seen very little open sky in the last few days, and he took the opportunity to reacquaint himself with the topography. Harte Tower, its right skyline painted red by the sharp light of evening, cut deeply into a sky of dark blue. He could just see the bottom of the North Glacier they had traveled down, but the peaks beyond were still enveloped with clouds.

"Look," Ethan said as he pointed to the panorama.

Joe sat up, balancing on his good arm, just in time to take in the views Ethan enjoyed. The hard work of the day had dulled the fever's intensity and eased some of the stiffness in his leg. He was aware that he had caused more damage to his leg during the climb up the ramp. He lost count of how many times he'd bumped his boot against rocks, feeling the bones shift within, like razors cutting at him from the inside.

"The more they beat me down…the more reverence I have," Joe panted.

"Do you think God is telling us something?"

"I wouldn't have a clue as to what He is thinking."

"Not a believer?"

"Wouldn't say that. Only thing I know of Him is that He is a mystery. And those who claim to know Him best, are the most clueless."

Ethan figured the South Glacier was likely only another quarter mile ahead on the other side of the rib. Maybe they could make it to the tent by the end of the night. He took a moment to appreciate the moment, then said, "This doesn't seem to be a great place to sleep."

"I get the hint," replied Joe, staring blankly. His eyes betrayed the trepidation for the pain to come.

Ethan was too tired to empathize. He looked toward

Harte Tower.

"Alright. Help me up," Joe grunted.

"Oh, wait. Hand me the map," Ethan said. He took it and laid it on the ground before him. He found the rib they were on and could see that the gully they had just climbed was the apparent curve of contour lines intruding into its side. He didn't have a pen to mark their current spot, so he found a sharp little quartz rock in the gravel next to him, punched a small dot where they stood, and punched another small hole in the map where he thought their base camp and tent had to be. Then, he took his compass and oriented the map to point north. He next shot a bearing between the two points and spun the dial around to mark it for later use. In that way, if Ethan checked the map regularly and marked their path, he would know which direction camp was if clouds rolled in again and blocked their view. This could save them from endlessly wandering around the glacier looking for their tent in the fog and rain.

Once satisfied, Ethan put away the map and hung the compass around his neck. He helped Joe to his feet. They walked and hopped in the direction of their camp in hopes of finding an easy way onto the glacier. Traveling across the top of the rib was the most effortless navigation they'd encountered since the avalanche. For a change, the ground was windswept and free of large rocks. They made the opposite lip of the rib in an hour. The edge dropped off precipitously, almost vertically, for about one hundred feet, where it met the South Glacier. Ethan had read about bergschrunds, places where glaciers meet rock. It was one of the most volatile places in the mountains, known to kill climbers, often due to broken rock and jagged glacier edges. The ones they'd encountered before had been tame in comparison.

"Oh, lord," said Joe.

"Yeah, I'm not feeling it either."

"Should it make us feel better...that we don't have a choice?"

"True." But Ethan wasn't worried for himself. "It's getting late, and I don't see anywhere for us to try and sleep."

Joe leaned, trying to find the correct posture to ease the pressure on his ribs, which were sore from all the tugging from Ethan all day. "We'll get blasted up here. And exposed if the rain comes back." Then he peered down into the gaping bergschrund. "That's no place to linger. We'll get crushed."

"Can you push on through the night on your leg?"

Joe paused and thought for a moment. "I'll have to," he replied.

Ethan tried to look up the glacier to their camp. Their yellow tent was still out of sight, but he figured it was just over the rise. Or perhaps it was too hard to make out in the gray light. Glaciers make it difficult to judge distance because they have no recognizable features to compare to.

"We could make camp tomorrow," Ethan said. The thoughts of his warm sleeping bag and their large cache of food perked him up. "I could live with that."

They located a rounded crack system near the edge and placed two cams. Neither minded leaving them since it would be the last time they'd need any rock gear. In fact, it meant they'd have less to carry up the glacier. Ethan uncoiled the rope and fed the middle through the carabiners, then tossed both ends far out above the glacier, where they floated down into the moat.

Joe worked both strands of the rope through his belay device. The danger of the task sent a shot of adrenaline through the old man, returning a sense of heightened awareness.

"Don't you want me to lower you instead?" asked Ethan.

"I need to control the speed...in case a rock comes loose."

"Are you sure? Remember the rib?"

"Of course. You beat me up on that lower. I'll take my chances this time."

Joe carefully inched down the wall, trying to push out on his one good leg and protect his injured one. He encountered a few loose blocks along the way and pried them off with one hand while he held the brake strand with the other so as not to leave something for Ethan to knock down onto him once he was below. He found a safe stance between the rock and ice to wait for Ethan to lead them up from there. The ends of the rope were just barely long enough to get him to a block to stand on out of the way. He leaned to the side so he would be clear of rocks being kicked down from Ethan as he rappelled.

"Off," Joe said, but his voice was too weak to travel up that high. Ethan felt the rope go limp, forced two loops through his belay device, worked slowly down the broken wall, and carefully joined Joe at the bottom.

Joe watched as Ethan took himself off the rappel and began pulling one end of the rope to clean it from the anchor above.

"Your father taught you well," Joe said.

"He had a good teacher."

Once Ethan had pulled the rope and flaked it on the boulder, Joe pointed to the route he thought would be best. "Up there," he said weakly.

"Sounds like as good a plan as any." Ethan retrieved

the rock hammer he'd found in the Harte Brothers' mine from his pack. Then, he tied into one end of the rope and headed up. The crevasse floor ramped up at a gentle enough angle to not be too treacherous, and half a foot of crusty, old snow in the bottom helped with his footing. He deliberately cut steps close together with the hammer so Joe could use them when he followed. The old man would have a hard time, even with a tight belay.

Ethan reached the top quickly but found the glacier's surface too slick for him to have a firm stance. If Joe fell, his weight would rip both of them off the glacier and into the bergschrund. Ethan looked down the crack he had climbed up and saw Joe looking up at him.

"I can't find a good place to belay from, so I'll have to walk a little out of sight. I'll let you know when I'm in position," he called down.

Joe nodded, and Ethan continued his search. About fifty feet from the exit, he found that the glacier ice had softened and transitioned from deep blue to white again, more like old snow than ice. He turned back toward the exit of the crevasse and stomped two holes in the soggy ice, then took off his backpack and placed it under him to sit on. He holstered the hammer in the gear loop of his harness and took a seat. He leaned back in a strong position and pulled the slack until it came tight.

"ON BELAY!"

Ethan belayed, pulling the rope tight to help Joe get up the crevasse as smoothly as possible. Joe struggled to make it without Ethan's arm around him pulling him along, like he had the last few days, and hopping on one leg inside an icy crevasse was less than ideal. Joe tried to brace himself against the ice walls, but they were too smooth to offer much assistance, and the force of pushing outward hurt his ribs when he did find purchase. He wanted to pull on the rope for balance but didn't want to yank Ethan off his stance since he knew he had nothing solid up there from which to anchor. The hopelessness of the moment sank in. Desperation overwhelmed him, and he quietly sobbed, standing on his one leg and arms stretched out to his sides, his palms against the ice walls.

Ethan grew cold sitting on the ice for so long. He noticed the snow below him was softer than he had first thought. He kept sinking, little by little, deeper into the soggy surface of the glacier. He wanted to stand up and find a better spot, but he knew that if Joe fell while he was standing, he would likely be ripped from the top. He needed to stay here and brace himself for a few more minutes.

In an instant, the ice and snow surrounding Ethan dropped away, and he was flushed into the depths of a wide crevasse. He fell backward and would have been dumped into the bowels of the glacier along with the several tons of ice he had been sitting on if he hadn't held the brake strand of the rope. What had been a lifeline for Joe was now holding Ethan precariously above certain death. Ethan's momentum plucked Joe off his feet and pulled him to within a few feet of the top of the crevasse. Only the friction of the rope melting into the lip of the glacier stopped Ethan from plummeting to the bottom and taking Joe with him.

Ethan's adrenaline had taken over, and his death grip on the brake strand held him. He swung around wildly until his back crashed against the inside of the crevasse. His mind rushed to take stock of what had happened. He had unknowingly set up to belay on top of a snow bridge. He was angry with himself for being so careless. However, he had no probe to gauge the depth of the snow, even if he had wanted to.

Ethan's hands were already cold, even in his thin leather gloves, and he knew his grip on the brake wouldn't last much longer. He needed to ensure he didn't slide down the rope any farther. He didn't know any fancy tricks for this, so he held the brake strand hard with his left hand while tying an overhand knot with his right. He had difficulty tightening the knot with one hand, so he put the loop in his mouth and pulled with his teeth while yanking the other strand down with his right hand. Satisfied, he lowered himself onto the knot and allowed the belay plate to slide up against it, bringing him to a halt.

"NO MORE!" Ethan screamed desperately as he pounded his fists against the crevasse wall. "I CAN'T TAKE ANYMORE!" Ethan hung, near sobbing, and tried to calm down and think. He was so tired. Too tired.

Now what? he asked himself. He looked up and could see he was only twenty feet from the rim of the crevasse. *You better get your ass out of here before the old man comes sliding in on top of you. That's what.*

Ethan had spent a lot of time watching the guides, including Joe, teach and reteach rope skills to their teams in Talkeetna. He helped the clients practice until they were confident in their ability to tie the most complex knots and hitches while wearing their bulky gloves and mittens. Taking them off in deep cold while high on the mountain, even for a moment, could result in losing a fingertip to frostbite.

Teammates first learned how to tie in together with the rope so that if one person broke through a crevasse, then the others would hopefully catch them before they all were pulled to their deaths. Also, the climber who fell in, once his or her fall was arrested, would have to know how to ascend the rope using nothing more than Prusik cords and carabiners. The guide company kept a rope hanging from a thick Birch tree branch for all of them to practice ascending. These skills had saved many lives, but not all were that lucky. Plenty of climbers over the years had walked away from the tent alone to get snow to melt for water or empty their bladders and had broken through a lightly covered crevasse, never to be seen again.

Joe had told Ethan to rehearse these skills, reminding him that they could save his life one day. Ethan had memorized each knot, and then he had practiced tying them all with one hand. The most essential hitch was the trusty Prusik, which would allow him to ascend a rope.

Ethan searched his harness in the near darkness. He could barely feel anything with his cold hands and was afraid he would drop the gear needed to get out. He managed to unclip a sling with both hands, wrap it in a Prusik around the taut rope above him, and then clip it to his harness with a carabiner. He found a second sling and did the same just above the first one. Joe had taught him to clip another sling into the lower Prusik to put a foot into, but he was out of slings.

Shit, Ethan despaired. *Maybe one is in my backpack.* He reached to unstrap his backpack, but it wasn't there. Then he remembered he was sitting on it when the ice bridge collapsed. It would be sitting at the bottom of the crevasse. He peered down into the darkness but could not see the floor of the monster crack he was dangling in. He could see the free strand of rope trailing down into the darkness.

I'll just use the rope, Ethan decided. He pulled up some of the slack rope and made a two-foot-tall loop with an overhand knot. He clipped the loop into the lower Prusik, slid his foot into it, and stood up on it. He unweighted the upper Prusik and slid it up the rope a couple of feet. Then he weighted the upper Prusik and slid the lower Prusik until it hit the upper one.

"It works!" Ethan thankfully proclaimed. He was going to live, and even better, he was saving himself.

The walls of the crevasse muffled all sound, and Joe had no way of knowing what Ethan was up to. But he started to feel the vibrations in the tight rope as Ethan began to ascend it. The stimulus of the last hour had mentally exhausted him. Joe could feel reality slipping away. Delirium was taking over his thoughts. He struggled to remember why he was lying next to a crevasse.

Ethan continued the process of stepping up on the lower Prusik and sliding the upper Prusik, and he neared the lip after twenty minutes of hard work. But here, he ran into trouble. The rope had cut a deep groove through the top of the glacier that his Prusik knots couldn't pass through. The rope was effectively buried in the edge of the glacier. He was now stuck five feet from the top. He searched for answers. He looked behind him, and the opposite edge was ten feet away. He wouldn't be able to chimney his way out of this.

Maybe I can just climb it, Ethan said to himself. He stood as high as he could and clawed at the soft snow around the rope. His hands grew cold and wet very quickly, but he kept at it, desperate to get out of the hole. He suddenly remembered the hammer in his gear loop and used it to swing into the slushy snow. Finally, Ethan cleared enough snow and ice around the rope to grab it with his hands and drag himself up while desperately kicking his feet into the crevasse's side for some traction.

When Ethan got half of his body on top, Joe's weight pulled him the rest of the way up. He flopped onto the top, depleted and half-frozen.

Ethan slowly pushed himself up on his knees and stared at Joe without saying anything, still struggling to catch his breath. Ethan struggled to control the pain that convulsed over him as the cold blood and lactic acid flushed from his hands.

"Ya did good, Chris," Joe said. "Ya did real good, son."

29. THE LONGEST DAY

Brooks Range, Alaska
July 2017
3 days until pickup

Joe took Ethan's wet gloves off and put them into his chest pocket to warm them. Then he unzipped his jacket and brought Ethan's hands into his own armpits. Joe's actions were automatic, ingrained from years of work in the mountains caring for fellow climbers and clients.

"Can't have you gettin' frostbite," whispered Joe. Ethan noticed that his ice-cold hands on Joe's torso didn't shock Joe.

Ethan was thankful for Joe's help, but confused and worried. Joe had clearly called him "Chris," his father's name. Was it just an honest mistake from a tired man? Or was it something more? Joe had grown paler and even more depleted. His eyes sank in, and his cheeks thinned. He'd lost the confident aura that had always enveloped him.

Their faces were close together, so Ethan could see the tears well in his grandfather's eyes as Joe said, "I'm sorry. I've always pushed things too far. I've always gotten away with it. The debt's bein' paid."

Ethan shook his head. "No, this isn't your fault. I'm the one who didn't check that hold and cut the rope."

Joe put his arms around Ethan and hugged him lightly with the little strength he had. "If I don't make it," he said as he jabbed a finger into Ethan's chest, "you have to get to the plane."

"You will make it. We'll both make it. I'll make sure of that." Ethan didn't want to dwell. "My hands are warm enough now. We should go. We could be back in camp by the end of the day."

Ethan coiled half of the rope around his body and tied an overhand knot to attach to his harness with a locking carabiner. Joe was still tied into the other end. They had no other option but to move separately at either end of the rope, for if they walked together, they risked falling into a crevasse right alongside each other. They needed to disperse their weight and provide safety for the other. In Talkeetna, Joe had shown Ethan how to tie butterfly knots every ten feet, and Ethan did just that with their rope. The knots were meant to act as a brake by catching in the groove cut by the rope at the lip of a crevasse.

Ethan felt a stab of pain in his abdomen. His body was starving and on the verge of open rebellion. He rubbed his belly and felt his ribs and abdominal muscles in more detail than he ever had. He removed his helmet, rubbed the matted mop of hair on his head, and tried to straighten the tangles. It soothed him somehow. Looking up and around the vast, empty amphitheater, he realized he had seen Harte Tower from every angle. He felt as though he knew it intimately, like an old friend, or perhaps more accurately, an adversary with whom he had grown up knowing. His emotions had fluctuated in response to the mood the towering obelisk projected. Clouds drawn to its gravitational pull darkened his spirit, while even the slightest beam of light illuminating its surface lifted him out of despair.

Whether it was his deep, primal hunger or the stillness of the cold mountain air, he did not know, but his senses were heightened. The hair on his arm detected the slightest breeze washing down the glacier. His eyesight was almost avian in its clarity, and he could hear each tiny ice crystal breaking under the weight of his boots. He felt the mountain's vibrations resonating on a secret wavelength previously hidden from him.

Ethan checked his map and compass to get his bearings, then set out carefully, looking for sagging areas that could indicate a crevasse lurking beneath a snow bridge. When the rope came tight, Joe began crawling. It was the only way they could imagine traveling since they couldn't walk together. Ethan tried to pull as much as he could to help Joe along. The frequency of crevasses decreased once they moved past the outer edge and into thicker ice.

Soon, the day warmed up the glacier's surface and made for easier traction for Ethan, but it was harder for Joe to slide his body across. The coarse surface of the ice ground away at his thin climbing pants, creating holes that allowed the ice to punish his skin. He all but gave up on the thought of keeping warm once his clothes were soaked from the melting snow. All he knew at that point was misery and pain. They pushed as far as they could before taking a break to eat snow to rehydrate, fueled by the hope of reaching camp soon.

His father's words came back to Ethan once more.

Believe the line will go.

The surface conditions wore on Ethan more than he realized. His boots sank deeper into the soft snow, draining his energy with every step. Joe was crawling as best he could, but Ethan was pulling half of Joe's weight on the rope. Sweat poured from Ethan's body, sapping him of the precious salts needed for his muscles and brain to function properly—salts that could not be replaced without a savory meal. His grasp on reality began to slip, and his perception of time blurred. He felt as if he had always been on the mountain. Though he had been on Harte Tower for just over a week, it was hard to recall a time when he hadn't been there. Memories of his mother and Camila had faded so much that he could barely picture their faces. He felt that he was now a part of the mountain—and it, a part of him.

His thoughts went to the future, both as an escape from the pain and discomfort and as a goal to push himself toward. His mother had done so much for him, but he wondered if he had shown her enough appreciation. He tried to recall a time when he showed an understanding of her pain or acknowledged her patience with him, but he couldn't. He wanted another chance; he couldn't leave things as they were.

And Camila. She had no reason to waste her time with him. He couldn't fathom the depth of kindness in her heart to carry him when he most needed it. He had to get out of here if only so that he could show her how much he appreciated her. It was time for him to grow up; he just had to escape this place first.

Ethan made a surprise discovery in the middle of the glacier. There at his feet was a torn wrapper. It startled him, and he thought hard about what it meant. Was he hallucinating? He picked it up and recognized the brand. It was from their box of snack bars they brought with them, three of which were their cherished last meals in the previous days. He was embarrassed. He must have carelessly put aside a wrapper instead of throwing it in the trash bag at camp. Joe would be upset if he found out, so Ethan put the wrapper in his pocket and leaned back into the rope to continue dragging his grandfather along the soggy glacier.

Fifteen minutes later, he came across something much more startling. There in the snow were massive tracks bigger than his feet, with noticeable claw marks as long as his fingers. Grizzly bear. The tracks headed up toward their camp. He turned around and pulled the rope to help Joe catch up to him.

Joe pulled up to the bear print, positioned it right between his extended arms, and had to stare at it momentarily for his beleaguered brain to comprehend its meaning. "'At's a big boy," he said through heavy breaths. He stared fixedly in the direction of their camp.

Ethan slowly took out the torn wrapper he'd found and held it in the air for his grandfather to see. Joe sat back on his good leg, a look of resignation mixed with total exhaustion on his face. "The hits keep coming." He rolled over onto his back, the only position he could truly rest, and shoved his half-frozen hands into his armpits to warm them for a few moments.

"Do you think he's still up there?" Ethan glanced around the glacier nervously, expecting a big, brown monster to appear from any direction.

Joe closed his eyes and nodded his head slowly. "Possible."

Ethan looked up the glacier toward camp and then back the way they came. He considered his options. He knew they'd be sitting ducks if they continued to camp and the bear was still there, especially Joe. And, if they went back to the rib, they'd spend another night exposed, and Joe didn't seem capable of surviving that.

"If we cross him," muttered Joe. "Leave me. Run back to the rib."

Ethan pulled out the compass and found his bearing toward their camp. Three hundred and twenty-five degrees. He untied from his end of the rope and stacked it neatly. He then stomped out a shallow indentation the size of Joe's body and helped his grandfather slide into it. He tried not to think of how much the hole resembled a grave.

He kneeled down next to Joe and patted his shoulder. "Stay right here for a little while. I'll be right back."

Joe grabbed his hand and looked up to him through glazed eyes. "It's okay. They'll understand."

"I'm not leaving you. Just stay here."

He remembered hearing that bears didn't like human sounds, so he turned on his phone. The battery was at twenty-eight percent. He scrolled through his downloaded music, selected a heavy-metal playlist, and cranked it as loud as it would go. He set it in his chest pocket so that the noise would travel as far as possible.

Ethan continued up the glacier toward camp. He didn't know which to be more afraid of, falling into a glacier unroped or getting mauled by a bear. His mind got away from him for a moment, and he found himself debating which would be a worse death, imagining the details of each. He was leaning toward a bear when he forced himself to stop thinking and focus on his breathing and listening.

He stepped lightly and tried not to make any more noise than necessary. Still, the crunch of the snow was impossible to silence. He stopped periodically and listened for any sign that the bear was still in their camp. Finally, he heard the flapping of their tent in the breeze. He grabbed the hammer from his harness and held it firmly, as it was his only defense. He was struck by the absurdity of fighting a grizzly with a hundred-year-old rock hammer. Fear washed over him in waves, and he nearly turned around, but each time he reminded himself that he needed supplies if Joe was going to have a chance.

Even from a distance, he could tell the camp had been destroyed. Litter had blown all about, and broken tent poles jutted up from their carefully crafted kitchen site. He stood alert for signs of the bear for several minutes before approaching.

The camp was a complete disaster. Every bit of food had either been eaten or shredded. It was littered with cans punctured with incisors and squeezed the way Popeye ate his spinach. What the bear didn't eat, he stomped. Ethan checked the buried "refrigerator" at the edge of the camp, and it too had been hit. Raven tracks told him the birds had eaten anything the bear didn't get to. A giant pile of bear dung sat beside the campsite.

The bear's massive claws had punctured the air mats. Ethan thought back to the conversation they had about the reason for having a backup foam pad for each of them. He grabbed them both, then dug out the pistol and bear spray. No more half measures. He found the big puffy jackets they had worn in camp, and he folded up the probe to bring along so he could search for hidden crevasses at their new site.

The small tent had not been damaged, so he pulled it out and unzipped one of the doors. He threw all the supplies and the tent poles inside and zipped the door shut. He holstered the heavy pistol in his pocket; it rubbed uncomfortably against his leg, but he didn't care. He used a carabiner to clip one of the corner tie downs to his harness so he could drag the tent behind him, and slowly made his way back to Joe.

It was early evening before they retraced their steps back to the edge of the glacier, and both were tired beyond exhaustion. The extra night of moving without sleep caught up to them once they stopped moving, and the anticipation of getting to camp evaporated. Joe had lain on his least injured side and curled up, shaking from the cold of lying on ice. Ethan pitched the small tent. Then he spread out their foam pads and pulled out their sleeping bags. He rolled Joe into his bag and zipped him up. Although he was shivering, Joe sweated heavily.

They had been moving continuously for a day and a half.

30. NEW SMELLS

Brooks Range, Alaska

July 2017

—The Bear—

The Bear had never ventured this far out onto the ice before. His only excursions onto the glacier were to chase an occasional ground squirrel or marmot seeking refuge from his deadly swipes. The surface was soft and crunched under his weight. His big paws acted like snowshoes to keep him afloat. He stopped often to sniff the air and to listen. Still no sign of the men. Big cracks and fissures in the ice were easy for him to avoid, and he was lucky not to drop into a hidden hole.

His nose brought him to the tent, and he circled it, sniffing and listening. He growled to stoke fear into any animal that might be hidden, reminding them he alone sat atop the food chain in the cirque. He shoved at the strange fabric a few times to test it, then tore at it with his claws. It came apart easily, to his satisfaction, and he began snorting around, tearing through packages, investigating with his nose. He tore open a box of cookies and devoured the contents. Then a loaf of bread left out on the snow table. He kicked the cans of food around curiously, then stomped one, and soup sprayed him. He liked the taste. He crushed the rest in his teeth and licked away the salty liquids. He had never tasted anything so delicious. A jab of fear pierced his primal brain and reminded him of the dangers of letting his guard down. He stood up on his back legs and sniffed the air, while scanning the horizon in all directions. He caught a whiff of meat somewhere close by. He followed the scent and found lunch meats and packages of chicken buried in the snow.

The Bear's belly had not been this full since killing the caribou a few weeks ago. It had been frail, wounded, and limping. He went back to the tent and rooted around for the few things he'd missed and licked up the crumbs and drops in the snow. When he finished rooting through everything, he waddled back outside and lay down and licked his lips, satisfied with the meal he'd found. The sweet and savory tastes were like nothing he'd encountered. The quick rush of energy excited him at first, but then he grew tired, almost drunk from the powerful punch of highly refined energy he'd nearly inhaled. He sprawled out a short walk above the tent and fell quickly asleep.

A strange, screeching, metallic noise awoke him. It was still far away, but the sound traveled easily across the ice. He raised his head toward the direction it came. He didn't like the sound, and it angered him, but he also felt fear. The same fear he had felt when the giant, shiny bird flew over him days ago, and the fear he had felt when his mother was killed by the stick that brought lightning. Finally, the smell of man touched his nose, and his primal brain weighed his response. He could attack quickly, charging across the open glacier. But there was no cover for him. His mother had tried the same maneuver, and that was the end of her. The Bear remembered that he had eaten all the food here. There was nothing for him to protect. The risk of confronting the foul-smelling man was not worth the consequences. He hesitated for a moment, then lurched away in the opposite direction and made his way back to the rocky moraine beside the glacier and slept the night in his cave while the rain fell heavily outside.

The rain had stopped by morning. He emerged from his cave and stretched his legs in the gray mist. His belly still full. He returned to the darkness of his den and slumbered the day away.

He knew his hunger would return tomorrow, and he hoped to find more of the new tastes and smells he had discovered.

31. WAITING

Fairbanks, Alaska
July 2017
1 day until pickup

—Sandy—

It was cold for summer, even for Fairbanks. Sandy woke early and drove to work under cloudy skies. She knew the airfield would not likely run flights into the mountains that day. Even with modern technology, pilots can't land or fly where they can't see. The backcountry is littered with bush planes of bold pilots who braved bad weather only to pay the ultimate price. Mountain pilots have many similarities to mountain climbers. Both revel in risk and like to push the line. But sometimes, even the best don't get away with it. She never could tell which group was crazier.

Since dropping Joe and Ethan off a little over a week ago, she had thought about them every day. Katherine had called her each of the last four days to ask about their status, and she had to keep telling her she had not received a call or message from them. Katherine was in near panic the last time she called. She and Ethan's mother were ready to book flights to Fairbanks at a moment's notice. Sandy felt helpless sitting in Fairbanks waiting for the clouds to lift.

Sandy and the other pilots used the downtime for routine maintenance. They left the big-ticket items to the mechanics, but there was plenty of small stuff for them to take care of that didn't require much expertise. Sandy set out to change the tires on one of the Cessnas, which had been worn down by rough landings in the backcountry. She cranked up one wheel with the manual hydraulic jack, removed the outer bearing assembly, and slid the wheel off.

"Excuse me, would you happen to be Sandy?"

Sandy turned, still hunched over the wheel and tire, which she was about to roll toward the shop for removal. A gray-haired woman with a friendly face stood smiling at her. A face that Sandy didn't recognize as anyone she knew, but her voice sounded familiar.

"Yes, ma'am, that would be me. I'd shake your hand, but mine is covered in bearing grease."

"Oh, that's okay, I won't bother you long." Sandy noticed that her eyes looked tired, and she guessed her friendly smile was concealing something. "I'm Katherine. We spoke on the phone."

"Oh, of course. I knew I heard your voice before." Sandy propped the wheel against the struts so that she could stand and talk and pulled the shop rag from her back pocket to wipe some of the grease from her hands. "What brings you up here? I thought you were in Talkeetna."

"Well, I was too worried to stay home, so I drove up last night."

"That's not a short drive," replied Sandy. She put her rag back in her pocket and stood with her hands on her hips.

"No, it's not," agreed Katherine. "This isn't the first time Joe has been unable to call, but this feels different."

Sandy nodded her head. She felt the same but didn't know how much of her concerns she should voice to Katherine. There was a good chance that things had gone wrong for Joe and Ethan. She also knew that no amount of worrying would help at that point. The weather made the rules.

"I don't feel good about it either. I was actually thinking of you this morning." Sandy glanced past the mountains at the gray, cloudy skies, as if hoping to see a chance of them clearing. "There's just nothing we can do until those clouds lift."

"I understand." Katherine's eyes watered, and Sandy couldn't tell if it was welling tears or just a lack of sleep affecting her.

"Are you staying in Fairbanks? I can call you as soon as I get clearance to fly."

"Yes, I have a hotel room not far away. I can be here in no time at all."

"That's good."

Katherine awkwardly shifted her stance to the other leg. "Do you think I could fly in with you? I could help look for them while you fly."

Sandy thought about how to answer that. She could easily fit Katherine into the four-seater plane and still have room for the boys and their gear. However, adding another body to the equation complicated things. Flying into spotty weather was always dangerous, and endangering another life should be avoided. A search for two climbers could quickly escalate to a search for two climbers, a pilot, and one passenger.

"I think that will have to depend on the forecast."

32. DELAYED

Brooks Range, Alaska
July 2017
1 day before pickup

"Grandpa, what's the longest you ever waited for a bush plane?" Joe didn't seem to hear him, although they were lying next to each other in the small tent, so Ethan asked again. He thought the mental exercise might be good for him. Might keep him tethered to this world in some way. Although he didn't admit it to himself, Ethan also wanted to check that Joe was still alive and conscious.

No answer. Ethan hoped the rest would help Joe fight the infection until the weather broke and their ride out showed up.

They had followed their footsteps back toward the rib and found a flat spot on the glacier a few hundred yards from the hole where he broke through. He probed the area diligently before setting up the tent and carefully placing Joe into his sleeping bag. His grandfather had been sleeping when he returned from the wrecked campsite with their tent and what gear he could scrounge up. He simply rolled Joe onto the tent, tied him to it as best he could, and dragged him down the ice. It wasn't so hard sliding downhill.

Ethan woke in the night to the sound of hard rain beating on the tent. Big heavy drops. Soon, little streams of water coursed into the tent under the exterior wall and wet his sleeping bag and would have rendered the down useless for warmth if he hadn't caught it in time. He laid his bag on top of Joe to make room to work, then used the rock hammer to carve a trench in the icy crust of the glacier, which was now their floor. The trench diverted the incoming water along the edge of the tent and out the lower end near the entrance. He lay back down. The patter of rain helped him sleep.

***

Ethan unzipped his sleeping bag the next morning and sat up to find a closed world outside the tent door. Fog so thick he couldn't see a hundred feet had enveloped their camp. Due to exhaustion and hunger, Ethan slept so hard through the night that he didn't notice the drop in temperature. He was lost in dreams and nightmares and cocooned in his zero-degree sleeping bag.

Throughout the day, the sky sometimes looked like it was clearing, only for the fog to roll right back in. It was the day Sandy was scheduled to pick them up, but the weather was not cooperating.

The weather didn't change much the next day either. Joe tossed about in agony, sometimes receding into the confines of his bag to shake out the cold, then bursting out in boiling desperation. His groans became almost childish, reminding Ethan of when he had the flu in third grade and his mother sat by him all night, giving him medicine and damp rags for his forehead. Except, Ethan had nothing to help Joe. White and yellow fluid spilled out of his wound when Ethan checked, and Joe's fever was constant. The lower leg was solidly red and black, and the infection was moving up his leg in black streaks, reaching its poisonous grip toward the heart. Even the most potent dose of antibiotics wouldn't help him if it went that far. In a brief moment of alertness, Joe grabbed the boy's wrist tightly and, with eyes still shut, muttered, "We got you back. We got you back."

Ethan felt weaker than he had ever felt and couldn't remember how many days it had been since he'd eaten. He tightened his belt by another hole, so he knew he was still losing weight. He also noticed the last night was colder than the others, and he could only guess it was because he had less fat to keep him warm.

Ethan picked up his grandfather's copy of *Lonesome Dove*, which he found in the pocket of Joe's down jacket. He tried to read it to distract himself from their grim reality but had to read the opening paragraph three times to comprehend what it was saying. He gave up and was about to throw it into the hole in the glacier when he noticed the light was bright enough to make him want his glacier glasses. He unzipped the tent door and saw the sun breaking through the clouds.

"Look!"

Ethan left the tent and stood to watch the clouds thin out, revealing an open, blue sky above and Harte Tower standing triumphantly.

"This could do it," Ethan said happily and looked down at Joe's unmoving sleeping bag.

33. FADING

Brooks Range, Alaska
July 2017
1 day past scheduled pickup

—Joe—

What is that godawful flapping? Joe erupted from the sleeping bag, slinging his right arm out to his side and rolling onto his back. Through the haze, he watched the unzipped tent door rustle in the light breeze. Katherine must have left the door open. Or one of the kids. They'll be back soon.

He repositioned his arm to cover his eyes with the crook of his elbow. His heart beat out of his chest, and his breaths were rapid and shallow. *I guess I'll zip it up myself. I just need a break first. Have to rest.* He drifted off to sleep. In and out. *That's better.*

He'd been there before. In first grade. He was burning up. His throat hurt so bad, worn coarse like sandpaper, but he couldn't stop coughing. His mother piled the blankets on him. He sweated through all of them. "The only way to beat a fever is to burn it out." When his fever finally broke, she made him a fried bologna sandwich and tomato soup.

A cool breeze swept over him. *I feel better. It doesn't hurt anymore. Just a little more sleep.*

A slight smile graced his face as he fell backward into a more profound slumber than he had ever felt. The orange glow of the tent faded, and, slowly, even the sound of the tent fabric flapping in the breeze waned.

34. GUNSHOT PASS

Brooks Range, Alaska
July 2017
1 day past scheduled pickup

—Sandy—

Sandy departed Fairbanks with partly cloudy skies, nervously watching the weather out west and hoping it would stay clear enough to enter the mountains. She speedily refueled in Coldfoot and was back in the air as soon as she was cleared to do so by the tower. She wanted a full tank in case she needed more time to look for the boys. If they weren't at the tent site, then she would buzz Harte Tower and the glacier below it in search of traces of them. Their climbing plans had seemed straightforward enough when Joe explained them to her. Go up, then come right back down. Money in the bank.

"I hope those clouds are high enough," said Katherine over the headset.

Sandy didn't call Katherine when she woke to clear skies. She planned to have the flight operator call her once she'd taken off, but Katherine was parked at the front door when she arrived. She was dressed in work pants, boots, and a hoodie and carrying her coat. It wouldn't be her first time hopping out of a plane onto a glacier. Sandy didn't have much choice but to allow her to ride, especially after she agreed to pay a passenger fee.

"It looks like we have a shot, but it'll be close."

Sandy had two options for approaching the boy's camp in such cloudy weather. She could fly high above the range and try to drop into the valley from the other side, but that would require an open sky above Harte Tower, which was impossible to know from so far away. Her second option was to fly in low, up the valleys, and pop into their cirque from one of the mountain passes. With option one, she might waste precious time and miss an opportunity to fly in under the weather. The cloud level sat on top of the highest peaks of the range, like a giant top hat, so she made the call to go low and hope that Gunshot Pass was clear.

Sandy's boss had ordered her to turn back if the ceiling was lower than the highest peaks. She saw that the highest summits were chopped off by the clouds, so she should technically turn around, but she pressed on in defiance of her orders.

Her engine roared as she clawed her way up in altitude toward Gunshot Pass, the low point in the long ridgeline running to the north. If she could make it over Gunshot, she could drop right into the valley and land on the South Glacier of Harte Tower. If Gunshot wasn't clear, she would have to quickly turn back and come around from the north or, worse yet, fly back to Fairbanks and wait for better weather.

She still had a feeling things were not okay. Joe should have called from his satellite phone by now, but he hadn't. Sure, batteries could go dead, or the clouds could have been too thick to get a call out, but she doubted Joe would have forgotten extra batteries or that he wouldn't have found even a short break in the weather to check in.

Sandy took a right out of the gentle Alatna Valley and followed the small stream toward Gunshot.

"This part might get rough," Sandy said, not looking away from the windshield. Katherine tightened her seatbelt and searched for the best grip on her seat.

The clouds seemed to be just high enough for Sandy to make the pass, so she continued past her last easy bailout. She was only a mile from where she would bank a hard left over the pass and down into the next valley, where the clouds were only a hundred feet above. She would typically turn back when it was that close, because it wasn't worth the risk. But, knowing the boys could be in trouble, she decided, against her better judgment, to give it a chance. She banked hard left and entered the pass only a hundred feet above the ground, aiming to thread the needle between the pass and the low clouds. Her heart raced as she roared over the ridge and glanced down at the rocks so close she could almost reach out and touch them.

In a moment of terror, she glanced upward only to find herself engulfed in a suffocating fog that had crept from the west side of the ridge. She was blinded, surrounded by nothing but an impenetrable gray abyss. Her only choice was to ascend, to desperately claw her way above the cloud cover, clinging to the hope of escape. Katherine closed her eyes.

Sandy pulled back hard on the yoke, her eyes straining into the void for any sign of the world beyond her windshield. She gained altitude rapidly, glimpsing the first hints that the sky was lightening. But through the mist, the ghastly silhouettes of rocks emerged. She was hurtling straight toward a jagged wall. She instinctively jerked the plane upward and to the left, the engine howling in protest. Her grip on the yoke was wooden. Her heart pounding was the only sound she could hear over the engine's scream, and she braced for the collision that seemed destined to claim them.

35. DELIVERANCE

Brooks Range, Alaska
July 2017
1 day past scheduled pickup

Ethan lay outside on his sleeping bag with the pistol next to him, cherishing the sun's warmth. He kept a watchful eye out for the bear and listened for the purr of a plane engine. Above him, Harte Tower shone in all its brilliance. The storm had frosted the summit. Ethan desperately hoped this was the weather they needed for the plane to land. The sky above was all blue, but clouds still lingered along the edges of the valley. Hopefully, the heat would burn those off as well.

Ethan worried about how much longer Joe could last. When he woke him to check his wound, Joe looked at him as if he'd never seen him before. He didn't wake the second time he checked in, even when Ethan zipped down his bag to look at his leg again. Even bundled up in his bag, Joe was still shivering cold. Ethan's mother had told him about some of her patients with harmful infections who needed antibiotics to break their fever. He knew he didn't have any medicine to give Joe. Their only hope was for the plane to show up and take him to the hospital. Until then, Ethan could only lie back on his bag and dream about food and a hot shower. It wasn't long before he faded off to sleep too.

From somewhere came a high-pitched whine, like a lawnmower motor with the throttle wide open. The sound pulled Ethan from his nap and sat him up, alert. It was still far enough away that Ethan couldn't at first place the direction it came from. The sound echoed off the surrounding walls, and he started to think he was just hallucinating in his malnourished state. He was losing track of what was real and imagined. Was he still sleeping?

Then, to the east, he saw a tiny, white speck approaching him from the clouds on the rim of the cirque.

"It's Sandy!" Ethan shouted. "She's coming!"

The boy stood and instinctively waved his arms for her to see them, even though she was still a couple of miles away. He couldn't control the tears running down his cheeks and tried to dry them with his jacket sleeves. But his rush of joy dissipated as the plane flew past them and continued up the glacier to the old camp.

"She didn't see us."

***

Sandy and Katherine fought to shake off the adrenaline rush from their near-miss at the pass and focus on the task at hand. Sandy remembered precisely where the boys were camped and lined up to land next to it just as she had when she dropped them off. She hoped they would remember to stay out of her way.

"Wait, something isn't right," said Katherine over the headset.

Sandy pulled the plane up, punched the throttle to regain altitude, and eyed the destruction of the camp as they passed. “Bear musta torn into it,” replied Sandy. “I didn’t see anybody; did you?”

Katherine shook her head as tears welled up. “No, I didn’t.”

Sandy dipped her left wing and circled back. “We have enough fuel for a couple passes, then we’ll need to head back. We can radio to Search and Rescue if we don’t find them.”

Sandy slowed the plane and flew toward the south face of Harte Tower to inspect the boys’ intended climbing route.

“I don’t see a thing,” said Katherine.

As they neared the wall, Sandy cut a hard right, veering to the east and over the rib before pointing back south. She glanced at the fuel gauge and started calculating how much time they had left before heading back. She knew that she could always stop at Coldfoot on the way back to Fairbanks for more fuel if they needed to look longer. A search team would be better equipped to scan the immense terrain than the two of them, but she would circle until the gauge said otherwise.

“There they are!” shouted Katherine. In the excitement, she forgot to hold down the button, so Sandy only saw her flapping her arms wildly and pointing down to their right. But the smile on her face said it all. Sandy rolled the plane right and looked out Katherine’s window and saw a speck of red on the ice. And someone swinging a sleeping bag around in the air. It was Ethan.

They didn’t see Joe but figured he must be in the tent packing things up. Sandy dropped elevation and flew out over the bottom of the valley before turning around and dumping speed as she climbed back up to the glacier.

They both saw the bear at the same time. Katherine

pointed to the big, brown animal climbing onto the edge of the glacier, up a rib of soft snow between two gullies of broken ice. He was only a few hundred yards below the tent and obviously stalking them. Sandy nodded her head in acknowledgment and pointed the nose of her Cessna right at him. They watched him cower at first, then, as the noise of the engine grew louder over his shoulder, he peered back to see them bearing down on him. He bolted straight down the slushy slope and barreled through the boulder field at full throttle. The ladies laughed joyously, and Katherine clapped and bounced in her seat like she was a young girl again.

Sandy pulled back the yoke until the plane nearly matched the angle of the glacier. Crevasses flew by underneath until she was in the soft middle of the glacier, where she could safely land. The touchdown was perfect. She eased the gas forward, spun around, ready for the downhill takeoff, killed the engine, and hopped out. She'd stopped the plane a couple of hundred yards above their tent to avoid the broken edge of the glacier. Ethan jogged toward them slowly.

"Looks like your camp got a visit," she shouted to him as he approached. "Smokey the Bear made quite a mess."

Katherine emerged from her door as Ethan pulled up out of breath. "Thank god you're okay, Ethan. Your mother has been worried to death." She then realized Joe hadn't left the tent. "What's wrong with him?"

"He broke his leg. He's had a fever for a few days and won't wake up today."

While Ethan summarized their ordeal, Sandy and Katherine hiked to the tent. The weight of the situation sank in. Katherine went to Joe and unzipped his bag. She felt his forehead.

"Oh, lord, Joe, you're on fire." Katherine looked up at Ethan. "Help me get him out of the bag so I can see his leg."

She pulled up his bloody pant leg and saw the pus running from the open fracture wound and the red and black bruising. The putrid smell made her stomach turn.

"Oh, good lord, he needs a hospital fast. Let's get him on the plane."

They zipped Joe back up, and each gripped the hood of his mummy bag and dragged him back to the plane. Ethan was very weak but tried his best to help Joe get into the back seat. Leaning over from the cockpit, Sandy had to struggle with all her strength to help pull him in, while Katherine and Ethan pushed from below. The weight Joe had lost over the last week helped.

"Forget about the rest of it, kid; we gotta go now!" Sandy demanded as she started up the engine. Ethan crawled into the front seat while Katherine buckled in next to Joe in the back, just in time for Sandy to gun it down the glacier. They were airborne, and Sandy took a hard right, veering far south of the storm front she had flown through. Harte Tower faded behind as Sandy hit a cruising altitude at the highest speed she could maintain. She radioed ahead to Fairbanks and filled them in on what had happened. An ambulance met them at the airfield to rush them to the hospital. Sandy's director of operations called Julia, who booked the next available flight out of Denver.

Ethan and Joe rode in the same ambulance to the hospital while Katherine drove her car to meet them. The paramedic briefly took Ethan's vital signs and annotated them but was otherwise focused on stabilizing Joe. He radioed ahead to page the trauma surgeon.

When they arrived at the hospital, Joe was whisked away for surgery. Ethan was separated into his own room. Katherine checked on him to make sure he was in good hands, then walked back to the intensive care unit to be by Joe's side.

Sandy joined them at the hospital after she parked her plane and completed her post-flight list. The nurse at the ER desk didn't seem to want to let her through to see Ethan until Sandy exaggerated her position by claiming to be a long-time family friend.

"How are you doing?" asked Sandy as she entered Ethan's room.

"I'm okay." An IV was stuck in his left arm, and a fresh roll of gauze was taped on the inside of his right. "Yeah, they stuck me a few times already." He raised his arms for further proof. "The doctor is worried about my kidneys and liver, so he took some blood to test. He said it's not natural to put the body through so much without enough food and water."

"That sounds like a good idea to me."

"Yeah. They gave me some good painkillers, too."

"I bet that's nice."

"Not as good as lying down on a real bed, though. I forgot how much I missed that. Even if it's just a hospital bed, it's a lot better than sleeping on ice."

Sandy nodded and smiled, then turned serious. "Did you hear anything about Joe?"

Ethan tilted his head. "He's in a coma. The doctor put him on some strong antibiotics and said he has a thirty percent chance of making it through. He'll also lose the leg. I don't think he'll like that, but it doesn't seem like there's any options."

Sandy took a deep breath at the news. "That tells me

Joe has a fighting chance. Luckily, he's a fighter."

Ethan nodded in agreement. "I don't think he came this far to give up now."

She smiled. "Kid, you need a shower. And a cheeseburger, most likely. Get yourself cleaned up, and I'll be back in an hour with some grub."

Sandy drove back to the airfield while Ethan showered in his hospital room. She found some extra clothes one of the former employees had left in his locker a few months back, and they were a close enough fit, so she packed them in her bag. She grabbed them both a cheeseburger, a shake, and fries at a fast-food drive-through on the way back.

Ethan lay in the hospital bed, wearing the thin gown they had given him, and looked out the second-story window at the tops of the trees just outside. The nurse had removed his IV, allowing him to truly relax for the first time in days. Seeing the vibrant green of the tree canopy reminded him that he hadn't seen that color in over a week, and he hadn't realized how much his eyes had been starved of it until then. Just then, Sandy walked in, tossed a bag of clothes onto the bed, pulled up a chair, and began divvying up their lukewarm dinner.

"Oh my god, that smells so good." Ethan scooted down and joined her at the end of the bed.

"I bet it does. Here you go. Enjoy it, hero." Ethan took a big bite and closed his eyes while appreciating every flavor.

"Back in my twenties," began Sandy, "before I started flying, I volunteered for search and rescue in Valdez. Ever skied there?"

"No, I'm not much of a skier," answered Ethan.

"Good ice climbing there, too. Anyway, we got plenty

of calls for missing skiers up on Thompson Pass. Snowmobilers too. Avalanches are serious there. Sometimes they get buried so deep we don't find them 'til summer melts all the snow. One time, we got a call for an overdue snowmobiler. He'd separated from his friends to check out a different bowl, and they didn't see him again. Visibility was low, and the place was already tracked out. No one could tell which were his. He'd already spent a night out, so we searched hard all day to keep him from spending another out there. *If* he was still alive. Didn't find him anywhere, so we figured an avalanche buried him. We took the sleds out the second day and looked again, but no luck. Cloud cover was still too low to get a heli in there to help look. We started losing light, so we called it. Took a shortcut down a different draw than we'd taken the day before to get to the road to get the sleds back on the trailers. And there he was. Wasn't a mile from the road. Said his skidoo ran out of gas, so he sat down right there and waited to be found. Two nights and two days. Lost three toes and a pinky."

"Ouch."

"Yeah. Ouch. One of the guys asked him why he didn't even try to wade through the snow to the road. You could literally hear the cars driving by. Said he was tired."

Ethan shook his head.

"Makes me wonder," said Sandy, "why there are people like that who just leave it all up to fate, but then there's people like you and Joe who fight like hell."

"Do you think you would have found us over there on the north side?"

Sandy shrugged her shoulders. "Maybe. But, maybe not."

Ethan looked out the window, gazing far off in the distance. At the pillowy tops of Birch mixed with the pointed jabs of Spruce, sprinkled between the tops of buildings. "Guess I just got tired of losing things."

They sat together in silence for another couple of minutes until the nurse returned to recheck his vitals. Ethan told Sandy it was the most incredible cheeseburger he'd ever eaten, and that was the truth.

36. HARD TO KILL

Talkeetna, Alaska
Late Summer 2017, Spring 2018

—Joe—

Joe's doctor in Fairbanks feared complications and flew him to Anchorage, where they were better equipped to handle cases like his. Katherine was by his side when he awoke eleven days later.

Aside from Ethan's brave actions, doctors credited Joe's active lifestyle with saving his life. The high level of infection coursing through Joe's blood should have sent him into cardiac arrest, but decades of hard-charging in the mountains had likely steeled his body and made him too hard to kill. The road to recovery was a long one, however. His infected leg was left to fester so long that the tissue around the wound could not be treated. The surgeon made the first amputation just below the knee, but the infection was stubborn, and several more surgeries were required to clean the dead tissue and stop the infection from spreading to his bones.

Every few weeks, he would make the return trip for his checkup, and they would take more. The pain was sometimes worse than what he experienced on Harte Tower, and he often wished Ethan had left him behind. In his medicated dreams, he could still walk and run like he always had, and then all of a sudden, he would remember what happened and fall on his face. He worried how much of him would be left when they were done carving him up. Ultimately, he was left with a stump just above the knee. Six months later, the swelling had subsided enough to be fitted for a prosthetic. The doctors told Joe that rock climbing and mountaineering were likely out of the picture for him. But they didn't know Joe.

He had to learn to walk all over again with the new leg. Fortunately, his physical therapist was patient with Joe and understood his frustrations at starting all over again so late in life. Joe was also aware of the irony of how the same war that took his only son was also the catalyst for the innovative new prosthetics that now allowed him to walk again. He would far rather have his son, he thought. In a way, the plastic and carbon leg was a double reminder of his two most significant losses.

By early spring, Joe was venturing out alone for increasingly longer walks along the plowed roads of Talkeetna. He used the quiet strolls on his new leg to meditate on his new life. He took his cane and moved carefully, trying to synchronize his steps into a natural stride. One early March day, Joe wandered slowly from their house at noon with no destination in mind. He ended up at the bank of the river and found a cold rock to sit on, next to Katherine's parked car. He watched the stirring current in a small, ice-free eddy. Constantly swirling and turning. The deep chill of the air seemed to mirror the feeling in his soul.

Katherine's voice carried from across the river as if

she were standing next to him. "You can join if you like. They're biting."

Joe looked up with only a half smile. "I didn't bring a pole."

"There's an extra in the roof box."

Joe grabbed the fishing rod plus a camp chair from the back of the car, then made his way carefully across the frozen surface of the river.

"Nice of you to finally join me."

Joe baited the hook with a minnow. "Thanks for the loaner."

"I've packed that spare for years, hoping you'd use it."

The breakup would come in a few weeks, and spring warmth would release the rivers from their icy tombs. Leaves would eventually return to the Birch and Aspen. Joe knew he had many springs left to enjoy. And he would be by her side for as many as possible.

37. CLARITY

Colorado Springs, Colorado
December 2017

Ethan lobbed the rake and shears into the back of the work truck and piled the bags of leaves on the curb. The worn magnet reading "Thomas Landscaping" was peeling off the tailgate, so he pulled it and tossed it back with the tools. It was only 4:00, but the sun was already setting behind Pikes Peak. He joined Bill in the cab and put his hands to the heater vent.

"Damn, it got cold quick," said Ethan.

"Cold front moving in. Winter's here for a while."

Bill put the truck in drive and pulled away. Ethan hated how bleak the neighborhoods looked this time of year, with their dead, leafless trees in the gray light. It was better in the mountains. He went for hikes there often, driving up alone in the car he'd bought with the money he earned working for Bill. The work was steady until now. Not much landscaping to do when everything was dead. Surprisingly, he felt no desire to climb solo in the canyon again. When he glimpsed the golden walls and spires from his walks, he even felt a pain of remorse and guilt for the careless days spent there, seemingly in a different life. Not long ago, he had felt a sense of freedom and rebelliousness when climbing there, but that had been replaced by the sometimes-crushing weight of responsibility. He knew he would eventually return to climbing, but it wouldn't be like it was before. He could never be that selfish again. The mountains deserved more respect than that. Those he loved did as well.

"You and your mom have a good Thanksgiving?"

"Yeah, it was alright. Just us and David."

Bill merged onto the highway heading south. He still picked up Ethan from the townhome every day and dropped him off, even though Ethan had his own car. Bill lived close, and Ethan didn't mind the company. Sometimes, while driving to a job site, Bill told stories of Ethan's dad and the guys they worked with.

As Bill pulled up and parked at Ethan's condo, he started to speak, then stopped. Then he asked quietly, "You guys do anything for the anniversary?"

Ethan nodded, looking out the window. "We went for a hike in the canyon and spread some of Dad's ashes. He always liked it there."

"That's good. Still can't believe it's already been a year. A lot's happened since then."

"Yes, sir, it has," he agreed as he got out of the truck.

The townhomes were quieter now that Camila was gone. He spoke with her often. She was enjoying her new life in Texas. She found the classes challenging, especially while working part-time to pay as much of her tuition as she could. A small scholarship helped her, but it didn't pay for it all. She told him all about the books she was reading and the new friends she'd met. He was proud of her but also felt left behind. He felt the distance between them growing, and he knew that she would soon forget to return his calls and texts. It was understandable.

Julia pulled into her parking spot as Ethan fumbled for his keys. He unlocked the front door and waited to open it for her.

"Oh, thank you, it's freezing."

David's jacket saddled the chair at the end of the table. Julia surreptitiously slid it off, dropped it into the coat closet, and hung hers from a hanger.

"It's okay, you know."

"What's that?"

"I'm glad you have him—have each other."

Julia smiled and hugged him. "Thank you, Ethan. I'm lucky to have you both in my life."

They talked about their days over a rewarmed Thanksgiving meal. Julia made her plate orderly, with each item well-spaced and separated. Ethan tossed all the ingredients into a bowl and stirred them up.

"Well, anyways, enough of my work drama. How's Bill?

"He's fine. Heading out of town for a few weeks while we're slow."

"Things are finally slowing down, huh?"

"More than that. It died. Won't have any work around here until spring, most likely. But Bill has a friend in Ouray who needs someone to shovel snow and drive a plow."

"And you'd be in the mountains. Sounds like your kind of job."

"Mateo texted me. He'll be there too for a few months, guiding. Says he'll teach me how to ice climb."

"Who's this Mateo, again?" asked Julia, with a hint of motherly protection.

"He's one of the guides Grandpa knows in Alaska.

They worked together."

Ethan helped himself to another slice of cornbread. He'd eaten very little all day and was hungrier than he thought.

"Have you talked to Camila? Does she still like it out there?"

"She likes it. Said she'll need a new roommate next semester. Hers decided college wasn't for her."

"Are you thinking about that?"

"A little." Ethan forked the last bite of his food into a pile. "What do you think I should do?"

Julia took a few moments before speaking. "I like Camila. And I know you like her. You're a mountain guy at heart, but mountains will always be there. I think you'll choose the right direction for you."

In the middle of December, Ethan loaded his old beater of a car in the dark of morning and pointed it away from the mountains, toward Dallas. When the blood-red sun crested the endless horizon of the high plains, only the snow-capped summits of the highest peaks of the front range were still visible in his rear view.

38. THE COMPASS

Afghanistan
November 1, 2016

My Son,

Things have been hectic this time around, but not as bad as they were last time I was here, or Iraq in 07. Keep working hard in school and be good for your mom.

I thought about you a lot today. The seasons don't change here much. It's always dry and brown and there's little green to turn gold in the fall. I imagine the leaves have all turned in Colorado by now. I hope you appreciate those changes of season.

There's something about being a father and seeing my boy grow and experience life that brings up buried memories of when I stumbled through adolescence. I like to think I've learned a few things in that process, and I've tried to pass that hard-earned wisdom on to you when I could. I do remember when I was your age I thought I knew everything there was to know about the world, and I thought my own dad was clueless. Oh how things have changed.

This morning I remembered a trip we took one summer to visit my uncle and his family in the Ozarks. I believe I was 13, a bit younger than you are now. It was hot and humid, and they had all kinds of bugs that drove me nuts, but at least they didn't have grizzlies to worry about.

My cousin had a nice little single-shot 20-gauge shotgun we used to hunt rabbits and squirrels with. One day, I wanted to walk in the woods and see what we could scare up, but all he wanted to do was go swimming in the lake, so I decided to go on my own. Looking back, I think I was a bit full of myself. I grew up roaming the big Alaska mountains with my parents, and those little Arkansas hills were nothing I needed to worry about. Or so I thought.

I walked for an hour before jumping up a great big red squirrel. I brought up the shotgun but couldn't get a clear shot before he disappeared into his hole high up in an oak tree. Typically, we would have walked on and looked for another. But, since I was alone I decided to try to wait him out. I think I wanted to really show my cousin I was right about hunting and that he missed out by not coming along. I sat down on a log and resisted every temptation to move. Flies and mosquitoes tore me up, but I didn't dare budge to swat them away. Clouds started to roll in while I waited and cooled things off a little, which I was thankful for.

After an eternity, that sucker crawled out of his hole. I caught him with one shot as he inched his way up the side of the tree. He was a fat boy and I couldn't wait to show the family and tell them the story. I tied him to one of my belt loops with some string and headed back to the farmhouse.

I soon realized I had hiked for too long and should have been back by then. I looked around but the woods all looked the same. Unlike Alaska, there were no mountains to use for direction and I couldn't use the sun because it was covered by the clouds. I was lost. I spent an hour thrashing through thick brush and crossing ravines. I even climbed up a tree trying to look for the farm but the canopy was just too dense.

I finally settled on one direction that felt right and decided I would either make it to the farm or I would hit a road or the lake eventually. I finally popped out at the far end of my uncle's pasture. By then I was all scratched up and tired, and even worse, the squirrel must have gotten torn off me in the brush. I had nothing to show for it, but I was just happy to be back on familiar ground.

By now you're probably wondering why I'm telling you this, and you might be wondering why my old compass is in the box this letter came in.

It seems like you get bigger and stronger every day, and with that comes independence and confidence. I feel lucky for every minute I have spent with you, and I've tried my best to give you the best chance at life. But of course my job has kept me away from you for more time than I like. There will come a time when I am not around to help you when you need it.

I want you to have my M2 compass. I barely use it anymore since everything is digital and satellite-based anyway. I've had it since basic training, and it's seen a lot of action around the world. It's faded now from the sun, and the desert sand really took its toll on the hinges. It might be old and heavier than some of these newer plastic models, but it will last. We'll take it out for a spin when I get back.

Life can get messy, and it's easy to get lost in the brush. You won't always have high peaks or the sun's warmth to guide you. But just remember, you can always find your way if you start with true north.

Love always,

Your Dad

ABOUT THE AUTHOR

Phil Wortmann is a lifelong climber, Army veteran, and twenty-year high school teacher based in Colorado Springs. Since 1999, he's logged significant first ascents, worked part-time as a mountain guide and avalanche safety instructor, and competed nationally in ice climbing. His writing has been featured in the American Alpine Journal, and he has shared his stories across podcasts, and magazines. His blog series, *The Alpine Ethos,* which documents the mountain culture of Southern Colorado, as well as his other published works, can be found at his website: philwortmann.com.

If you enjoyed this book, please consider leaving a review on Amazon.

Also By Phil Wortmann:

Alpine Adventures on Pikes Peak America's Mountain

www.ingramcontent.com/pod-product-compliance
Lightning Source LLC
LaVergne TN
LVHW040216110826
845146LV00005B/1310

* 9 7 9 8 9 9 5 0 0 8 6 1 3 *